ELIZABETH CRANE

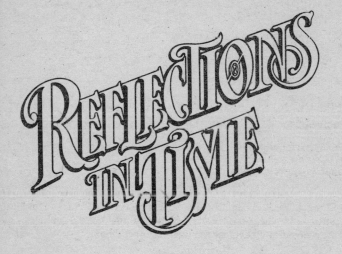

REFLECTIONS IN TIME

LOVE SPELL   NEW YORK CITY

LOVE SPELL®

April 1996

Published by

Dorchester Publishing Co., Inc.
276 Fifth Avenue
New York, NY 10001

Printed in the United States of America.

REFLECTIONS IN TIME

Chapter One

Renata O'Neal told herself she wouldn't go there that day. She spent the morning straightening her apartment and washing her hair, all the time telling herself she wouldn't go there that day. By noon she knew she was lying to herself.

She couldn't have said what it was about that particular graveyard that was so fascinating to her. Although she had lived in Lorain, Louisiana, most of her adult life, none of her family was buried there. They were all in her hometown of Joachin, Texas, and those who were still living would have been surprised at her new pastime of graveyard roaming.

At first she had simply been fascinated by the lichen-covered headstones and the inscriptions on the older graves. Because Lorain was well inland, the graves there were all beneath the surface, unlike the above-ground tombs in New Orleans. Renata had recently passed her thirtieth birthday, and during a private birthday party for her, her fiancé, Bob Symons, had said this peculiar quirk of hers was likely nothing more than an early onset of her midlife crisis. At the time Renata had laughed at him, but now she wasn't so sure.

"Just a short walk," she told herself. "Once or twice around the block, and then I'll come home and read."

She pulled a knit cap over her short, dark hair and reached for her coat. Winter had not yet released its grip on the south and the day was blustery. There had even been snow that year, only an inch or two, but nevertheless a rarity in Lorain.

She let herself out and checked to make sure her apartment door had locked behind her. The crime rate in Lorain was negligible, but she had no intention of making her place an easy target for thieves. It was that same feeling of vulnerability that had persuaded her to take a course in self-defense in Baton Rouge the previous summer. The drive to Baton Rouge had been a long one, but after the course, she felt more secure.

Since graduating from college Renata had lived alone. Though she wasn't the sort to enjoy being alone, it had just worked out that way. All her friends from high school and college were married and had completed their families for the most part. At her last high school class reunion, she had been one of only three women in her graduating class who had never married. Of the other two, one was unattractive and the other was unabashedly gay. She

8

told herself that discovering she was a part of such an idiosyncratic group wasn't the reason she had agreed to marry Bob shortly after her return from the reunion, but she wasn't convinced deep in her heart.

Bob Symons was likeable, if a bit dull. He had a good job with an accounting firm and the promise of someday becoming a full partner. Renata was also an accountant, and he had talked of someday opening a firm called Symons and Symons. She had teased him that she would agree if the first Symons in the title referred to herself. Bob hadn't been all that amused; they both knew that Renata was the better accountant of the two.

As a child she had loved Saturdays and had tried to make them last forever. Now, without effort, they stretched long and empty and boring. Bob jogged most every morning including the weekends, then lounged in his easy chair all afternoon watching whatever weekend sporting event was currently in season. Renata knew she needed a hobby or new friends to fill her empty hours, but it wasn't going to be easy. Her closest friend had recently been transferred to Houston, and she had never been particularly good at making new acquaintances, a holdover from her shyness in school, she supposed, though Bob sometimes complained that she was too assertive or pushy, as he called it.

Renata turned the corner and started up the

windy street. Dry leaves rattled over the pavement, scurrying ahead of her. To protect herself against the blustery chill, she buttoned her coat.

Not for the first time, she questioned whether she loved Bob. The thought made her feel guilty. Of course she loved him. They were going to be married. There was no one else she would rather marry, and Bob was a nice person. She frowned because that sounded so dull. Was Bob really so boring?

To get her mind on more pleasant thoughts, she crossed the street to a small chapel on the opposite corner. Lately, she had made a habit of going inside when there were no other cars about. Renata wasn't of the Catholic faith, and she didn't want to offend those who were. Finding the building again deserted, she went in.

In the serenity of the chapel, she felt her cares wash away. It was a small building with only a few rows of pews. The narrow windows along both sides were filled with stained glass in varying shades of green. A vine outside, now leafless, grew over one of the windows like a tracery of lace.

Renata sat in one of the pews and gazed at the altar. What was she going to do with the rest of her life? The thought wasn't a new one. She had been asking herself that ever since she had attended that accursed class reunion. On the surface she knew the answer. She would marry Bob, and someday they would have the best accounting firm in Lorain. They would make a handsome living, perhaps even become wealthy. She enjoyed being an accountant and had loved this town ever since she moved here. So why wasn't she happy?

Bob had been urging her to set the date for their wedding. As he kept saying, her biological clock was ticking since she was already 30. He wanted a son to carry on after him, convinced that any child he fathered would be a son. Renata wanted children, too. She wanted more than one and didn't care which sex they were, yet somehow she had never had the time to have a family. Getting her degree and becoming established in town had occupied all her days. Before she knew it, years had passed.

Did she love Bob? The disturbing question wouldn't leave her alone, even in the peaceful chapel. The fact that she asked it so often told her the answer. She had heard that a person who is in love knows it beyond a shadow of a doubt. If the question came up, the answer was no. Renata wasn't sure she agreed with that, for to do so would mean admitting she had never been in love before in her entire life. She was not a virgin and hadn't been for a long time, but that was different. Surely love was more than physical enjoyment. But if so, she wasn't sure she could marry Bob with a clear conscience.

Bob loved her. She was pretty sure of that. He didn't spend a lot of time saying he did, but that was fine with her. She prided herself on being pragmatic. He had said he loved her once and that should be enough—but was it? If they were really in love wouldn't they both want to express it often?

She looked up at the stained glass circle above the altar. The sunshine slanting through it cast a pale green glow onto the altar's white cloth. Had she not known the altar cloth was white, seeing it in this light might have made her think it was green instead. Things weren't always what they seemed to be. She had more questions than she could answer or even comfortably ask.

There was no use putting it off. She had known where she was going when she left the house. As she left the chapel, she doubled back alongside it and entered its adjoining cemetery through the side gate.

The cemetery with its mossy headstones no longer bright nor entirely straight in the earth folded about the small chapel as if to serve as a guardian to its flank. Many of Lorain's earliest inhabitants rested here. The latest grave had been dug nearly 40 years ago, while the earliest bore the faded numbers, 1779. Enormous live oak trees stretched their verdant boughs over the graves, but the grass beneath was a grayish brown and matted from winter. In the spring the ground would be covered with wild flowers, but now there was no hint of life anywhere. Some might have found the setting a bit depressing, but to Renata it was only peaceful.

She had discovered the cemetery months before. It lay behind a wall and was almost invisible to traffic. Only on foot could it be glimpsed. At first she had been afraid she would be viewed as a trespasser, but she had come here often and no one had ever told her to leave. She closed the gate and walked down the brick path that circled the back of the church. Clearly the path once had been heavily used as it was worn and had sunken beneath the level of the grass, but as far as Renata could tell, it was now used only by the caretakers.

She had systematically crisscrossed the grave yard in the past months, pausing to read each inscription. At times she felt as if she were looking for something in particular, but she knew that was impossible. No one she knew was buried here, the last grave having been dug before she was born.

As usual she started in the back corner and began working her way forward in a pattern that would pass every grave. She had the sensation of viewing time backward as the newer graves were the farthest from the church. The older ones huddled beside the church as if for shelter. The newer graves were more or less arranged in neat rows, but the older ones seemed to have been laid out somewhat randomly. Families were grouped together, making the paths wind and twist and finally disappear. Here and there among the older graves were tall pinnacles of white marble and smaller ones at the bases. Some headstones were topped with stone angels or lambs; others held poems or mournful phrases or expressions of hope. Renata's heart went out to the multitude of babies and small children who had been laid to rest there.

Near the church was a plot which was surrounded by a black iron fence whose forbidding spikes had kept her out previously. She had tried to read the inscriptions on the headstones, but always from outside the fence because she had felt that to go inside would indeed be trespassing. Again she viewed the enclosed graves with growing curiosity. Finally, with determination, she walked to the wrought-iron fence and tested the gate.

With a bit of effort, she was able to swing it open. Inside were several headstones, all bearing the surnames Blue and Graham. Obviously they were all of the same family since they were enclosed within the fence. Renata stooped closer, trying to make out the names and dates in the dim light. Applying a bit of reasoning and logic to the dates, she decided that Ida and William Graham had been married and would have been of an age to have been parents to most of the others. There were graves for several babies and one for a boy in his early teens. Renata wondered if he had died of illness or an accident and whether modern medicine could have saved him.

The other two graves had matching headstones which read: "Callie Blue, Beloved Wife" and "Nathan Blue, Devoted Husband."

Renata felt a strong sense of *déjà vu*, and she knelt to read the dates. Callie had died young at the age of 25. Renata speculated that she might have died in childbirth. Nathan had lived another 54 years. According to his headstone, and the absence of another which might have been that of a second wife, he had never remarried. Tears stung her eyes at such a sign of devotion.

Renata wiped her eyes and told herself she was being silly. She had no connection with these people. Though Blue wasn't an unusual name in this area, she had never known anyone with that name, at least not on a personal basis. It was obvious that caretakers saw to it that all the plots in the cemetery were weeded and mowed in season, but these particular graves had a lonesome air about them, as if the family's survivors had either moved away or lost interest in maintaining them. There were no shrubs or rose bushes planted here as there were on some of the other graves. There was no only a twisted and aging crepe myrtle whose trunk looked slick and white without its flowers to brighten it.

Slowly Renata sat down. She wrapped her arms about her knees and gazed at the two tombstones. Bob was right. She had been looking for something, and she had just found it. Unfortunately she had no idea what she had found or why two old graves should have any meaning for her. She stayed there until the early evening shadows told her that it was time for her to go home and get ready for her date with Bob.

The next day was Sunday, and Renata went back to the cemetery after the worshipers had had time to leave the chapel. She had tried to tell Bob about the graves and how they had affected her, but he had thought she was kidding and had laughed at her earnestness.

With painstaking care, Renata planted some bulbs she had brought with her around the headstones. This spring the graves would have a cared-for look again.

When she was finished, Renata began to question her actions. At the time, it had seemed perfectly reasonable to buy and plant bulbs. Now it had a macabre note. She had never been moved to do anything like this before and wasn't sure she liked the fact that she had done such a thing. Bob was right. She was being ghoulish.

"That does it," she said firmly. "I won't be back." She realized she was talking aloud to herself and frowned. She didn't know what was happening to her, but she was becoming uneasy.

By the time she reached her apartment, Bob was waiting for her. She had given him a key soon after he had given her the engagement ring, and lately he had started dropping over without calling first.

"Hi. Where have you been?" he asked when she walked in.

Renata took off her coat and hung it on the brass coat rack. "Walking. I didn't know you were coming over this afternoon."

"I started to call, but I was going out anyway so I thought I'd drop by and wait for you if you were gone." He pressed the remote control and switched the television from the sports channel he had been watching. "There's a good movie on."

Renata glanced at the screen where a car skidded across a street, slammed into a parked car and exploded. She shook her head. "I've seen it. Can you stay for dinner?"

Bob grinned. "You twisted my arm. What are we having?"

She tried to think what her pantry held. "I can whip up a casserole or nuke something in the microwave."

"I need to buy you a cookbook," Bob complained. "I never knew any woman who liked to cook less."

"I just have other interests."

He pulled her down beside him on the couch. "Like what? Walking? Where did you go today?"

Renata tried to stand back up. "I just walked."

Bob narrowed his eyes. "You didn't go back to that cemetery, did you? The one you were going on and on about last night?"

Elizabeth Crane

"It's on my way. It's only a block from here. I pass it all the time." She didn't meet his eyes.

"You didn't go in, did you?"

"So what if I did? Why does it matter to you? It's peaceful in there."

Bob put his arm around her shoulder. "It's weird, baby. You never used to do things like that. What is it about that place that keeps pulling you back to it?"

She frowned. "I'm not sure. There's nothing wrong with me, though. I'm positive of that."

"I never said there was."

"I mean, I'm not depressed or anything. I'm not going off the deep end."

Bob looked at her with a raised eyebrow but said nothing.

"Okay. So I'm having trouble sleeping. A lot of people do, and it doesn't mean anything."

"Maybe you're not getting enough exercise." He grinned and leaned forward to kiss her.

"I'll go see about dinner." She moved away and pretended not to have noticed his intention. For some reason she didn't want Bob to kiss her, not at the moment.

In her small kitchen she dug through the pantry but found little. She had been putting off going to the grocery store for almost two weeks, so her choices were limited. There were two boxes of noodles, a few cans of vegetables, and one of salmon. None of it looked especially inviting.

Bob had followed her and was lounging in

the doorway. "I don't know why you don't just move in with me. We'll be married soon, and there's no sense in paying two rents."

"I thought we had discussed that already."

"We did, but I didn't like the answer. It just makes sense. We could ride to work together and save gas. Your office is only a couple of blocks from mine. We could meet for lunch."

"I'm not ready for that yet."

"Then why don't we set our wedding date?"

"Later. Would you look in the freezer and see if I still have any spinach?"

Bob opened the freezer door and frosty air billowed into the kitchen. "There's one package."

"That's all I need." She took out the package of noodles and got a large pot from beneath her countertop to boil them in. "I'll make that casserole you like."

"Why don't you want to set the date? I thought the woman was always the one who was anxious to get everything settled."

"You watch too many old movies. I'm in no rush to settle down."

"That's news to me. I was under the impression you were at least as anxious as I am. You certainly seemed to be at the time I proposed."

"Was I?" She leaned against the sink as water flowed into the pot. "I don't remember."

"Mother is beginning to ask why we are still waiting since neither of us has any reason to postpone the wedding."

"She called again?" One of the things Renata liked least about Bob was his attachment to his mother. She didn't know any other grown man who so frequently visited his mother's house and called her at least twice a day. The woman didn't particularly like Renata, but Bob was unable to see that.

"I called her. She said her sciatica is acting up again and her rheumatism is bothering her. Poor thing. I don't know how much longer she will be able to live alone."

Renata glanced at him. "You sound as if she's a hundred years old. She's still young. She just needs more to keep her busy."

When Bob didn't answer, she knew she had angered him. Almost any reference to his mother could start an argument. "Will you turn on the oven for me?" She put the water on to boil and carried the frozen spinach to the microwave.

"Mother's health has gone down since Father passed away. In a way that's what I want to talk to you about. I found a house I think you'll like."

"You've been house hunting? Without me?"

"You were out on one of your walks. It's in the Kingwood addition."

"Not the one by your mother's house." She turned and stared at him.

"Sure. Why not? They are all new houses, and it's close by Mother's in case she needs me."

"I don't want a new house. We discussed this already." She sprinkled some salt into the pot of water. "I would rather wait until we can buy exactly what we want. Like that house over on Stovall Street, for instance."

"You can't want that. It's a hundred years old if it's a day," Bob objected, "and it's all the way across town."

"I like old houses. The new ones seem too slick, and they all look alike."

"No, they don't. At least come see this house. It has three bedrooms. One for us, one for the baby, and one extra."

"For an office? I'm glad to leave my work behind at five o'clock."

Bob looked down at the floor. "One in case Mother gets to the point where she can't live alone."

"What? You mean she intends to live with us?" His words had taken her by surprise so that she forgot to be diplomatic.

"Who else but us? My brother and sister both live out of state, and she wouldn't be happy anywhere else."

"Bob, your mother is only fifty-six years old. She has half her life left."

"No one in my family has ever lived to be one hundred and twelve years old," he said stiffly. "I thought you understood that's why I want a one story house that's near the hospital."

Renata didn't know what to say. "You're choosing a house for her, not for me."

"I thought you'd be bigger about this. Most women would be glad to see a son who lives up to his responsibility."

"This goes beyond that." She was afraid to delve too deeply into what he had meant by his responsibility. "I'm glad you're loyal to your mother and I know you love her, but what about us? Don't we matter at all? I don't want a house in that addition. Every third one has the same floor plan, and the yards don't have trees in them."

"We can plant a tree. It's near the school as well as the hospital. Our son can walk to school."

"And that's another thing. What if I want more than one baby? And what if we have a girl? There's a fifty-fifty chance, you know."

"You're just upset, probably because you haven't been sleeping properly. Have you tried sleeping pills?"

"I'm not going to take sleeping pills. Everybody has insomnia at one time or another. I'll start sleeping again." She wished she could sound more convincing. Her lack of sleep *was* making her edgy at work as well as with Bob. "Remember that psychologist Betty Frankenheim went to see? Maybe I should go to him."

"A psychologist? I don't know." Bob shook his head doubtfully. "Lorain is so small; word would get around."

"Dr. McIntyre isn't a witch doctor, for goodness sake. He's a trained professional."

"You know how people talk. It might get around that you have something wrong with you. You know, up here." He tapped his forehead. "It could hurt your business."

"I can't believe we're having this conversation. If I want to go see a psychologist, I'll see one, and that's all there is to it." She dumped the noodles into the boiling water. "This isn't the middle ages, you know."

"I know, but folks here in Lorain still have a narrow mind about some things."

Renata frowned. "Now I know I'm going to make an appointment with him. I do need some help with my sleep problems, and lately I've felt the need to get some counseling."

"Your walks in the cemetery, you mean."

She didn't look at him. "I suppose I could talk to Dr. McIntyre about them. I know it bothers you that I like to go there," she said as she stirred the noodles unnecessarily hard. "Bob, I can't explain what it is about that place. It was almost as if I was looking for it. First I went to all the graveyards in town, then I found that one and lost interest in the others. Yesterday when I discovered those two graves—well, I can't explain it. Something happened to me inside."

"If you ask me, *you're* the one who has been seeing too many old movies. You sound like the girl does just after she meets the vampire."

"Don't be silly. There's nothing there to scare

anyone. Come with me and I'll show you."

"No, thanks. I plan to eat my dinner and find a good movie to watch."

Renata sighed. "We rarely talk. Have you ever noticed that? When we do, we end up fighting."

"We aren't fighting. What are you talking about?"

"Never mind." She tested the noodles against the side of the pot to see if they were done.

After dinner Renata put the dishes in the dishwasher and then joined Bob in the living room. The TV was throwing flashes of light against the dark walls. Bob always liked to watch TV in a darkened room. It often gave Renata a headache, but she seldom mentioned it since Bob didn't believe in headaches.

The movie was one about teenagers who seemed to be bent on destroying their high school and whichever members of society got in their way. Renata detested movies like that. It occurred to her that if they were married she could take a book to the bedroom and have several hours of uninterrupted reading, which was appealing. Then she paused mentally. Reading a book alone in bed was nothing to look forward to in a marriage. Not for the first time she wondered if she was making a mistake in marrying Bob.

She could see him from the corner of her

eye. He was chuckling at the movie, thoroughly engrossed in it. How did she really feel about him? The better she came to know him, the less they had in common. What did she really expect to gain from this marriage? Children? Bob only wanted one, and it had to be male. Security? She could supply her own security as well as Bob could. Companionship? Reading alone in bed or watching a boring TV movie could hardly qualify as companionship.

For a minute she considered calling her own mother, but her mother had been so excited at the prospect of finally having Renata married that she hated to burst her bubble. To her mother, marriage was synonymous with happiness and success. She thought wryly that her mother was better suited for Bob than she was. Once he had even suggested that after they were married, she should quit work. Renata had made it abundantly clear that she wouldn't consider such a thing.

Would Bob be happy with her? She had never thought of it from that angle, and she was rather appalled to discover that she doubted that he would be happy at all. She knew he had never considered this, or if he had, he had arrived at the opposite conclusion. Nevertheless, there it was. She wasn't suited for him.

She wondered what she should do. Everyone they knew had been informed of the engagement, and it was generally assumed that the wedding would take place in a few months, if not before. She had worn his engagement ring for almost a year. They had picked out china and silver plate and bought a piece for each other for birthdays and Christmas and other special occasions. She had a dress hanging in her closet that her mother had sent especially for the ceremony—not a long one with lace and flounces, but a dignified cream-white suit that she could use afterwards as well. It was a logical wedding dress.

Renata wasn't sure she wanted to be logical. In fact, slowly but surely, she was becoming convinced that she didn't want to be logical at all—not about this. Logic said she should marry Bob and make everyone but his mother happy. Renata found she wanted more out of life than this. But what?

It was as if a clock were ticking in her ear. She was 30. Middle age was just around the corner, then retirement, then . . . what? She didn't know, but she was positive she wanted to look back on a life that had been more exciting than hers had been up to this point. It struck her as ludicrous that her one deviant behavior in her entire life was that she had started taking walks in a graveyard. She had to smile.

Bob saw her and grinned back. He obviously thought she was laughing at the movie, and Renata let him think what he wished. She decided that she had to make that appointment with Dr. McIntyre as soon as possible, if for no other reason than to reassure herself that she wasn't having some sort of nervous breakdown.

She made a genuine effort to become interested in the ridiculous movie.

Chapter Two

Renata felt nervous as she walked through the door of Dr. Boyd McIntyre's office, despite the pleasant surroundings. The waiting room was tastefully done in soothing pastel colors. A large plant stood in one corner, a rack for magazines in another. Renata tried to look as if she were here for reasons other than seeking professional help as she gave her name to the receptionist behind the glass window.

She sat across from the two women who were already waiting and selected a magazine at random. She knew it was silly to be so nervous, but she had never spoken to a psychologist other than at a party, and Bob had been extremely upset when she had told him she was coming. A glance at the other women told her they were strangers to her and that they seemed far more at ease. Obviously this wasn't their first visit. She wondered why they were here and whether they were to see Dr. McIntyre or one of the other doctors who shared this reception area.

After what seemed to be an interminable time, Renata heard her name called and she rose and followed the woman through the inner door and down the hall. She was led to an office decorated in shades of blue and beige with burgundy accents. Another large plant loomed by the window, and tasteful prints adorned the walls. Along with a large walnut desk which dominated the room, there were a leather recliner and two comfortable-looking chairs in a conversational grouping. When the door closed behind her, the man behind the desk stood up and offered her his hand.

"Boyd McIntyre. What can I do for you?"

Renata tried to smile. She had assumed he would have read the voluminous application form she had filled out while she waited. "I'm Renata O'Neal. I'm here because I've been having trouble sleeping. A friend of mine, Betty Frankenheim, said you helped her stop smoking."

"Ah, yes. Betty. She was here last year. Not smoking again, is she?"

"I don't know. She moved recently, but I don't think she is."

He nodded as he came around the desk and sat in one of the chairs. He motioned for her to do the same. Renata chose the recliner and found herself wondering if this choice might mean something Freudian to Dr. McIntyre.

"You seem nervous. Is this your first visit to a psychologist?"

Elizabeth Crane

"I had hoped it didn't show. Yes, it is. I have to admit my fiancé tried to talk me out of coming." Since she found it remarkably easy to talk to the man, because he was fatherly and had a way of listening as if he were really interested in hearing what she might say, she relaxed somewhat.

"We still get that occasionally, especially in a town the size of Lorain. So how long have you been having trouble sleeping?"

"About three months, off and on. Lately it's been getting worse."

"Often a person is sleeping more than she thinks—little catnaps off and on, naps during the afternoon. Think that may be the case with you?"

"I work all day, so I'm not sleeping then. Usually at night when I can't sleep I turn on the light and read or watch TV. I don't notice any time lapses, so I assume I'm staying awake."

"How about the rest of your life? Job secure?"

"Perfectly. No, I'm not worried about work." She was getting accustomed to his partial sentences.

"How about your fiancé?"

Now he had hit on a nerve, and she shifted in the chair. "Bob is a nice person." There was that word again. "I know that sounds insipid, but it's true. He really is nice."

Dr. McIntyre waited.

"He has good job potential. We're both ac-

30

countants. Our future is compatible."

"You haven't mentioned love."

"Well, of course I love him." Her voice sounded strained, even to her. "I only came to get help for my insomnia, and I don't want to take pills. I understand you use hypnosis?"

"Yes, that's correct. I've had a great deal of success with that method." He looked as if he would rather continue talking about her relationship with Bob. "You do, however, need to deal with the issues that have caused the insomnia. If it's being caused by a physical illness, you need to treat it. When I put you under, I'll give you a post-hypnotic suggestion that if the problem is physiologic, the hypnotism won't work." He smiled. "In that case, it probably wouldn't anyway unless you're an unusually good subject."

"It wouldn't?"

"Hypnotism is subtle. It can't make you do anything against your will, for instance. Some people can't be hypnotized at all, while some go under fast. It depends on your will power and your ability to concentrate. A lot of people doubt they have been under at all until the post-hypnotic suggestion makes the cigarettes taste bitter or food look unappetizing."

"I hope it works. I'm exhausted."

Dr. McIntyre pointed to a lever on the side of the recliner. "Why don't you get comfortable, as if you were going to take a nap. Take off your shoes if you wish, and loosen your belt if it's noticeably tight. Just relax."

Renata slipped her feet out of her shoes and leaned the recliner back. She closed her eyes and felt thoroughly ridiculous.

Dr. McIntyre began to talk to her in a soothing voice. She recognized the technique. Her office had provided a seminar for its employees on meditation techniques, and this wasn't appreciably different. Once she was thoroughly relaxed, he began to count backward, suggesting that she was falling deeper and deeper asleep; that she was allowing herself to be surrounded by feelings of love, that she was floating deeper and deeper to the very core of this feeling.

Renata felt her body relaxing more than she thought possible. Nothing seemed to matter except the doctor's soothing voice and the floating sensation. Time seemed to stand still, and she surrendered completely.

At first she thought the voices she was hearing were outside the office door, but then she realized they were all around her. Barely audible at first, they grew in volume until they were speaking in a normal volume. In her mind she saw the people who were speaking, as if she were in a play.

"Are you listening to me?" a woman with graying, blond hair said.

"I'm listening," Renata said. It seemed natural for her to answer the woman. When she did, the room came into focus. She was in a Victorian bedroom and was gazing out the second-story window.

"This is your wedding day, and I have to tell you what to expect."

Renata had to smile. She wasn't sure why Dr. McIntyre used a technique like this, but she had to admit it was interesting. She turned to face the direction from which the voice was coming.

A woman was standing there, wearing a long dress such as Renata had seen in pictures made in the 1880's. When she looked down at herself, she saw she was indeed wearing a white wedding dress with yards of ruffles and lace and satin roses. She had to admit that the doctor's hypnotism was certainly thorough.

"Callie, pay attention." The woman seemed nervous about what she was about to say. "Nathan is a good man, and you have nothing to fear from him. Love grows in a marriage."

"I love him already," she heard herself say. She was enjoying this.

The woman shook her head impatiently as if she didn't believe Renata. "Tonight when he takes you to his bed . . . all wives go through this. It will hurt more the first time than it will after that."

Renata had to struggle not to laugh. She was no stranger to sex.

"You just be obedient. Do what he tells you to do and he will see to the rest." The woman seemed to think this was instruction enough because she sighed in relief. "Just use that time to plan what you will cook for the next day or think about pleasant memories. It doesn't last very long."

Renata nodded, since she didn't trust herself to speak. Laughter was too close to the surface. She wondered how this was supposed to make her sleep better at night.

"Come on. Everyone is waiting. Molly, you go down between Callie and myself."

Renata noticed a girl in her late teens had come into the room. She wondered why the older woman insisted on calling her Callie. Had Dr. McIntyre misunderstood her name? Yet for some reason the name sounded very familiar.

The woman went to the door and opened it, braced her shoulders and went out. Molly waited a few seconds and followed her. Renata did the same. The upper hall was papered in a hideous print of maroon and navy medallions on a brown background. A side table held a chimneyed lamp, the glass of which was slightly smoky as if it were actually used.

At the head of the stairs Molly paused and let their mother precede them into a room to the left of the entry. Molly leaned toward Renata and whispered, "What did Mama tell you after she sent me out of the room?"

Renata wasn't sure what to say. "She told me to relax and think of England."

Molly frowned. "Why would you want to think about England?"

"I'm kidding. It's what Queen Victoria supposedly told her daughters on their wedding days."

"What does a queen have to do with this? What do you mean 'kidding?' Callie, have you been into the cooking sherry?"

Renata was puzzled and looked around uneasily. This was certainly a vivid fantasy. There were objects in the vestibule below that she would never have thought of for herself.

"Come on. Everyone will think you're having second thoughts." Molly preceded her down the stairs.

Renata paused. "Dr. McIntyre?" she whispered. As if from a long way off she heard a reassuring murmur. As she went down the stairs she wondered why his voice sounded farther away than those around her.

Molly led her into a parlor where several guests were seated in rows of wooden chairs. At the far side of the room stood a man in a dark suit holding a Bible, undoubtedly the preacher. Then she saw Nathan.

He was tall, much taller than the preacher, and he was young and handsome. His hair was black and was longer than Bob had ever worn his, and even though she wasn't close enough to see the color of his eyes, she somehow knew they were a warm brown. His skin was tanned, and he moved as if the suit he wore made him feel uncomfortable, as if he were more at home in a field than in a parlor.

And Renata knew she loved him. The emotion rocked her to the depths of her soul. She had never believed in love at first sight, until now. It was as if she had been created to love this man and no other. They had yet to exchange a word, but she knew she loved him. When his eyes met hers and he smiled, Renata thought her heart would burst.

Slowly she walked down the aisle made by the folding chairs, never taking her eyes from his. A touch at her elbow made her realize an older man had fallen into step with her. Until now she had been unaware of his presence.

Just before reaching the preacher, the older man signaled her to stop. In response to the preacher's question, he announced he was giving the bride to be married.

Renata glanced up at the groom. As she had known, his eyes were brown, a soft brown that held dreams and warmth. She smiled. The older man squeezed her elbow as he stepped away to join the older woman in the front row.

Renata tried to put her mind on the preacher and what he was saying. Who was this man beside her? How had she ever manufactured him out of her psyche? One thing was for certain—she knew now that she didn't love Bob and couldn't marry him. How had Dr. McIntyre known to lead her into a dream like this? Why had he dared do so when she had more or less told him she was there for sleep therapy, not to discuss Bob? It occurred to her that this wasn't ethical, but at the moment she didn't mind.

"Do you, Nathan, take this woman to wed?" the preacher was saying.

"I do," the man replied.

Nathan. His name was Nathan. Somehow she had already known that. She listened while he promised to love and honor her until death would separate them.

"Do you, Callie, take this man to be your husband?"

She nodded as if she were in a dream, her eyes on Nathan. "I do."

"Do you promise to love, honor and obey him? To cleave only unto him until death do you part?"

Renata started to object. She didn't like the obey part, especially since Nathan hadn't been required to do the same. To object seemed out of the question, however, so she said, "I do." The room was growing fuzzy, and the preacher's voice was receding. Only Nathan's face was clear. She leaned toward him to tell him that she would remember, that she would never forget.

"Renata? Are you awake?"

She opened her eyes and sat up. The chair clicked into a sitting position. Dr. McIntyre was leaning over her, the strange expression on his face telling her of his concern. Renata rubbed her forehead as she looked around. Where was the preacher? Where were the people and the fussy Victorian room? Most important, where was Nathan?

"Renata, are you okay?"

She blinked and nodded. "I'm all right, I think."

Dr. McIntyre sat down in his chair, looking both relieved and elated. "I can't believe this. I can't believe what a run of good luck."

"What? What did you say?" She tried to focus her attention on him, but her mind was full of Nathan.

"Do you remember anything?"

"Of course. I saw someone—no, it was me—being married. I was in an old house, but it seemed as if everything was new. There were people and someone named Molly." Her voice drifted. "And Nathan."

The doctor nodded vigorously. "I know. I have it on tape. I always tape my hypnotism sessions in case there are questions later about what was said. I have everything you said right here."

"What time is it? How long have I been here?"

He consulted his watch. "You were under ten minutes."

"Ten minutes? All that took place in ten minutes? That's not possible. I was upstairs longer than that."

"Your voice did fade in and out a bit and you

were talking quite rapidly, but the mind can work so quickly—and of course all this was in your mind, not real time."

"I'm confused." She rubbed her forehead again. She felt as if she were out of place here.

Dr. McIntyre stood, went to a coffee pot and poured two cupfuls. "Cream or sugar?"

"No." Renata glanced around. She had the unsettling sensation that *this* was a dream, not reality. Nathan had been more real to her than was this room. "No, I drink it black."

He handed her a styrofoam cup, and gingerly she sipped it. He said, "Do you realize what a breakthrough this is? We seem to have tapped directly into your subconscious."

"What are you talking about? I only saw the meditation fantasy you led me through."

"But I didn't. I didn't have time to do that. All at once you started talking, describing a scene that must lie dormant in your subconscious wishes. What does this house symbolize for you?"

"Nothing. I saw an actual house. You make it sound as if I were dreaming."

Dr. McIntyre smiled as if he were humoring her. "But you know it couldn't have been an actual house, don't you? I mean, you never left my office. Describe your parents' house to me."

She shifted impatiently. "It's a brick ranch-style, one story, and no one has ever been married in the living room."

"I see, I see." He tapped his front teeth with the end of his pen. "Nathan. What does that name call up for you?"

"He was the groom."

"No, no, no. I mean do you have an uncle or some other family member by that name? Has a Nathan ever been employed by your parents?"

"Never. I've never known anyone by that name. I also don't know anyone named Molly, and if I was going to fantasize a wedding, I would see myself and my fiancé. And what does all this have to do with insomnia?"

McIntyre made a distracted humming noise as he seemed to be trying to come up with some sort of connection. "The mind is very complex. It defies a simple explanation in almost every instance. At some time you must have read about this scene you described, or perhaps you saw it in a movie. Subconsciously, you filed it away, and now the memory of it is exerting itself."

She stared at him. "That doesn't make any sense at all." She shook her head. "I'm sorry, but I don't believe in all that. Did you cure my insomnia or not?"

"I have no idea." He made a shooing motion with his hand as if her objections were wearing his patience thin. "Listen." He pressed a button to rewind the tape recorder and another to make it play back.

The woman's voice was unlike Renata's. It was softer and had a more southern cadence.

She was describing the scene Renata had just witnessed.

"Who is that?" she demanded. "That's not me."

"Yes, it is. I thought you might be a difficult subject, so I spent more time than usual in talking you under. All at once you started to talk, and you can hear the results."

"How can that be me? What does it mean? I'm confused."

"We all sound odd to ourselves on tape. I've often heard voices that alter remarkably when the subject is under hypnotism. What we have to figure out is what it means to you."

Renata frowned. "It means nothing to me. I don't understand it at all."

"It must. You can hear yourself talking. There's no one else it could mean anything to in the least. Do you want to hear it again?"

"No." Renata looked at the black tape recorder. It looked like any other one as far as she could tell. "Maybe it recorded wrong or . . ."

"I'm telling you, it's your voice. It was coming out of your mouth."

Renata didn't know what to say. To deny it further seemed futile, especially since the vision had seemed so real to her. She *had* stood beside Nathan and looked into his eyes. She had fallen in love with him.

"I want you to come back." Dr. McIntyre was thumbing through his desk calendar. "My earliest appointment is next Tuesday. Two o'clock."

"I have to work then. My job, remember?"

"Yes, I forgot about that. After hours then? I could stay late on . . ." He ruffled the pages. "On Wednesday. Could you come Wednesday at, say, six o'clock? We wouldn't be as rushed then. I have no appointments that night."

"I don't know. I still feel confused. I feel as if I belong in that other time."

"I believe you've tapped into some important symbology. I've never seen anyone do it so quickly. In my opinion your insomnia is the symptom of some deeper problem. You're wise to tackle it before it tackles you." He smiled and light reflected off his glasses. "Metaphorically speaking. Think again. You've never known a Molly or a Nathan? Surely you've heard these names before. In what context?"

"I'm not kin to anyone named Molly, and none of my family ever lived in Lorain as these people seem to do. I'm from Joachin, Texas. I'm positive the house I was seeing is here in Lorain." She paused. "How do I know that? I've never seen that house before."

"What about this Nathan? He would seem to be the most important. Are you positive he doesn't ring a bell?"

Did he ever, she thought. Love at first sight rings bells all over the place. To the doctor she said, "The name is vaguely familiar, but I can't recall why. So is the name Callie." Suddenly a light went on in her head. "The graves! Their names are on the graves."

Dr. McIntyre frowned. "What graves?"

"It's silly, really. I like to walk in graveyards." She noticed he maintained his professional calm. "I found a particularly interesting one behind the chapel near my apartment. There are graves there marked Nathan and Callie Blue. I'm sure it must be the same people." She felt a sharp pain. Nathan was dead?

"And you go there often?"

"Occasionally," she hedged. "It's just something I do." She caught her breath. "Could I have been this Callie person in another life?"

Dr. McIntyre shook his head firmly. "No, no. I can't buy reincarnation. Not at all."

"You can't believe in reincarnation and yet you think I'm dredging up subconscious scenes complete with names, faces and all five senses? Give me a break!"

"I think the best thing will be to put you under again. Wednesday, if possible. Then let's see what we have."

Renata stood. Her legs felt shaky, but otherwise she was fine. "Wednesday, then." As she left the office she saw the doctor go to his desk and begin scrawling notes on a yellow pad. She shook her head. She hoped he wasn't a mental case himself. Subconscious, indeed.

At dinner that night Bob asked, "How did it go? Did he cure your sleep problem?"

"How should I know? I haven't been to bed

yet. I'm sorry. I didn't mean to snap at you. I have something on my mind."

"The good doctor didn't make a pass at you, did he?" Bob sounded as if he were only half-teasing.

"No, of course not. Nothing like that." She paused. "While I was under I began to talk in a different voice. He has it all on tape."

"A different voice? You mean as in a split personality?"

"No, he said it was my subconscious. I seemed to be in a house and that it was all happening a hundred years ago." She smiled. "You should have heard the premarital advice my 'mother' gave me. It's no wonder Victorian women weren't particularly happy sexual partners."

"What do you mean, your mother? You dreamed about Mrs. O'Neal?"

"Not my real mother now. Another woman. I had never seen her before." Renata laughed and pushed her plate away. "According to Dr. McIntyre, she has probably been dead seventy years or so."

"Are we talking ghosts here? What kind of doctor is he?"

"I don't know what happened. He counted me down, and suddenly I was somehow describing a wedding that took place a hundred years ago." Her voice trailed off. She couldn't explain Nathan to Bob. The memory was too precious to her to risk Bob's ridicule. She stood and began removing the dishes. Bob made no move to help her.

"I told you he was a quack. Next time maybe you'll listen to me. He sounds like a nut."

"But it was so real. Bob, I used the names on those graves I told you about."

"Now it's beginning to make sense. Those names are in your brain and so are the dates when those people lived. He did something wrong when he counted you down, and you supplied the names and a scene to go with them. A wedding, did you say? That's explainable, too. You're engaged, and we will be married in the near future. As for the house, you keep saying you want a Victorian monstrosity. What could be plainer? I'm a better shrink than Dr. McWhatever."

Renata had to admit that what Bob said made sense. It was logical. It didn't explain Molly, whose grave she had never seen. She didn't know if Callie had even had a sister or not. Nor did it explain the presence of objects that Renata couldn't identify, such as a scissor-looking contraption on the dresser and a wooden frame that had been suspended from the ceiling in the back parlor.

Renata almost dropped the plates. How had she known about that wooden frame? She hadn't been anywhere near the back parlor. Bob's logical explanations suddenly seemed to lose their credibility, because now that she tried, she could remember several other rooms in that house and she didn't seem to be imagining them. Certainly she would never have thought up that hideous wallpaper in the upper hall. She decided to keep her appointment for the coming Wednesday after all.

That night Renata had a dream. She was living in a large farmhouse and could hear a rooster crowing out back. Again she wore a long skirt, this time a dark green one, and a white cotton blouse that fit high at the neck and covered her wrists. She was drawing water from a well inside a wide side porch.

As she hummed a song Renata had never heard before, a man's arms slipped around her waist, and she laughed as he kissed her on the neck. "Nathan, stop that," she pretended to scold. "I'll spill this whole bucket of water."

Nathan drew back and easily lifted the heavy bucket from her hands. Renata felt herself smile at him, and although she wanted to put her arms around him and kiss him, she made herself walk beside him into the house. Nathan put the bucket on the cupboard counter and looked at the stove. "Beans again?"

"They smell good, don't they?" In her dream Renata circled around the table so it stood between Nathan and herself. "Are you hungry?"

His eyes told her he was hungry for her rather than for the beans. "Are you in a hurry to eat?"

The words came spilling out of her mouth. "Now, Nathan, don't start that at this time of day. Why, it's still daylight out. If you eat fast, you'll have time to mend my clothesline before dark." Renata wanted to take back the words, but a veil had already fallen in place behind his eyes.

"All right."

She put the beans and a pan of golden cornbread on the table, sat down and began to eat. All the time she was screaming inside that she wanted to hold him and kiss him and that she didn't care if the clothesline never got fixed. Instead she ate methodically and in silence. Nathan did the same. When he was finished, he went outside. She put down her fork and lowered her face into her hands and cried without making a sound, because she knew she was doing everything wrong and couldn't seem to stop herself.

Renata awoke with her face damp with tears. For a long time she lay there staring up at the ceiling. The dream had been so real. It was as if she had been another person, a woman named Callie, and she still ached to hold Nathan. Why hadn't she kissed him while she had the chance? She seemed to have been stopped not by her own inclination, but rather by convention, as if she thought he would disapprove of it. But Renata could tell he had wanted her to make love with him and would have swept her away to the bedroom if she had given him the slightest encouragement.

She sat up and drew her knees up under the covers. Why was she thinking all of this as if the dream had been real? Bob would blame it on the chop suey they had eaten at dinner. Even in a dream it wasn't like Renata to deny her feelings. Why had she acted as if she were someone else?

She lay back down and curled into a knot on her side. At least she could report to Dr. McIntyre that she had slept, but she almost wished she hadn't. Her body ached for Nathan, and she didn't even know who he was.

Chapter Three

After dreaming of Nathan for four nights in a row, Renata decided she had to know more about this man and his wife. A search of the parish courthouse records revealed their marriage had taken place in 1884. Based on the birth dates on their tombstones, Nathan would have been 24 and Callie 22 at that time. The thought brought a smile to her face. It was obvious from the attitude Callie's mother had shown prior to the wedding that she had considered her daughter to be an old maid and was thankful Callie had found a husband at all. Renata wondered what the mother would have thought about her being 30 and not able to decide whether or not to marry a successful man.

"Times have changed," she murmured to herself. When an office clerk looked up, Renata pretended to have been reading aloud from the records. Talking to herself was becoming a bad habit and one she would have to break if she intended to marry Bob.

Lately that had become more doubtful. She

had been edgy with him the last few days. The little irritating things he did had become magnified, and she was heartily sick of hearing what his mother thought about everything, especially how much his mother had liked the house Bob had picked out, which Renata still had not seen. She knew Bob wasn't doing anything that he hadn't done before, but now these things bothered her more than she would have thought possible. The fact of the matter was that Bob wasn't Nathan.

As Renata replaced the record book on the shelf, she decided she had to forget about Nathan. Not only was he inaccessible to her, he was inaccessible to everyone. He had been dead 53 years.

She checked her wristwatch and decided she could still make it to the library since it was open late on Fridays. Tucking her purse under her arm, she thanked the clerk and was on her way.

The library was only three blocks away, but since it was on the way home, there was no reason to walk, especially since she was wearing new heels that hurt her feet and the air was damp and chilly. As soon as she was in the car, she slipped her feet out of the shoes and rubbed her toes. Renata had never liked wearing heels, and she promised herself that when and if she ever had her own accounting firm, she would have a less stringent dress code for herself and her employees.

She parked near the door of the library and hurried in out of the cold. The librarian looked up and smiled in recognition.

"Hi, Jean. Do you have any way to trace a family that used to live here in town?"

"We usually just ask the relatives. Most families have an oral history. What family is it?"

"Callie and Nathan Blue. I don't think there are any relatives." It had never occurred to her that their descendants might live in Lorain. "Callie died in 1887 and Nathan in 1939."

"Let's see what we can find."

After an hour's search Renata had learned that Callie and Nathan had died childless, as she had assumed, and that he indeed had never remarried. Callie's sister Molly had married, but the name of her husband was smudged and unreadable. She had given birth to five children, three of whom lived to adulthood. Her eldest daughter had married a man in Lorain, the other daughter and son marrying out of state.

"Can we find this daughter?" Renata asked. "She seems to have stayed in Lorain at least for a while."

The librarian nodded. "I've always liked genealogical research. It's like unraveling a mystery." She glanced at the clock on the wall. "We have two hours before closing. Let's give it a try."

By the time the library closed, Renata had the name of Molly's eldest daughter and her husband. Their second son had stayed in Lorain, as had two of his children. One of the children was still alive and lived on Main Street.

Renata sat in her car and reread the information several times. Molly's great-granddaughter was named Emma Blanders and would be 71 now. That meant she was almost 18 years-old when Nathan died. Renata's fingers felt cold, but she knew it had nothing to do with the weather. Emma Blanders would have known Nathan personally.

She rested her forehead on the steering wheel. Did she dare intrude on Emma's life? She had no reason to bother the woman except curiosity. What if Emma became upset that Renata had been looking into her family history? Renata told herself that was silly; the records had been in the library and were public knowledge. Still, people had a right to their privacy. It was one thing to do research and another to contact a stranger with personal questions.

Renata was to go to Bob's house after dinner. As she ate a sandwich, she watched the evening news. Then she brushed her teeth, switched off the TV and slipped on her jacket. Her tennis shoes made almost no noise on the metal steps outside of her apartment. She could see a few of the brighter stars past the silent glare of the lights in the parking lot and was glad she had moved to Lorain rather than to a city. In a city the stars would be all but invisible.

Bob also lived in an apartment, but his was in a newer unit. Bob liked everything as modern as possible. At one time Renata had found this amusing and had teased him that he would eventually recycle her as well. Bob hadn't found that funny, and Renata no longer did either.

She used her key to his door and called out as she stepped in. "Are you here?"

"Come on in."

She found Bob in the bedroom he used as a den. As usual, he was watching TV. "What's on?"

"*Night Child.* It's a mystery. If you want a piece of pie, there's one in the refrigerator." He glanced at her and smiled.

"No, thanks. When did you start baking pies?"

"Mother brought it over."

Renata wisely made no comment. She slipped out of her jacket and sat on the couch beside him. He automatically put his arm around her, and she slid down until she could rest her head on his shoulder. The movie looked as if it would have been good had she caught the first of it, but it was half over. Try as she might, she couldn't understand the plot, and when the mystery was solved, the killer turned out to be someone she had only seen briefly.

"That was a good one," Bob commented as a commercial came on.

"I wish I had seen the beginning of it. How was your day?"

"Fine. Tax season is already starting. We'll be swamped in a couple of weeks."

"Tell me about it," she said wryly. "My office works around the clock between now and the deadline." She smiled. "Guess what I found out today."

"You're pregnant and we have to get married right away."

"Be serious."

"I'm no good at guessing. What?"

"Molly Graham's great-granddaughter is still alive and lives right here in Lorain."

"Who's Molly Graham? I never heard of her."

"She was Callie Blue's sister. This Emma Blanders would have know Nathan Blue."

Bob stopped smiling. "Are you back on that again?"

"But it's fascinating. I can't understand why you aren't interested."

"Renata," he said in a strained voice, "all this business about the Blues is nonsense. Okay. So there was a Callie and a Nathan Blue. So what? Your subconscious supplied a story for McIntyre and he ran with it. Big deal."

"It wasn't like that. I'm telling you I actually heard what was going on, and I saw things from Callie's eyes."

"Right. And Bridey Murphy is your first cousin."

"I'm serious about this, Bob. I wish you would be, too."

"I told you not to go to that jerk in the first

place. Betty Frankenheim may be a friend of yours, but she has some pretty far out ideas. Remember when she told you she had seen a UFO?"

"I don't see why you have to be so close-minded on everything. Can't you admit there may be something beyond what you can see and touch?"

"Okay, so now that you know the name of Emma Blanders what do you intend to do? Go see her? Tell her about her great-grandparents' wedding?"

"Callie and Nathan were her aunt and uncle. She's descended from Molly." Renata's voice was stiff; she was trying hard not to lose her temper.

"I just hope you don't have any intention of bothering that woman. She'll think you're crazy."

"Like you do?"

Bob paused. "Let's not fight. You know how I detest arguments."

"I don't enjoy them either, but sometimes they're necessary." She glared at him.

"Maybe we should call it an early evening."

Renata glared at him. "You're telling me to go home?" she demanded.

"No, I'm trying to keep peace."

Renata abruptly stood up and grabbed her jacket off the chair. "Fine. You stay here and enjoy your peace and quiet. I'm going home." She hesitated at the doorway. "Has it ever occurred to you that when we are married we will be confined to the same house whether you want peace or not?"

Bob's frown deepened, and Renata left him with his thoughts.

She knew she was going to see Emma Blanders from the time Bob told her not to do it. The street was one that meandered through the center of town, and her address was easy to find. Renata looked at the house from the window of her car, trying to decide whether she was making a mistake. Before she could change her mind, she opened the car door and headed up the walk.

Emma Blanders answered the door. "Yes?" she said.

"Mrs. Blanders, you don't know me. My name is Renata O'Neal, and I'm interested in your family history. Would you mind talking to me?"

Emma hesitated. "Why are you interested in my family?"

This was the question Renata had dreaded. "I moved to Lorain about ten years ago, and I've been interested in its history ever since. I understand your family has been in this town for quite a while."

Emma opened the screen door. "Come in. Have a seat. Yes, my family was one of Lorain's founders. You've come to the right place."

Renata smiled. "The period I'm most interested in are the years after the Civil War."

"You certainly came to the right place. My great-grandmother was a dedicated correspondent. I have a trunk full of her letters upstairs. She kept not only the ones she received, but the first draft of all the ones she wrote. I started to do away with them a few years back, but then I decided to will them to the library after I die. Somebody may be interested in them one day." Her wrinkled face smiled. "And here you are."

"I know this is a great imposition on you, but if I could read the letters, I would be so grateful." She could hardly believe her good fortune.

"Of course you may. Naturally I have to insist that the letters remain here in my house, but you are welcome to read them here. What are you planning to do? Write a book?"

"Perhaps," Renata answered evasively.

"Just spell the names right. You can't know how exasperating it is to have your name misspelled." Emma laughed. "I guess it comes from being a retired English teacher."

Renata followed her up the stairs. The house was comfortable but not expensively furnished. It was exactly the sort of home she had pictured Molly's great-granddaughter as having. She wondered why she thought that. Several times in the past few days she seemed to have known facts that she couldn't recall having known before.

"If I'm not mistaken, your great-grandmother was Molly Graham," Renata said as casually as possible.

"That's right. Molly Irene Graham. Her parents were Ida Wilson Graham and William Graham. Sometimes the 'Wilson' and 'William' confuse people. Wilson was her maiden name, you see." She pushed open a door at the top of the stairs. The room was scrupulously clean and smelled of lavender sachet. "That's the trunk. I'll let you wrestle with it. The cold gets in my bones these days. If it's too chilly up here, plug in that heater over there."

"Thank you." Renata was staring at the trunk. For some reason it looked familiar to her. She went to it and slowly lifted the lid. The interior was lined in green rather than in pink as she had expected, but the paper seemed newer than the trunk. She heard Emma leave to go back downstairs, but she didn't turn her head. Half-memories were rushing at her. Although she tried, she couldn't quite catch one of them. She sat on the floor and opened the first letter.

Emma had been right. Molly had kept every scrap of correspondence. Most of the letters were the inconsequential type that could have been thrown away without any great loss. When she opened one addressed to an Alma Graham, she knew it had been worth the search.

Reflections in Time

My Dear Alma,

It seems like so long ago since you were here. I hope Aunt Ellie and Uncle Dodd are well. Mother sends you all her Love.

We have a sadness, I'm afraid. Callie is no longer expecting a child. Jemima Blue was here yesterday, and she told me more than Mother ever would have dared. You know how Jemima is. It seems Callie lifted a heavy basket of wash and it was too much for her. We are all quite distraut as it seemed this time she would become a mother. Jemima has been quite a source of information, and I'm sure she would be in great trouble if anyone knew she told me all this. At any rate, Callie's hopes are dashed again. Please don't be angry at me for writing in such a forthright manner, but I knew you would want to know.

"I've found a new recipe for rose water—

Renata stopped reading and shook her head. Hadn't Callie known not to overextend at a time like that? She recalled the marital advice Ida had given her and knew Callie had probably had no better instructions as to how to take care of herself during pregnancy.

Renata lay the letter down. She felt strange reading something from the pen of the teenager she had seen at the wedding. At the same time, she felt as if she knew Molly and maybe Alma as well. Was Bob right in saying she was fabricating this entire story? What if Dr. McIntyre had given her some sort of post-hypnotic instruction to make her imagine these things? She knew that was impossible when she thought about it, because the entire session was on tape and she had listened to it all.

Could it be that there really was something to reincarnation? Renata had never given it much thought. She didn't disbelieve in it; she just had never been interested enough to consider it. If it was true, wasn't it likely that she had been Callie Blue in a past life? The idea felt so right that she shivered. She felt as if she were on the brink of a great discovery. Picking up another letter she read:

Dear Cousin Alma,

I know you will say I am fickle and laugh at me for it, but I have quite forgotten Albert Downs and have a new beau altogether. His name is Ennis Hite, and he is quite unlike Albert. He is a bit older than I am so you can see why I find him fascinating. He has black hair and a remarkable moustache. Callie is quite against my seeing him, but she refuses to say why. At one time Ennis showed some interest in her, but that was a long time ago and she is a married woman now. I never would have thought Callie could be the jealous type. Would you?

I can hardly wait for you to meet Ennis. Will you come to Lorain soon?"

Best Wishes,
Molly

Renata returned the letter to its envelope. From other references Callie didn't appear to have been small-minded enough to dislike the romance for that reason, but then again Renata knew of no other reason.

On one side of the box, as if it had been hastily thrust in, was a letter folded and penned in Molly's slanted handwriting. Renata was into the letter before she realized what she was reading

Dear Alma,

I have dreadful news. Mother and Father are beside themselves and have asked me to write and tell you of our sorrow. There has been a terrible accident and we have lost our Callie. I know this is a shock to you, but I know of no other way in which to tell you.

Three days ago Ennis and I had planned an outing with Callie and Nathan. As I told you in an earlier letter, Ennis has bought a parcel of land adjoining Nathan's land, and we were to build a house there and be neighbors. We had planned a picnic on our land, and the men were to mark off the

foundation of the house.

I'm still not entirely sure what happened. Callie mounted her horse and rode away, I think to look at the site from a different angle. We believe the horse threw her. Ennis went to search for her when we saw the horse returning alone. By the time I reached her side, she was gone. A large rock lay by her head, and Ennis said she must have struck it when she fell.

Please forgive me for delivering this dreadful news in so frank a manner, but we are all shocked by our loss and I can think of no other words to use to tell you.

My heart goes out to Nathan. I have never seen a man so broken by grief. If it is indeed possible to die of a broken heart, then Nathan will soon be gone as well.

Sorrowfully,
Molly

Renata sat back. Her stomach was knotted, and tears filled her eyes. Because Renata wasn't a woman to cry easily, she impatiently brushed the tears away. She reminded herself that Callie had died over 100 years ago and that it was foolish to cry for her now. Nevertheless, she felt a personal anguish.

She reread the letter again. Something about it did not ring true, but she was not sure what bothered her about it. True, Nathan was only mentioned as having been included in the outing, but he might have returned to his house for some reason and been gone when Molly and Ennis found Callie's body— or perhaps he was present and Molly simply had not mentioned him. Judging by the way the handwriting wavered, Molly was indeed affected by shock. Her tone was more than sad, however. It seemed to be withdrawn, as if she were repeating phrases she found necessary but abhorrent. Renata told herself that was understandable under the circumstances.

The dates on the letters suddenly skipped almost a full year. Renata thumbed through the remaining letters to see if any were out of place, but there weren't.

Renata read through the remaining ones. For no apparent reason the friendly, happy tone of the letters was altered. Molly had apparently been widowed and was about to remarry. The groom wasn't named and the letter, which was from Alma, sounded stilted and more formal than any of the previous ones. Had the cousins had an argument? Renata thought it was likely though no disagreement was mentioned. After that time the letters became more infrequent and ended in 1929 when Molly died.

Renata put the letters back in the trunk in order. She still didn't know much about Callie and Nathan other than what Molly had been willing to tell her cousin. She remembered the courthouse records where the name of

Molly's husband had been smeared. Now the man wasn't mentioned at all. She shook her head. Surely she was reading more into it than the matter warranted. Many records from the 1800's were less well-documented than this.

When she went back downstairs, Emma was waiting for her in the front room. "Did you enjoy reading the letters?" the older woman said.

"Yes, thank you. I can't begin to tell you what this has meant to me." She hesitated since the next part was tricky. "A Nathan Blue is mentioned. His wife was Callie? Do you recall ever meeting him?"

Emma laughed. "Uncle Nat? Why, sure. He was my favorite uncle. Great-great uncle, I should say. He didn't die until I was a senior in high school. He was seventy-nine and was as sharp as a tack and never lost his hair or his eyesight. His hair was the prettiest silver-gray I ever saw. A tall man. Well over six feet. There will never be another one like him, more's the pity."

"What about Callie?"

"She died young, poor thing. I gather Uncle Nat loved her to distraction because he never married again. He was sought after by the ladies, I can tell you—right up to the end, in fact—but he never gave one of them a second glance. I never knew Callie, of course—I don't even have a picture of her—but according to family stories she was reckoned to be a beauty."

Renata's heart leaped into her throat. "Na-than—do you have a photo of Nathan?"

"Why, as a matter of fact, I do." Emma led the way back into the part of the house she used most often. "I haven't looked at the photo album in years, but I know it's here." She studied a cluttered bookshelf that took up most of one wall in the small den. "Here it is." She reached up and pulled out an old album.

Renata sat beside her on the couch. Her heart was racing at the prospect of seeing Nathan's picture. If he looked like the man she had seen under hypnotism she could be sure something out of the ordinary had happened in Dr. McIntyre's office.

Emma turned the yellowed pages slowly. "So many memories. This is my mother. She died when I was only seven. I can barely remember her, but I recall Uncle Nat saying she reminded him of Molly."

Renata studied the picture, but it was blurry as if the camera had moved as the shutter was being triggered. She could see no resemblance between this woman and the teenager she'd seen in the Victorian house. Doubts began to creep in.

"This one is of my stepmother. She was good to us. She was one of the Brockfields from over in Baton Rouge." She turned more pages. "I know it's here somewhere."

The page turned and Renata saw a man with silver hair and great dignity. Her heart leaped into her throat. He looked older and tired, but his eyes were still the warm brown she remembered, and his mouth looked as if he were accustomed to smiling often.

"That's him," Emma said triumphantly. "Didn't I tell you he was handsome?"

"Yes," Renata whispered, "he was certainly handsome." The tears were threatening her again so she stood up. "I want to thank you again for letting me read the letters and see the photos. I can't tell you how much help you've been."

"Glad to oblige. People these days don't put much stock in family, but I was raised in a different generation, a different time altogether." She shook her head as she walked Renata to the front door.

Thoughts were flooding into Renata's head. She had known what Nathan looked like! She had seen him and it had been no fabrication of her imagination. Again she wondered if reincarnation was the answer to this puzzle. If so, then she was talking to her own great-great niece. Renata looked at Emma with interest but she could see no resemblance to anyone she had seen during her trance.

As she drove home, Renata wondered at how it all fit together—Callie being married at home, not in a church; Nathan looking the way she had known he would. What did it mean, and most of all what would happen now? She counted off the days until she could return to McIntyre's office. How could she wait until the middle of the week to try and return to Nathan?

She wasn't going to tell Bob what she had learned. In the first place he still wouldn't believe her, and in the second, he would be upset over her going to Emma's house.

When she reached her apartment her phone was ringing. When she raced to answer it, she found Bob on the other end.

"I was about to give up. What are you doing this afternoon?"

"I don't know, Bob. I guess I'll clean house and catch up on my reading."

"I have a better idea. Let's go see that house I told you about."

Renata hesitated. She didn't want to see it; she wanted to think about Nathan, but she could hardly tell Bob that. "Okay. When will you pick me up?"

"I can be there in fifteen minutes."

"All right. I'll be waiting." She hung up and tried not to be disgruntled over spending the afternoon with the man she had promised to marry.

As he had promised, Bob arrived in exactly fifteen minutes. Punctuality was important to him. She got in the car, and they drove to the Kingwood addition. As she had said, every third or fourth house was built to the same floor plan, although the facades varied.

"I like this one. It's Colonial." Bob parked on the mud-spattered driveway.

"Somehow I couldn't see you choosing the Spanish or Tudor style." She studied the house. It was made of the type brick that was supposed to look antique, and the trim was painted white. Green plastic shutters flanked the front windows, and an empty window box hung beneath the kitchen window. The lawn was raw earth that had been sodded in patches of St. Augustine grass, and a spindly maple tree was guy-wired to stand erect.

"It's great, isn't it?" Bob was already getting out of the car and walking toward the house.

"Are we going inside? Is it open?"

"Sure, come on. The workmen are still finishing the interior."

She followed him into the house. It smelled new. The walls were all an off-white, and the carpet was beige. The tiny living room had a crystal light fixture and traces of spray paint on the windows. The entry was paved in terra cotta tile, and overhead was a smaller replica of the light fixture in the living room.

"I can put my bookcase over there," Bob explained, "and my living room furniture will fit perfectly in here." He enthusiastically led her farther into the house. "Look at this den!"

The room was large, with a fireplace in one corner and a sliding glass door on the back wall. At the far end was a counter top which divided the den from the kitchen. The flooring was one of the no-wax sheet vinyls in shades of beige and tan. The walls were paneled on two sides in imitation oak, and there were built-in bookshelves on either side of the fireplace. The other solid wall was the off-white. Renata made no comment. For a new house it was pretty, if predictable.

The kitchen was all electric, and the cabinets were an odd shade of yellow. She remembered to smile.

"The bedrooms are back here," Bob said. He dodged a painter coming down the hall and motioned for Renata to follow him.

"I thought this one would be good for the baby." Bob pulled at his lower lip as he always did when he was planning something. "This larger one will be Mother's"

"Then she really is planning to move in here?"

"Not at first, of course. I'm referring to the years ahead."

"It seems to me that our baby, assuming we have one, should have the larger room. Babies have toys and need room to play."

"But Mother has all that furniture and things she can never bear to part with. She will be crowded in here as it is."

Renata kept quiet, although she was beginning to do a slow burn.

"Our room is down here." He led her past an off-white bathroom into the largest room. "My bed will go there, my dresser there."

"Where will mine go?" she asked.

"What?"

"Just teasing." She couldn't make herself smile. The bedroom windows looked over the bare backyard. A scrawny Chinese tallow tree was propped up to one side.

"Look in here," Bob called from beyond the opposite door.

Renata went after him and saw a large pass-through closet that led to another off-white bathroom. "I think I'm getting snow blind," she said. "Don't people use color any more?"

"We can use colorful accents."

"Your furniture is shades of brown and your bedspread is beige."

"Not everyone wants to live in a crayon rainbow like you do. I like my color scheme."

"Bob, I have to think about this. I'm not sure I like this house."

"What? How can you not like it? It's a great house," he said defensively. "It's perfect."

"Can't you see that I want us to pick out one together? I don't want you to make all the decisions and tell me what we're going to do. The house is pretty, but it has no personality or charm."

"You think charm requires rotting wood and crumbly gingerbread trim."

"That's not true. I would love to live in an old house, but if you are set against it, I'm willing to compromise." She waved her arm at the off-white walls. "This isn't compromise."

"I told the owner that I'd let him know if we want it today."

Renata frowned at him. "Why did you do that? I don't want to rush into an important decision like this. I haven't seen any other houses to compare this one with."

"I have, and this one is not only pretty—it's a steal. If we wait it will be snapped up by someone else."

"I say we let them have it."

"I say we buy it." He set his jaw and glared at her.

Renata sighed. "Bob, listen to us. We can't even choose a house without arguing. Maybe we're making a mistake."

Bob took her into his arms and kissed the side of her head. "You're overworked, that's all. Brides always have the jitters, I hear. Everything will be fine after we're married."

Renata no longer believed him.

Chapter Four

McIntyre was so excited he could hardly contain himself. "You're positive? This Nathan Blue looked exactly like the photo you saw?"

"He was older, but yes. It was Nathan."

"This is wonderful! Stupendous! Do you have any idea what this means? We can tap in on any time in history."

"I don't see where you get that. I'm telling you, I think I saw what I did because I must have been Callie Blue in a previous life."

McIntyre nodded impatiently. It was evident that he didn't agree with her. "Let's get to it. Lie back in the recliner. I'm going to count you down deeper than before."

Renata lay back willingly and tried to become calm. She was going to see Nathan again.

The doctor began, first relaxing her, then talking her into a deep hypnotic state. She heard his voice growing fainter and fainter. He was saying something about Williamsburg and the Declaration of Independence, but she fastened her mind on Nathan. She was going to see Nathan again.

First she heard the birds and after that the stream as it gurgled along over rocks and mossy logs. Renata opened her eyes.

She was standing beside a stream and next to her was a black iron pot lying on its side. A large basket of wet clothes was at her feet, and when the breeze shifted directions, smoke from the remains of a fire filled her nostrils and momentarily stung her eyes. Renata felt dizzy and vaguely nauseated. Slowly she sat down on a log and waited to see if she was going to be sick.

She held out her hand and stared at it. Her fingers were shorter, and her nails, no longer painted, were cut short in smooth crescents. On the ring finger of her left hand she saw a plain gold wedding band. Renata shook her head, hoping to clear her muddled thoughts. She didn't recall feeling disoriented the time before when she saw the wedding. Then she had been able to hear McIntyre's voice when she felt panicky. "Dr. McIntyre?" she whispered. There was no response.

Looking around, Renata found she was at the edge of some woods, and beyond she could see a sloping meadow where green grass waved in a breeze and wildflowers nodded at its passing. On the crest of the hill was a farmhouse. She had no idea where she was.

"Callie?" a voice called out.

She wheeled so fast she almost fell off the log. Nathan was standing behind her, watching her with a concerned expression on his face.

"Are you all right?"

"Yes," she stammered. "I just didn't hear you come up behind me."

"Are you finished washing the clothes?"

She looked at the basket and at the iron pot. "Yes, I'm finished." She hoped it was true because she had no idea how to go about washing clothes in a stream.

Nathan kicked more dirt on the dying fire and picked up the large basket of wet clothes. "You shouldn't be carrying such a heavy load. I thought we agreed you would make several trips instead."

"I was in a hurry," she said, hoping her answer made sense to him. She still had that odd sensation as if time were speeding by her, yet she felt curiously suspended in it.

He turned and began walking toward the meadow. Renata studied the house atop the hill more closely. Since no other house was in sight, she assumed this was where Callie and Nathan lived. She had taken only a couple of steps when she stumbled. Callie's smaller body moved differently than Renata's taller one, and she wasn't used to keeping her long skirt from tangling in the weeds and briars. Quickly regaining her balance, she hurried to catch up with Nathan.

"I know you're worried about Molly," he said,

"but try not to let her know."

She had no idea what he was talking about. "How do you feel about it?" she fished.

"You know how I feel."

"Will you tell me again?"

"Ennis Hite has never been my friend. What you ever saw in him, I'll never know. I guess your families being friends and all made the difference, but I don't trust the man."

Renata was thankful she had managed to locate Emma Blanders and read Molly's letters so she had some clue as to who Nathan was talking about. "That was it. Mother always expected me to marry him."

Nathan laughed. "Since when do you call her 'Mother?' "

"I meant to say 'my mother.' " She cautioned herself to be more careful. She had been so attentive as to how to react about this Ennis that she had made a mistake. She wondered what Callie called her mother and what other mistakes she was likely to make before McIntyre counted her back. "Could you tell me what time it is?"

"Time?" He squinted at the sun. "Going on three o'clock, I'd say. Molly is always late. Don't worry so much."

So she would soon see Molly again. She wondered if her sister would notice the difference in her and whether Ennis would be with her. Even more important, why was Callie worrying about Molly?

"Aren't you going to ask why I'm back to the house so early?"

"I was just about to do that."

"Janie has already foaled. You have a little chestnut filly."

Renata had visited on her grandparents' farm in Texas enough to know he was talking about horses. "That's great. When can I see her?"

Nathan glanced down at her. "Any time you want to. You know the way to the barn."

"Of course. How silly of me." She could see several out buildings now that they were closer to the house. The larger one with a fence around it must be the one he meant. "If you came from the barn, why didn't I see you coming across the meadow?"

Again he gave her a searching look. "I spoke to you as I passed, and you answered me. I went to see if the fishing hole is low on water."

Another mistake! If she weren't careful, he would become suspicious, and then what would she do? She didn't want to spoil this. "Was it?" she ventured.

"Nope. Looks good. I saw an old catfish near the bottom. We can go fishing tomorrow if you'd like."

"Maybe. We'll see." Fishing wasn't high on her list of things she would like to do.

"You're still mad at me," he confirmed. "Callie, you stay mad longer than any woman I ever knew. If you'd just say what's on your mind, I swear we would get along better."

76

She didn't know how to answer this so she kept quiet in hopes he would give her a clue.

"I know you're still upset over losing that baby, but things like that happen. You weren't being punished for enjoying our lovemaking. That's all wrong."

Renata stared at him. She couldn't see how Callie or any other woman could be married to Nathan and not want to make love with him. She thought it was a pity she wouldn't be there long enough to lie beside him in the dark. The thought made her pulse race. She wanted to tell him how much she was attracted to him, but she didn't want to make matters any worse for Callie when she returned. Maybe Callie didn't want to make up with him.

Nathan carried the basket around the house to the clothes line out back. "I'll be in the toolshed."

As Renata reached for the bag of clothespins hanging on the line, she watched to see where Nathan was going so she would know which building was the toolshed. "Dr. McIntyre?" she whispered again. "Can you hear me?" As before there was no answer.

While pinning the clothes on the line, she tried to calculate how long she had been here. Surely this was longer than the time before. And she felt different, more as if she were *really* here and not just seeing things from Callie's perspective. A chilling thought touched her. What if she couldn't get back?

This had never occurred to her. She knew her body was lying asleep in Dr. McIntyre's office and that he was confident of being able to awaken her, but suddenly she wasn't so sure. He had said he had never known of anyone who had ever reached back into the past the way she had done.

Renata lowered her arms and rested her hands at her sides while inhaling a deep, relaxing breath. "Dr. McIntyre!" she called as loudly as she dared. A dog trotted around the corner of the house and sniffed in her direction. Renata paused. She had never owned a dog and wasn't comfortable around them. Her grandparents had a dog, but it was-mean tempered and she had never petted it.

The dog walked toward her, tentatively wagging its tail. Renata didn't dare move. What if the animal could tell she wasn't Callie? The dog came nearer and studied her more closely, then wagged its tail vigorously. Relieved, she reached down and gingerly patted its head. He licked her hand.

When all the clothes were on the line, Renata carried the empty basket into the shed nearest the back door. As she had guessed, this was the place where Callie stored the things she used to launder their clothes. On the shelf were bars of the same thick yellowish soap she had found in the bag hanging on the outside of the clothes basket, a length of clothesline and some paddles whose ends were stained dark from apparent use. What purpose the paddles might have, she couldn't fathom.

She hung the basket on a peg and went back outside. The dog was waiting for her. She kept a wary eye on him, but he seemed to have accepted her. Together, they went up the porch steps and Renata had a strong sense of *déjà vu*. The porch was the one she had seen in her dream.

The house was painted a pristine white, but the ceiling of the porch was as blue as a robin's egg. The support posts were elaborately turned, and gingerbread carvings with knobs and spindles filled the corners where they met the roof. At one end was a wooden swing suspended from chains. The yard beyond was bare dirt but with a pattern raked into it. Renata had never seen a scraped yard before, and she studied the pattern curiously.

A horse and buggy coming down the lane drew her attention. She walked closer to the end of the porch and narrowed her eyes to see. Since Renata had removed her contact lenses before Dr. McIntyre began the session, she was having trouble focusing at a distance.

It was a woman alone in the buggy, and when she saw Renata she waved. Renata waved back. This had to be Molly.

Molly tied the horse at a post at the boundary of the yard and energetically made her way across the flat, red rocks that served as a walkway to the front porch. "Mama says she has some honey for you, and Papa says to tell you to start eating more because you are too thin." She laughed. "He always says that. You look just fine to me."

Renata smiled. She had thought Callie could stand to lose a few pounds.

"Now, Callie, I know you don't like Ennis, and that you must still be angry with me, but I've come all the way out here to ask you not to stay mad."

"I don't feel angry at the moment," Renata said truthfully. What on earth was Callie so upset about? "I think we should go inside and talk about it."

Molly gave her an exasperated look. "I've been trying to get you to talk about it for months and you've refused."

Renata smiled. "I guess I feel like a different person today."

They went inside, and Renata looked around with far more curiosity than did Molly. The parlor was furnished with several chairs upholstered in tapestry cloth and a formidable-looking couch. The lamps had pale pink shades, and one had glass prisms around the bottom of the shade. Atop the mantel was a loud, ticking clock, and suspended above it by gold silk tassels was a large, beveled mirror. Renata could imagine Bob going into convulsions in such a room, but she rather liked it.

"Are we to sit in here?" Molly asked. "You're still mad at me. I knew it!"

"No, I'm not. I promise." There were three doors off the parlor, but as they were all closed, Renata had no idea which one led to a less formal sitting room.

Thankfully, Molly solved the problem for her by marching directly to the door opposite and pulling it open. Beyond was a room with chairs which looked more comfortable. The lamps here were ordinary tin ones, and the tabletops were covered with lacy doilies which matched the ones on the chair backs. The fireplace had exposed bricks and a plain mantel with a print of a pastoral scene above it. She started for a chair and realized Molly had the same one in mind. Renata veered toward the wooden rocking chair by the window.

Molly was staring at her. "Are you sure you're all right?"

"Why do people keep asking me that?" Renata asked testily. She felt as if she were making mistakes on every side.

"You haven't sat in that rocker since you lost the baby. Nathan and I have both remarked upon it."

"Never mind my choice in chairs. What do you want to talk to me about?"

Molly lifted her chin. "As you well know, Ennis and I are going to be married, and I want you to stop being on your high horse and accept it. That or tell me why you object to him. If I didn't know you so well, I'd say you're jealous."

"Jealous? Me? What on earth for?" She didn't see how any man could be more desirable than Nathan.

"Ennis was your beau, after all. Now he wants to marry me."

"I'm already married, and I love my husband." The words sounded strange in her mouth. "I'm certainly not jealous. I only want you to be happy."

Molly relaxed somewhat. "Then you'll stand up for me at my wedding? Mama says we can't possibly find anyone else at this late date, and it will be talked of if you refuse to come."

"All right. I'll be your witness. Tell me what you want me to do." She hoped Callie wouldn't be too upset when she returned and saw the changes Renata had made. "Do you really love Ennis?"

"Yes, of course I do. He's ever so smart, and I think it's wise for a girl to marry an older man. He is already settled in his business and has a nice house. The fact that our families are friends is another benefit, of course. It just makes sense for me to marry him."

"But do you really love him? More important, do you *like* him?"

"What an odd question. I just said I do. You're to wear your pink dress, the one with the satin ribbons and the rosebud print. Mama says there isn't time now to make you a new one and that will have to do. It was new for your wedding and that wasn't so long ago."

Renata wondered exactly how long ago it had been, but she saw no way of asking that question. "It is settled then."

Molly stood and went to a work basket beside another chair. She lifted out a length of white fabric with white embroidery. "When will my table runner be finished? You do such beautiful work. I know exactly where I'll put it. Ennis has a hall table in his vestibule where everyone will see it as soon as they come in the house." She smiled and lowered her gray eyes. "I suppose you are wondering how I know that."

Renata wasn't, but she nodded.

"Don't you dare tell Mama, but I've been inside his house!"

"Have you?" She smiled to think how innocent a time this had been. She had been in Bob's apartment long before they had begun to date seriously.

"He was a perfect gentleman, of course." Molly laughed and covered her mouth with her fingers. "Well, almost a gentleman. There now, I've shocked you."

"No, you really haven't."

"He kissed me. Not just on the cheek but a *real* kiss. His moustache is all bristly and not terribly pleasant. Be glad Nathan is clean-shaven. I wish Ennis would shave it off, but he would be offended if I so much as suggested such a thing." Her face clouded. "Does that make me too fast? To have kissed him, I mean? We are engaged and all."

"No, I think you should always kiss a man before you marry him." And a great deal more besides, she could have added.

"You kissed Nathan before? You didn't really!"

"Of course I did. Good heavens, Molly, everyone does, I should imagine."

"I don't think so. At least that's not what Mama said, and I'm sure Papa would agree with her. It's so important not to ruin one's reputation, you know. Barbara Downs is proof of that. Lidy Mae and Alma have said she wasn't so loose as she is now before she was divorced." Her voice dropped to a whisper on the last word as if were too scandalous to be spoken aloud. "I'd just die if I ever got divorced."

"It's not likely that you will." She wondered who Lidy Mae was. Alma was the name of the cousin that Molly had written to so diligently.

"Well, I should certainly think not." Molly put the table runner back into the work basket. She drew her chair closer to Renata and whispered, "What is it like to be married?"

Renata wasn't sure how to answer this since she had never been married. "I suppose it's not very different than not being married."

"It must be. Mama told me she would tell me on my wedding day, but that's a whole week away. I'm too curious to wait."

Remembering the advice Ida Graham had given Callie, Renata said, "All right, I'll tell you.

84

But you must promise never to tell Mama that I did."

Molly nodded solemnly and moved her chair even closer.

Renata suddenly realized she had no idea how to tell this girl about scx when Molly had evidently only kissed her fiancé one time. She didn't want to shock her, and anything but the unvarnished truth would be so vague as to be worse than saying nothing at all.

"Is it like what happens between Papa's bull and the cows?" Molly asked in all seriousness. "Don't you dare laugh at me if I'm wrong."

"Yes, that's more or less it," Renata replied with relief. "Only people usually do it facing each other."

"But not always?" Molly giggled. "I'm so embarrassed. I'm so glad you aren't mad at me any more and will tell me. I'm not sure Mama would have been so open. You know how she can be."

"I know. The first time it can hurt a little, especially if the man is inexperienced, but after that you should enjoy it."

"Enjoy it? No! Really?"

"I'm speaking from experience." Renata was glad to at last have a subject of conversation with which she was familiar.

"Tell me if I'm being too personal, but do you think you and Nathan will have another baby?"

"I don't know." Renata wished she could say

yes, but she already knew Callie had died child-less. "I hope so."

"You do? The last time I asked you, you said it wouldn't happen to you again, that there was only one sure way to prevent it, and that you were determined to do so. Since you told me about the other thing, can you tell me how not to have a baby?"

Renata was astounded. As far as she knew there was only one sure way for a woman in the 1880's not to get pregnant and that was abstinence. Could it really be true, after all, that Callie was refusing to make love with Nathan? "I was upset when I said that. Yes, there is a way, but it's too hard on a marriage. It's to not . . ." she paused and searched for words . . . "not do what Papa's bull does."

Molly nodded, her eyes round and her face serious. "Is this the same thing Mama calls doing her duty? If it is, I didn't think a wife was allowed not to do it."

"You and Ennis can work it out. Mama doesn't have to know anything about it."

"I suppose that's true. It's hardly something a lady would ask about. But I did, didn't I? Oh, Callie, I always seem to do everything wrong."

"No, you don't. I'm glad you asked me." She found she liked Molly, even if the girl was more innocent than any teenager Renata had ever known. Judging by Callie's premarital instructions, she had been equally uninformed. She found herself wondering how old Molly was.

A door slammed in the back of the house, and Renata knew Nathan was coming in. All her senses were attuned to his presence, even before his bulk filled the doorframe.

"Afternoon, Molly. You're wearing a new dress, I see."

"Yes, I am. And your wife never said a word about it." It was easy to see that Molly and Nathan were friends.

"I meant to comment on it," Renata said. "It's very pretty."

"I should have kept it for a part of my trousseau, I guess, but Alma is coming in today and I wanted to show it off."

"Is she? Tell her I said hello." Renata felt exhausted from having to stay constantly on guard.

"Callie has agreed to be in my wedding after all, and we have made up as if nothing at all has happened," Molly said. "Isn't that right, Callie?"

"That's right." She could feel Nathan's eyes on her, but she refused to look at him. "Sisters shouldn't argue at a time as happy as this."

Now both stared at her.

"The wedding, I mean," Renata faltered.

"I'm so glad to see you are happy at last," Molly said with a sigh. "We were all so worried about you. Mama even thought you might try something desperate."

Suicide? Renata's eyes widened. Had Callie really died by her own hand? Had the fall from a horse been simply a way for the family to explain it? "I promise I would never do anything like that. Be sure and tell Mama and Papa I said so."

"I will." Molly unhooked a small gold watch she wore on a brooch and consulted it. "Good heavens, but the time has flown. Alma will be at the train station before I am unless I hurry." She walked briskly from the room, and Renata followed her to a door in a small vestibule at the side of the house. Renata made a mental note to remember to use this one and not the front door. Molly kissed her on the cheek and smiled. "I'm so glad we are friends again. Let's not let anything come between us."

"I agree." Renata opened the door for her and waved as Molly climbed into the buggy and prepared to drive away.

She shut the door and turned to find Nathan watching her. "What's wrong? Did I do something wrong?"

"No, no. Nothing wrong. I've just never seen anyone make such a turn-about before. Until this afternoon you were adamant that you would never speak to Ennis again or to Molly if she married him. Now you're agreeing to stand by her at the wedding."

"I decided I was wrong." Renata hoped he wouldn't press her for details.

"It's the first time I've ever seen you stand firm on any issue."

"It is?"

"That's why I was becoming worried that there must really be something you had against Ennis and that Molly shouldn't marry him."

"I decided it's up to Molly whom she should marry. It's her life, after all."

"It was her life for the past two months and that hasn't mattered to you. What do you have against Ennis, anyway? Have you finally decided to tell me?"

"No, I haven't." Renata walked past him deeper into the house. She hoped he wouldn't follow her so she could see where the rooms lay. She heard him behind her.

The dining room was in the middle of the house, with rooms radiating off it like spokes in a wheel, and several of the rooms, the front and back parlors, for instance, had adjoining doors interconnecting them. Through open doors she could see the kitchen and a room with a treadle sewing machine. She circled the round oak table in the center of the room and went to the tall sideboard and pretended to be straightening the soup tureen and china pitcher. When she did, she saw herself in the mirror.

Taken by surprise at her reflection, she almost dropped the pitcher. She had assumed she and Callie looked alike. Now she realized nothing could be farther from the truth. Renata was tall and striking, but not technically a beauty. Callie was beautiful. She had light auburn hair and calm gray eyes, and her beauty was the dewy, wistful kind that decorated candy boxes.

A tendril of hair that had worked loose from the bun piled loosely on top of her head curled against her pale cheek. Renata could only stare at herself.

"Callie, if there's something about Ennis we should know, this is the time to say it," Nathan was telling her. "You can't keep quiet if you know something we don't."

"I don't know anything about him," Renata said in a voice barely louder than a whisper. She couldn't stop looking at the woman in the mirror, having great difficulty believing it was really her. Until now she had never thought how much her identity was tied to the physical appearance she had known all her life.

"You must have something against him—and don't leave the room like you always do whenever anybody brings the subject up."

Renata's eyes met his in the mirror. "I wasn't leaving."

"You have never once talked back to your parents, yet you've fought them all the way on this and have refused to tell me why. Now all of a sudden you seem to have forgotten all about it and are acting as if we're all one happy family."

"Aren't we?" she ventured.

Nathan looked away, then back at her reflection. "Don't tease me, Callie. I'm tired, and I'm in no mood for your evasions." As if the mirrored image gave him a safe base, he added softly, "I've tried so hard to make you happy.

Why is it you never smile any more?"

Renata's heart went out to him, and she wanted to go into his arms. However, he was already wondering at her behavior and this was probably something Callie wouldn't do. "I can't explain it. If I could, I would. I don't like to see you unhappy, either."

"I wish I could believe that. We started off so smoothly. I was sure we would grow to love each other and that we would have a big family and that we would prosper. So far, we've prospered, but nothing else."

Renata turned to look at him. It had never occurred to her that Callie and Nathan weren't in love when they married. She had assumed the overwhelming love she felt for him was coming from Callie's mind. Did that mean she, Renata, really had fallen in love with him at first sight? That her soul mate, the man she was born to love, had lived and died 100 years before her own time? A tear gathered and rolled silently down her cheek.

Nathan turned away and gruffly spoke as if he were trying to hide the fact he also felt like crying. "Now don't start that again. You know what that does to me."

"I'm sorry." Renata rubbed the tear away with the palm of her hand. She didn't know what to say to him, especially when she could leave at any moment and the real Callie would be back.

After an awkward moment, Nathan said,

without looking at her, "Let's eat dinner. I'm worn out."

Renata followed him into the kitchen and tried to collect her wits while he went out onto the service porch to wash his face and hands.

Chapter Five

Nathan watched his wife, wondering what was wrong with her now. Callie often seemed half-afraid of everything, but this time she seemed more confused than frightened. He didn't know why she was like that. Before they married, he had seen her as frail and needing protection, and he had liked the idea that he could be her protector. But Callie seemed to need protection against everything from loud noises and mice to crowds in the general store. After having worked hard in the fields all day, he didn't want to come home to hear she had been afraid to go alone to the creek to wash clothes or that she was positive that she had heard strange noises upstairs and, afraid to investigate, had stayed downstairs all day.

Now she had added a new wrinkle to her peculiarities. She was looking around the kitchen as if she had never seen it before. "Well? Are we going to have supper or not?"

"Of course we are going to have supper," she said a bit too brightly. She went to the stove and put out her hand as if she were going to touch it.

"Careful!" he exclaimed automatically. "You'll burn yourself."

She jerked her hand back. "What do you want to eat?"

"Anything but those damned beans." He had eaten more beans since his marriage than he had in his entire life. Callie seemed unable to make anything else, and she usually burned those.

With a pot hook, she lifted each of the lids on the stove in turn and peered in as if she weren't sure what she would find. When she uncovered the back well, he smelled the distinct aroma of cooking beans and hoped that he was wrong. He tried not to be upset. Whenever he had words with her, Callie usually sulked and trembled for days. Hoping a more tactful approach would help, he said, "There's that ham in the smokehouse. That would be a nice change to go with the beans."

She looked relieved. "Would you get it for me?"

He nodded. Callie had apparently become afraid to cross the yard to the smokehouse, even before dark now. He didn't understand what she was afraid of, but there was no point in arguing about it, so he went out for her.

The smokehouse was in a row of outbuildings, one of which housed the chickens, another his workshop, one for storage of his farm implements, and the other for storage of the ears of corn that fed the chickens all year. He turned the wooden latch and went into the dim room where the pot in which the wood for curing the meat was burned. Even though the meat had been smoked weeks ago, the smell of wood remained strong. Although there were no windows, enough light came in through the door for him to find a pork ham. He unhooked it and carried it into the house.

In the meantime Callie had taken a jar of tomato sauce from the pantry and was mixing something in a bowl. "Here's the ham." He put it on the cutting board.

"Slice me off a bit, won't you?"

Nathan tried not to sigh. He wasn't as tired as he had led her to believe, but he had done a good day's work. Frowning, he did as she asked, slicing two slabs from the ham. He wrapped the remainder in an old, but clean, cup towel and carried it back out to the smokehouse. He told himself that it should be enough that Callie was at least trying to please him by cooking meat to go with the beans. Usually she said that one or the other was all she wanted to fix.

When he returned to the kitchen she was busy slicing the ham into tiny squares. "What on earth are you doing to the ham? Aren't you going to cook it?"

"Of course I am. Why don't you go do whatever you usually do at this time of evening and let me work?"

"That's fine with me." He went into the back parlor and selected a book from the mantel. After positioning his chair next to the fireplace, just so, he sat down and leaned back in the chair and braced his feet against the bricks. Something about Callie was different tonight, but he couldn't quite put his finger on it. He rubbed his eyes and told himself again that he didn't have it so bad.

When William Graham had given him Callie's hand, Nathan had been positive he was the happiest man alive, but his high hopes and dreams hadn't panned out. He knew Callie tried, but what had been delightful in a fiancée had become tedious in a wife. It was one thing for Callie to have smiled up at him shyly and put her hand in his before she could go into a room full of people, and another when she couldn't go shopping alone because of the crowd. Lorain was hardly a town, let alone a bustling city, and he knew Callie had never seen a real crowd in her life.

Then there was the fact that she had not come to his marriage bed as a virgin, even though she claimed to be. Nathan gazed into the fire as he remembered. Her explanation was that she had ridden astride when she was a girl, but he wasn't so sure that held up. He had heard such an excuse before and knew a lot of people who were willing to accept that it could be true, but he couldn't for the life of him see why riding astride would rob a girl of her virginity. He had pretended to believe her because he had little choice, but he had been shocked. Callie had never let him do more than kiss her on the lips before their marriage, and she wasn't fond of making love.

Thinking of that brought a familiar ache to his loins. She had seemed to be trying to make him happy, but he couldn't take pleasure in lovemaking when he knew she was miserable. He had hoped the baby would remedy that, but when Callie miscarried, she became worse than ever. Now, she made it clear that she didn't want him to touch her.

When Callie finally called him to come and eat, he begrudgingly put the book he had wanted to read back on the mantel. He hadn't been able to concentrate enough to read a single word. All that he could think about was how his high hopes of a happy marriage and children seemed to have flown out the window.

She had set the table, but the plates were opposite each other instead of his being at the end of the table as usual. She had put napkins alongside the plates, and the silverware was divided out as if they were expecting company. He made no comment until she placed a single dish of what appeared to be cornbread on the table. "What's this?"

"It's a ham casserole. You said you're tired of beans, so I thought I'd dress them up a little."

He had never heard of a casserole, but as he was accustomed to humoring Callie, he spooned some onto his plate without question. Beneath a cornbread crust, he found a mixture of beans and ham in a tomato sauce. Cautiously, he took a bite, and to his surprise, it tasted better than he had expected.

"Do you like it? Is it seasoned all right?"

"Tastes good. Where did you learn to cook it?"

"I heard the recipe somewhere, I guess."

He made no comment. The casserole, as she called it, was actually quite good, cutting the taste of the red beans that he had come to despise. He wondered why she had never tried this before.

"So how was your day?" she asked as she served herself.

Nathan tried not to stare. Callie almost never sat down and ate at the same time he did. Normally, she insisted on puttering about the kitchen, staying up to pour him more tea or fetch more food, as her mother did for her father. Above all, she had always maintained silence during their meals. Now that he had finally become accustomed to the routine, she was switching it all around. "What do you mean, how was my day?"

"What did you do? Did you work hard?"

"Of course. Today was the same as always. I plowed the corn field in the back and put in the watermelons on the hill. Then I helped

Janie bear her colt. Why do you ask?"

"Tell me about the colt. You said it's a chestnut filly?"

"That's right. I'm surprised you haven't gone to the barn to see it as much as you've worried about it."

"I haven't had time. Molly came and then I had to cook dinner."

"This is supper. Are you sure you're feeling well?" He studied her face. There was something different about her. It was strange to think such a thing, but he was almost sure her eyes had changed. They were still gray, of course, but it was as if someone else were looking out of them. He told himself he was being foolish.

"I feel fine. The kitchen is hot, that's all."

"If you think it's hot now, wait until summer. It won't be long before we will have to move the table out onto the porch."

"Yes," she said vaguely.

Nathan ate the rest of the casserole and looked around expectantly. "Did you make a pie?" he asked, still hungry.

"I found . . . I mean I made one. It's in that cupboard." She pointed to the screened pie safe.

Nathan watched with growing curiosity as she went to get the pie. Why had she called it a cupboard, and why had she told him where it was as if this was an unusual place for it to be? Was she coming down with some illness? When she put the pie on the table and got down two saucers and clean forks instead of just cutting a piece onto his plate, he put his hand on her forehead. "Have you taken a fever?"

"No, why do you ask?"

"No reason." He ate the pie slowly. One thing Callie always cooked right was pies. At times he thought that was all that had kept him from starving until she became brave enough to try other things besides beans. He had assumed her mother would have taught her to cook, but he learned after their wedding that her mother had never learned how to cook and always had hired help to do it. Apparently she had never kept any of her help long enough for them to teach her daughters. He almost felt sorry for Ennis, since Molly didn't know any more about a kitchen than Callie.

After they finished, Nathan lifted the heavy pot of water from the back of the stove and poured some into the dishpan so Callie could wash dishes, then went out to the porch to draw more water for the heating pot. Through the window he could see her. She seemed to be searching hastily and furtively for something. Finally, she found the soap, and he thought he saw a look of relief on her face.

Nathan poured water from the well bucket to the kitchen bucket and wondered about Callie's odd behavior. If she were getting on in years, he would have thought she might be having a spell like one of his aunts had had when she would forget everything for a time.

No one had ever been able to explain why his aunt did that occasionally, but brain fever had been suspected. Callie, however, was only 25 years old and had always been in good health. He took the water inside and poured it into the large pot.

Callie washed the dishes and left them on a cup towel to drain instead of drying them and putting them away. Again Nathan took note but made no comment. When she forgot to bank the fire in the stove, he did it for her. She watched him from the doorway and turned away when he looked at her.

They went into the parlor where he again took up his book. Over the top of it he saw Callie looking around as if she didn't know where her knitting was. "It's over there by your chair where you left it," he said.

She jumped. "What is?"

"Your knitting. Isn't that what you're looking for?" He noticed she was sitting in the rocker that she had refused to sit in since she had lost the baby.

"I was thinking I might read a book instead."

He carefully laid down his book and frankly stared at her. "What did you say?"

"Why do you keep looking at me that way? Have I grown two heads all of a sudden?"

"The books are in the case. Help yourself." He pretended to be reading, but he was watching her over the top of the book. She stood and wandered toward the hall, opened the door to the guest bedroom and crossed to the door leading to the front parlor. What was wrong with her?

When she returned with a book, she went back to the rocker and tucked one foot under her, then opened it to read. He recognized it as being one he had recently read by Charles Dickens. He would have presumed that Callie could never wade through it. She was no reader by her own admission and shunned anything more taxing than her copy of *Mrs. Finch's Home Companion*.

After half an hour of wondering if she was really reading *Great Expectations*, he closed his book. By now it was completely dark outside, and he knew how early dawn would come. "Are you ready for bed?"

Her eyes met his, and he finally saw the startled, frightened look he usually associated with Callie. Without a word, she nodded and closed her book.

Renata had been dreading this moment, and hadn't expected it to come so soon. Why would he want to go to bed this early unless he wanted to make love? In her mind she called frantically for Dr. McIntyre to rescue her. She might think she loved this man and she might desire him, but he was still a stranger to her and she had never been one to tumble lightly into bed.

Nathan looked at her as if he expected her to do something in particular, but she had no idea what Callie's nightly ritual might be so she pretended to be busy hunting a piece of paper to use as a bookmark. By the looks of the pages, though, someone had developed the habit of turning down a corner rather than using a bookmark.

It also occurred to her that she had no idea where her bedroom might be.

As she continued to stall, waiting for Nathan to lead the way, Nathan went to the fireplace and rolled the logs toward the back and heaped ashes around them. Then he put a black screen over the opening. By comparison with the chrome and glass fire screen at her apartment, this simple one did not look very safe, and for a moment she had visions of them being burned alive. But Nathan evidently felt this was safe, and she hoped he was right.

Finally, Nathan lit a lamp and stepped toward the door which led to the short hall. Thankfully, she fell in line behind him, but then he stepped aside for her to precede him and handed her the lamp. She swept past as purposefully as if she knew where she was going, her mind racing. Off this hall were the doors to the dining room, the front door and a stairway. By process of elimination, she deduced the stairs must be the direction she should take.

At the bottom of the stairway, she gathered her long skirts and in doing so exposed a good bit of her leg. Apparently this was unlike Callie, because for a moment Nathan's eyes widened, then he covered his surprise with a look of nonchalance. Lowering the hem of her skirt, she hurried up the stairs.

At the top was a rather large landing with a bed on the far wall beneath the windows. She surmised this served as a bedroom, possibly for visitors' children or for nights when a breeze was needed. There was no air conditioning, of course, and she wondered how they could stand the summers without it.

Again she was faced with a choice of closed doors and knew that behind one of the three was the bedroom she was to share with Nathan. A faint hope lit her mind. This was the Victorian age. Might it not be possible that Nathan and Callie didn't share a room?

While Renata pretended to straighten a print of overblown fruit and flowers, Nathan crossed to one of the doors. "Aren't you coming?" he asked.

"Of course. I was only straightening the picture." She passed in front of him and into the room.

The bedroom was larger than she had expected, with windows on two sides. Covering the windows were white lace curtains that looked as if they had been starched. The walls were papered in a design of roses. The bed was brass and ornate with a white crocheted bedspread. A brightly colored quilt was folded across the foot of the bed, and a mound of pillows covered its head. Across from the bed was an oak dresser with Callie's hairbrush and other toiletries that Renata didn't immediately identify. In one corner stood a highboy and in another a folding screen.

When Nathan began unbuttoning his cuffs and shirt, Renata felt a constriction in her throat. He was pretending not to watch her, but she had the unsettling feeling that he was aware of her every move. She went to the highboy and tried to divine which drawer held Callie's nightgowns. Her first guess was wrong, but now she knew where to find Callie's stockings and underwear. She pretended to be straightening them, then opened the drawer below. To her relief, she found several neatly folded cotton gowns.

She took the gown on top and resolutely withdrew behind the screen. Though this behavior hardly seemed normal, Nathan didn't seem surprised, or at least if he was, he didn't say anything. Renata hurriedly began unbuttoning the blouse Callie had put on that morning, but found the bone buttons more difficult to get through the buttonholes than the plastic ones of her own time would have been. Nevertheless, she was thankful that she wasn't wearing a dress that fastened up the back because that would have required her to ask Nathan to help her undress.

Under the blouse and skirt Renata discovered she was wearing a thin cotton camisole, embroidered with delicate, little white flowers. She ran her hand over the embroidery and wondered if Callie had done the handiwork and, if so, whether she herself was skilled enough in needlework to pass if she were placed in a position of having to sew in front of anyone. Renata had always enjoyed needlework and could knit quite well, but the work she had seen so far had been of excellent quality and would be difficult for her to match.

Sitting on the stool behind the screen, Renata unlaced Callie's high-top kid shoes. They seemed small, but Renata noticed her feet fit into them comfortably. She still wasn't accustomed to Callie's smaller body. After rolling down her stockings and dropping them into the shoes, she untied the ribbon at her waist and stepped out of the bloomers. Finally, she pulled the camisole over her head, and suddenly she felt more naked than ever in her entire life. There was no mirror behind the screen so Renata explored her body with her hands. Her waist wasn't quite as small as Renata's and her hips were more rounded. Her breasts were larger than Renata had expected and were well-shaped. In spite of her shorter stature, Callie was beautifully built. After having spent her entire adolescence bemoaning her small breasts, Renata had to smile at the improvement there, but she still thought Callie could benefit from a diet. Renata had worked hard to get as thin as possible.

On the other side of the screen she could hear Nathan opening drawers and moving about. Was he putting on one of those nightshirts she had seen depicted in books? She fervently hoped so and reminded herself that Victorians were known for being prudes about nudity.

She pulled on the gown and fastened the buttons all the way up to the neck. With the sleeves covering her arms down to the wrist, her body was completely hidden behind yards of white cotton. As there was beautiful stitching on the bodice of the gown, Renata guessed the garment might have been part of Callie's trousseau.

She stepped cautiously around the screen and was thankful to see that Nathan was already in bed. She went to the other side and turned the covers back.

"Aren't you going to take down your hair?" he asked.

Renata's hands flew to her head. She was so accustomed to short hair that she forgot Callie's hair was long. She went to the dresser and stared at her unaccustomed reflection as she removed the pins. Once released, her hair cascaded down her shoulders and over her back exactly the way Renata had heard it described in romance novels. Turning slightly for a better look, she could see that it was even longer than she had expected, almost touching the stool on which she sat. When she leaned forward to pick up Callie's hairbrush, her light auburn hair waved and rippled around her, a new sensation that was surprisingly sensual. As she brushed her hair, Renata glanced over her shoulder in the mirror and saw Nathan watching her. At length, she put down the brush and went back to the bed.

"Aren't you going to blow out the light?" he asked. He was watching her closely.

"Of course. I was just turning the covers back," she replied more tartly than was needed. What else did Callie normally do before going to bed? She put her hand behind the lamp's chimney and blew as she had seen actors do in movies. The lamp went out, leaving only the one on Nathan's side of the bed glowing.

This time when she went to the bed he didn't say anything, and she was thankful. She stepped up on the stool and boosted herself onto the mattress, but because the mattress was stuffed with feathers and had no firm side, she promptly slid off the side of the bed. She refused to meet his eyes. Again she stepped on the stool and this time she launched herself farther onto the bed and hastily slid under the covers.

Renata's heart was pounding. Nathan seemed larger lying on the bed than he had standing up. She had always heard that people had been smaller in the preceding centuries, but Nathan proved that notion incorrect. She felt his presence in every atom of her body, and her blood was racing so fast she felt as if he must be able to hear it.

When Nathan raised up and leaned over to blow out the lamp on his side of the bed, Renata risked a look. He was naked, at least to the waist. His muscles were corded and looked hard. She found herself wanting to touch him and at the same time was afraid to do so. She had never known anyone who was so confidently masculine.

Suddenly, the room was plunged into darkness, and she felt him lie back down. The windows made paler rectangles, and she could see treetops like smudges behind them. Gradually her eyes became accustomed to the dark, but she was still afraid to move. She could hear his breathing in the darkness and was aware of every movement of his body. Her own body cried out for what she feared.

The covers rustled, and she knew he was turning toward her. She made herself be still and not do anything he might interpret as a sexual overture. What would Callie do? Wouldn't she reach for him and welcome his embrace? Renata tried to breathe more normally.

"What's wrong, Callie?" His voice was velvety and deep and stirred fires in her that she never knew existed. "Are you sure you are feeling all right?"

"I feel fine," she said, which wasn't entirely true. She was inordinately exhausted, and she assumed it had to do with her trip to the past.

And she was aching to make love to a man she scarcely knew.

"Did Molly say something to upset you? I know she often talks before she thinks, and she knows how you feel about her marrying Ennis."

"We made up. We had a sister-to-sister talk, and I'm all right about that now." Renata wondered again what Callie had against Ennis and whether her objections to the marriage were well-founded.

Nathan was quiet, but she knew he was still raised up on his elbow. She could see his silhouette against the window. Slowly she turned her body to face his. "Is something bothering you?" she asked, pretending she had noticed unusual behavior in him as well. "Are you still upset about Molly and Ennis?" She hoped he would give her some clue, but instead he sighed.

"I leave all that to you and Molly," he said. "You know I don't like him, but I figure it's none of my business. It wouldn't hurt for you to take the same attitude."

"I'm trying." She knew he could have no idea how hard she was trying.

Nathan reached out and touched her hair. "I like it loose like this. I'm glad you didn't braid it tonight."

So Callie usually braided her hair. Renata didn't know how to braid hair so she made no comment. It was enough to feel Nathan's fingers stroking her hair. The pace of her heartbeat doubled.

"So soft. I never knew anyone who had prettier hair than you do. I wish you would wear it down sometimes. I know it wouldn't be proper if we were having company, but we don't see many people out here. I've never understood why you won't leave it down once in a while."

"I guess it would get in my way. It's awfully long."

"I know. Remember how Jemima was jealous of it when she saw you washing it last summer? Her hair won't grow much past her shoulders, and she would give anything to have hair like yours."

Renata wondered who Jemima was and why she had been around when Callie was washing her hair. This society seemed too formal for that. "I think her hair is pretty," Callie said daringly.

"So do I, but she says it's too curly." He lifted a wavy tendril and let it curl around his finger. "I really don't want to talk about my sister. Do you?"

So—Jemima was his sister. She told herself not to forget the name. "No, I don't want to talk about her either."

Nathan was silent again. Renata wished she could read his thoughts. Was he wanting her as badly as she wanted him, or was he pondering some mistake she had made? Renata had never been married, but she knew it was expected for

111

husbands and wives to kiss good-night. She eased closer to him. What if he wanted more than a kiss? She could think of no other reason to come to bed so early.

He slipped his arm across her and drew her nearer. "Callie," he said in a tight voice. "Why do you torment me?"

"What do you mean?"

"You know as well as I do. Coming to bed with your hair loose and wearing the gown I like best. Talking to me in that soft voice. Are you trying to drive me mad?"

Renata didn't know how to answer. "I meant nothing by it. Really I didn't."

"I know you didn't. That's why it's so unfair." His arm tightened, and he pulled her against his body.

Renata caught her breath. His body was warm and muscular. Hers fit against it like a hand to a glove. Her breasts mounded against his chest, and she could feel the proof of his desire pressing her. Renata closed her eyes and put her arms around him. Her lips found his, and her fingers caressed his bare skin.

A groan rumbled from deep within his chest as he kissed her hungrily. At first Renata felt a surge of fear that seemed to be more Callie than herself, then she kissed him back. Nathan knew exactly how to kiss. His mouth was demanding but not hurtful. When she opened her lips beneath his, he moaned again. He nestled her body even closer to his, and Renata felt a surge of passion like she had never known before. Her love for this stranger intensified, and she was breathless. Somehow she was Callie and herself all at once, and they both loved Nathan.

Without warning, he released her. Renata could hear his ragged breathing in the darkness, and she knew he was wanting her as much as she wanted him. "Damn you, Callie," he ground out. "You'll push me too far some day." He rolled over and left her staring at his back in the dark.

Renata was astounded. He wanted her, but he was so sure of her ultimate rejection of him that he wasn't willing to try to make love with her. Renata lifted her hand but was afraid to touch him. She didn't know what was between Callie and Nathan, and she had already made too many mistakes. Callie might love him, but she obviously didn't want him to touch her. Renata thought of the miscarriage and Callie's insistence that she would never let that happen to her again. Evidently she was firm enough in her resolve that she had forced Nathan to live with her in abstinence.

Renata felt an emptiness in the pit of her stomach. She was not only trapped in the past but was caught up in a bad marriage as well. She recalled how Nathan had never remarried after Callie's death. At the time she had seen it as deathless love, but now she suspected it was because his marriage had been so disappointing. He had simply been unwilling to risk marriage again.

She rolled over so that her back shut him out. She felt like crying again, and she wondered at how she could be herself yet at the same time feel as if she were Callie, too. Reincarnation was the only explanation. She only wished she had access to Callie's memories as well as her body and her marriage.

Resolutely she closed her eyes. She wasn't trapped here. When she had been back before, she and Dr. McIntyre had discussed the way the passage of time in the past seemed to have no relevance to that in the present, and he had given her some confusing answer as to why that was. She must still be safely in his office, and it only seemed that she had been here for hours. Renata had read about hypnotism and knew the mind could do amazing things, and she also knew there was no danger of being stuck in a hypnotic state. At the worst she would fall asleep and when she woke up she would be back to normal. Therefore all she had to do was to fall asleep. She reminded herself to remember all she had seen so she could describe it to McIntyre and Bob. She smiled. Maybe not to Bob. She willed herself to go to sleep even though she wasn't sleepy at all. Finally she succeeded.

Chapter Six

Renata was resigning herself to the fact that she had no control over when or even if she would return to her natural time. When she had opened her eyes that first morning and found she was lying alone in Callie's bed, she had felt a burst of panic. As soon as she had figured out how to put on Callie's clothes and how to wrap her hair into a bun, she had gone far out into the woods and called Dr. McIntyre's name. She had shouted for him until she was hoarse, and when she became convinced that he couldn't hear her, she had called him some derogatory names Callie had probably never even heard of.

That was days ago. Renata had never been one to fight against the inevitable, so she was trying hard to adjust, for as long as would be necessary, to her new life. In some ways it was difficult. Nathan, for instance, never touched her, and she soon began to wonder if he ever would.

Callie's face was beautiful and her body

Elizabeth Crane

delectable. Renata had not only seen that in Nathan's eyes, but she could see that for herself in the tall cheval mirror in the bedroom. Granted, the honeymoon phase of Nathan and Callie's marriage was over, but Renata couldn't help but wonder why he never treated her as more than a sister. At times she could see the yearning in Nathan's eyes and sometimes his face seemed drawn and vulnerable, but never once, since that first night when he kissed her, had he intimated by word or deed that he desired her.

The day of Molly's wedding she awoke nervous and edgy. She had managed to fool Nathan, but today she would be around all Callie's family and her closest friends. Surely someone would realize she wasn't who she said she was.

She dressed carefully in the pink dress that Molly had asked her to wear. It was more frilly than anything she had ever worn before, but the mirror told her it suited Callie. Pink wasn't the best color with red hair, but Callie's hair was pale enough that the dress looked pretty on her. Renata still hadn't mastered the art of fixing her hair in a neat bun, however, and this took more of her time than she had expected.

Nathan came in as she was wrestling with her long hair. For a minute he watched her in silence, then he said, "Why aren't you doing it the way you usually do?"

"What do you mean?" Renata glared at Callie's image in the mirror and wondered what everyone would say if she cut her hair.

"You know, bend over and brush it like you always do and twist it up while it's hanging down."

Renata stared at him. That might work. She bent at the waist and brushed her hair toward the floor. Gathering it into a ponytail, she twisted it into a rope. With her face flushed, she stood up and coiled it into place on top of her head, pulling it looser about her face so the style wasn't so severe. She looked exactly the way Callie had the day she arrived. Wishing she could thank him but not daring to do so, Renata put the hairpins in place. To her surprise, she needed only half the pins she had used on the previous days.

Nathan was still watching her, the puzzled look back in his eyes.

"Yes?" she said coolly. She had become aware that he seldom verbalized his thoughts, and she expected him to walk away.

"I was noticing how you look in that dress. You haven't worn it very often since our wedding."

Renata looked down at the flounces. It did seem almost new, and it was dressier than would be suitable for a typical day on the farm. That must mean Callie and Nathan hadn't been married very long. She wondered again what year it was. "I guess I haven't."

"It's pretty on you. I wish you would wear it more often. It reminds me of the day I brought you home after our wedding."

Then she understood. This dress had been her "going away" dress. She had heard her grandmother refer to a dress by that term. She smiled hopefully. "Tell me more."

Nathan turned away. "We have to leave or we'll be late."

With a sigh Renata followed him out and down the stairs. The house was clean, but not as spotless as Callie had kept it. Renata had all she could do to keep it even this clean. Callie must have been a dynamo. She noticed the top of the sideboard needed dusting, a fact she had been unaware of when she stood beside it. Callie was so short she couldn't see to the top. If Nathan had noticed, he had made no comment.

Nathan had already hitched the horse to the buggy. He handed her up onto the seat, then came around and climbed up the other side. The buggy jiggled on its springs as he settled beside her. He spoke to the bay horse, and as if it understood him, it leaned into the harness.

Renata loved to ride in the buggy. She had only been in it once before and that had been when Nathan bought this horse and wanted her to see how it carried itself. She wondered how hard it would be for her to learn to drive a buggy and whether Callie knew how already. She assumed Callie must have known how since they were too far out to comfortably walk to town and since Molly had known how to drive her own buggy out for a visit. Therefore, there was no way Renata could ask Nathan to teach her.

She glanced sideways at him. Never had she known a man she found so intriguing. He was quieter than most of the men she had known, and he gave no sign of being surly or ill-tempered. If anything, he was just the opposite. She had seen him laugh aloud at the antics of Janie's new colt, and she had seen him playing with the litter of kittens that lived under the porch. Both times when he saw her watching, he had stopped laughing and had gone on about his business. She was aching to learn what had come between him and his wife and, if possible, to fix it.

His hands on the reins were strong, and the white cuffs of his shirt contrasted sharply with his tanned skin. He wore his best black suit and a tie that reminded Renata more of early Texans than of the way she pictured men dressing in Louisiana. On the other hand she didn't know that Nathan wasn't originally from Texas. There was so much she didn't know about him. He wore a hat since he was going to town, and his hair curled on the back of his neck below it. She had an almost irresistible urge to touch it and see if it was as soft as it looked.

His shoulders were broad under the coat. She knew that for a fact because she had seen them as he slept naked beside her. She had been curious that he wore nothing to bed, and after a surreptitious search of his clothing, she learned that such a practice was to be expected from him in the future as well, for he didn't own a single nightshirt. She didn't mind on principle, but now that she was no longer as afraid of him, she was finding it hard not to touch him. Certainly Bob had never excited her so much.

She thought of Bob and wondered how he was. She felt a little guilty that she hardly missed him. Bob deserved better. Next to Nathan, however, he paled significantly. As soon as she returned to her own time, she told herself, she was going to break off her engagement with Bob. After knowing Nathan, she couldn't settle for second-best.

After all these days as Callie, Renata was becoming used to the thought that the time she was spending as Callie was occurring at an incredibly accelerated pace, relative to the few minutes she was spending on Dr. McIntyre's couch, but it still left her with an odd, undefinable sensation of being disconnected. She had decided the weird feelings had to do with her being in a different time and body and that it was nothing to worry about. All she could do was to accept things as they were happening and make the best of it.

She turned to Nathan. "Why don't you ever talk to me?" she asked.

"I talk to you. What do you mean?" He glanced at her, then looked ahead again.

120

"No, you don't. You say what's necessary, like 'pass the peas' or 'don't let the cow out of the lot,' but we never really talk."

"I was under the impression that you didn't like to talk all that much. You never say a word at the supper table—or at least you didn't until the past few days. You always tell me to be quiet if I try to talk to you in bed. I know you don't like lovemaking," he said, the muscle tightening in his jaw, "but there are other things I want to say to you. If you're working at something or other you say it distracts you if I try to have a conversation with you. When have you decided you want to talk?"

Renata's stomach tightened. Had their marriage been as bad as that? "Surely you're exaggerating."

"You tell me. Which time was false?"

She stared at the road between the horse's ears. "I've changed my mind. I want to talk to you. I hadn't realized how impossible I've been. I enjoy talking to you."

Nathan gave her a searching look but said nothing.

"For instance, what are you thinking right now? Right this minute?"

"I was wondering why you've changed so much."

"Have I?" she faltered.

"You're like another person. I see you doing things that you've always done, but it's like you never did them before. Like milking the cow. I know you've never liked doing it, but you were always able to do it before. Why have you forgotten how?"

"I can't explain it. Maybe I've had a touch of brain fever," she added in inspiration.

"I never saw brain fever that didn't have a fever to go along with it."

"Then what's your explanation?"

"I don't have one. I do have to say this, though. You're easier to get along with these days. Now don't get mad at me for saying this, but you've been difficult for the last year or so."

"I have? For over a year?" So she and Nathan weren't newlyweds as she had assumed. "Why for a year, do you suppose?"

He looked at her before he said, "You know you miscarried the baby about then. That's when you stopped letting me touch you. You're teasing me again, and you know I don't like it."

"I wouldn't be so cruel."

"I wasn't saying you do it to be cruel. I guess you don't know how it hurts me, maybe. You seem to think you were the only one who mourned the baby, but I was as sad as you were. Only I got over it. And it doesn't mean I'm heartless like you say. I believe it's best to accept the things you can't change and to get on with life."

That was exactly Renata's attitude toward life. She wondered if, assuming she was the reincarnation of Callie, she had learned that lesson from Nathan. The idea put a smile on her lips.

"What have I said that was funny? It was your idea to talk, remember." His voice was defensive, and his face looked as if he thought she had lured him into making a fool of himself.

"I'm not laughing at you." Renata put her hand on his arm and felt him move as if to pull away. "Please don't pull away from me. You never want me to touch you, either. It's not just me."

"That's not true. I can't bear to have you touch me and not let me touch you in return. A man can take only so much, Callie."

Renata let her hand fall. There were too many hard feelings between Nathan and Callie for her to be able to solve it all in one buggy ride.

By the time they reached Callie's parents' house, several other buggies and horses were already tied out front. "I was afraid we were late," he said as he handed her down. "Go on in while I tie the horse."

There was nothing Renata wanted less than to go into that house full of strangers, but she had no choice. She squared her shoulders and lifted her chin. Somehow she would get through this. Her brain fever excuse hadn't worked. She wondered if these people had ever heard of amnesia.

The house was filled with more people than the number of buggies had implied. Most had evidently walked to the wedding. Renatà was accustomed to driving everywhere she went, even if it was only a block away. These people thought nothing of walking to a wedding. On the other hand, none of the women were wearing three inch heels.

She made her way through the crowd, smiling and nodding at the people who called her Callie, and trying to seem too busy to stop and talk to any one. A woman grabbed her arm and pulled her toward the stairs. "There you are! We had almost given you up. What do you mean being so late to your sister's wedding!"

"I'm sorry," Renata stammered. "We have a new horse and Nathan had some trouble hitching it to the buggy."

The woman made a snorting sound and looked at Renata as if Renata had lost her mind. "Hurry up. Your mama and Molly are beside themselves. We have been waiting for too long as it is."

Renata let the woman lead her upstairs and tried not to trip on her long skirts. She had no idea who the woman was and obviously couldn't ask. When they reached a room near the end of the upper hall, the woman stopped and opened the door. Inside Renata could see Molly and the woman she knew must be Callie's mother.

"Mama, Molly, I'm sorry I'm so late." She

hurried in and said to Molly, "You look love-ly."

Ida Graham frowned at her. "I think it's bad of you, Callie, to keep Molly waiting. I know you aren't in favor of her marrying Ennis, but this is really too much."

"I wasn't late for that reason," Renata object-ed. "I had trouble putting my hair up and we have a new horse and—"

"Never mind. Help me straighten the flounces on Molly's dress." Ida turned away and began pulling the lacy ruffles into place.

Renata knelt and did the same. She was accustomed to polyester blend fabrics that wouldn't wrinkle if a train ran over them, but she noticed the satin on Molly's dress had tiny wrinkles which the iron hadn't reached. She adjusted the lace to cover them.

"Callie, tell me you don't hate me for marry-ing Ennis," Molly said. "I can't bear it if you're angry with me."

"Nonsense, Molly. I couldn't care less if you marry him. What I mean is, I want you to be happy, and if Ennis is the right man for you, I will back you all the way."

Molly and her mother exchanged a shocked glance. "You haven't started betting, have you?" Ida demanded.

"No. It's just a manner of speaking. Now stand still. You'll wrinkle your dress if you turn about like that."

Molly stopped twisting so she could see

Renata. "I'm so nervous. What will I do, Mama? What if I don't make a good wife?"

"You will. Just look after Ennis and make him happy. Always put your husband first in all things and do what pleases him. You're the ship and your husband is the captain. He won't steer you wrong."

Renata suppressed a laugh. It was hard to believe the woman was serious. She was glad she had told Molly about sex. Otherwise the girl would have been in for a shock. She wondered if that was what had started Callie's marriage off on the wrong foot.

She straightened and helped Ida place a tiara and veil over Molly's blond hair. She had yet another feeling of *déjà vu* as she did so. The feeling was occurring more and more often these days. It was as if she dimly remembered some of Callie's life, though not on a conscious level.

"Am I pretty, Mama?" Molly asked shyly.

"You look quite respectable. Ennis will have no reason to be ashamed of you."

"You're beautiful," Renata assured her. "I'm proud to be your sister."

Molly smiled but her eyes were suspiciously bright. "Don't be sweet to me or I'll cry, and there's no worse luck than for a bride to cry on her wedding day."

"I hear the music," Ida said. "Let's go. Here, Molly. Take your Bible and remember to smile." She cast an appraising eye over her youngest daughter. "It's time." She turned as she opened

126

the door, and Renata was surprised to see tears in Ida's eyes. The woman wasn't as unfeeling as she seemed.

Ida led the way to the stairs with Renata behind her and Molly bringing up the rear. Renata couldn't help but notice the oppressively garish wallpaper and was glad Callie had not inherited her mother's sense of style. At the stairs, she paused to let Ida go down and into the parlor as she had seen Molly do at Callie's wedding.

"Callie? Am I really pretty? Will Ennis be pleased?" Molly whispered.

"You're beautiful. If Ennis isn't pleased, he must be crazy." She suddenly thought she shouldn't be too supportive of this Ennis or everyone would wonder. She still was puzzled why Callie, who apparently never took a stand on anything, had been so adamant that Molly shouldn't marry the man.

Ida went through the parlor door and the music swelled out. Renata began the slow trip down the stairs. She wished she had flowers or something to hold because she was visibly trembling. Surely someone would notice she wasn't really Callie when all their attention would be on her until Molly entered the room.

The parlor was the usual size, but Renata felt as if it was as long as a football field when she started between the rows of chairs. She looked for Nathan and found him in the second row on the left. Naturally he would be sitting with the bride's family, she thought. She looked at the preacher and recognized the man who had married Callie and Nathan. He was smiling and looking past her at Molly who had come in the door.

Ennis stood where Nathan had stood the other time Renata had been in this room. He wasn't looking at Molly but straight at her. When Renata's eyes met his, he winked.

Renata almost stumbled. That had been a wink, not a blink, and he was smirking at her in an unpleasant way. She suddenly felt sick. Who was he, and why was he affecting her so adversely? The part of her mind that had been Callie in this lifetime cringed with panic. Renata felt as if she were two people, and for a moment she thought Dr. McIntyre was about to pull her back to the present. She remained where she was, however, and her revulsion for Ennis continued to grow.

She took her place where the matron of honor would stand and looked back at Molly. She was smiling shyly beneath her transparent veil and glancing at Ennis. Her father had fallen into place beside her at the door, and her hand rested lightly on his. Renata risked another glance at Ennis and was relieved to see he was watching Molly.

Ennis wasn't bad looking. He was older than she had expected, but she knew it was acceptable for a woman to marry an older man during this time period. He had brown hair slicked to a darker sheen with pomade and a moustache in a lighter shade. His eyes were troubling, and she tried to tell herself it was because they were an unattractive shade of green, but that wasn't it. His eyes had no depth. Looking into them had reminded her of a shark she had seen once at Sea World. His eyes seemed perfectly flat and expressionless. Ennis seemed to be not only unpleasant to Callie, but perhaps downright dangerous.

When Molly reached the improvised altar, the preacher asked who brought this bride to be wed and her father answered that he had. Renata glanced at the man and saw where Callie had inherited her gray eyes. His hair was graying, but she thought it might have been the same auburn as Callie's when he was younger. He placed Molly's hand in Ennis' and went to sit by Ida.

The preacher began the ceremony. Renata clasped her hands in front of her and tried to stop trembling. This was the strongest of Callie's memories that she had experienced, and it wasn't pleasant. Ennis triggered a fear in her that Renata wouldn't have believed possible. Obviously Callie had been terrified of him. But why?

She tried to keep her mind on the wedding. Molly was marrying Ennis of her own free will, and her parents clearly were in favor of the match. What did Callie know that they did not? Renata could almost remember, but it kept slipping maddeningly away.

Once Molly and Ennis had repeated their vows, the preacher pronounced them man and wife, and Ennis lifted Molly's veil to kiss her. Renata watched with a sick feeling. Molly tilted her head up to him, and he put a chaste kiss on her lips. When his eyes met Renata's over Molly's shoulder, Renata took a step backward. This seemed to amuse Ennis, and he was smiling as he looked back at his bride.

The congregation rose and came forward to congratulate the bride and groom. Renata was relieved to find Nathan at her side. "Could we get some fresh air?" she whispered. "I need some space."

"Space? Let's go out the side door." He helped her maneuver toward a door that led out into the side garden.

Renata gulped in air. The scent of flowers was thick, and she could hear bees humming amid the blossoms. She wrapped her arms around herself and told herself not to hyperventilate.

"Are you all right? I thought you looked as if you might faint."

"I've never fainted in my life," Renata said. She was too upset to guard her words. "I didn't expect to be so upset by seeing Ennis."

"Do you still have tender feelings for him?" Nathan drew back as if he expected to hear an affirmative answer.

"Lord, no! I can't imagine that I ever did! I really used to date him?"

"Callie, are you well?"

She mentally chastised herself for being careless with her language. "I meant I don't see what I was attracted to in him."

"He's not bad looking. Certainly he has enough money. Everyone expected you to choose him over me."

"I'm not that foolish, surely." She still couldn't understand the strong negative feeling she had about Ennis. As much as she had loved Nathan at first sight, she had loathed Ennis. It seemed Callie's emotions were the strongest element she had passed to Renata. "You don't like him either. You've said so. What do you have against him?"

"It's hardly a fit subject to discuss with my wife and especially not at her sister's wedding."

"Don't give me that. Why don't you like him?"

"Even while he was courting you, he was keeping a woman over in Pier's Landing. He also frequents Barbara Downs' house. He won't be faithful to Molly."

The first thought that leaped to Renata's mind about Ennis' promiscuity was the risk of AIDS. Then she remembered that AIDS had not yet developed. Of course, at this time there were other sexually transmitted diseases that could be deadly without treatment, and she couldn't remember whether penicillin had been discovered yet. "Why didn't someone tell me? Would you all have let me marry him without telling me what sort of man he is?"

"It's Molly who married him," Nathan said to answer her question. "He hasn't changed."

"And you let her?"

"We both tried every way we could to talk her out of it. She wouldn't reconsider."

"Molly is such an innocent she probably doesn't know what it means to have a mistress, much less to know that he is seeing a whore!"

Nathan looked at her sharply, and Renata knew she had overstepped the bounds. "I'm sorry, but what else would you call Barbara Downs?"

"That's exactly what I would call her. I'm only amazed that you used the word. Besides, it's not unusual for an unmarried man to take care of his needs like that."

"Did you? Do you still?" she demanded.

Nathan smiled. "No, I don't. And didn't. That's not the only reason I dislike Ennis. He reminds me of something you might find under a rotten log."

Renata nodded. "Exactly. I guess there's nothing we can do now."

"Not a thing but be a friend to Molly. We had better go back inside before we are missed."

Renata dreaded returning to the stuffy parlor, but she knew he was right—especially since everyone must know Ennis and Callie had dated, or whatever the proper term might be. For her to stay away from the reception would make people think she was jealous. Renata wondered how Callie could have gone out with the man. Or was her revulsion of him a learned response, a reaction to Callie's experiences with the man?

When she worked her way to Molly's side, she kissed her sister's cheek and wished her happiness. Ennis was smiling in a way that made Renata want to slap him.

"What about the groom? Surely you can kiss your new brother."

Renata drew herself up. "I never heard of anyone but the bride getting kisses at a wedding. Welcome to our family," she made herself add. She had to be polite to the man or Molly would be upset with her.

"Callie," a voice said at her elbow, "I didn't see you come in. I was so relieved to see you stand up for Molly."

Renata turned to see a woman of about her own age. She reminded herself to smile. Was this a cousin? The woman had dark blond hair and hazel eyes and a slight resemblance to Ida. "We were late. I went directly upstairs. How are you?"

"Fine. It seems like we haven't visited in ages. Don't you ever come into town anymore?"

"Not as often as I'd like." Who was she? Did Callie avoid her as well?

"I saw Alma over by the punch bowl. She was wondering if you'd be here."

"I wouldn't miss my own sister's wedding, now would I?" So she wasn't Alma. Renata wondered what to say to her next.

"Hello, Lidy Mae," Nathan said from behind her. "You're looking pretty today."

Lidy Mae blushed and laughed. "Get out of here, Nathan Blue. You're a married man."

He laughed and winked at Renata. "You haven't been out to see us lately. Don't tell me you can't tear yourself away from your beau long enough to visit friends. How is Pete, anyway?"

"He's just fine. He couldn't make it today."

Renata gave Nathan a thankful smile. Naturally he couldn't have known she needed help, but inadvertently he had given her several clues.

"Oh? Why not?"

Lidy Mae leaned over and whispered in Renata's ear. "Mrs. Lucas is being delivered of her baby today."

Renata nodded. Lidy Mae must be seeing the local doctor. "Perhaps both of you could come see us next week."

"I'd like that. I want to get that quilting pattern from you."

"Quilting pattern?"

"You know, the Kentucky Star pattern. Don't you remember?"

"Actually I don't."

"I'm having a quilting party Monday week and you promised to help me set up the quilting frame and to bring the new pattern when you come."

"Oh, that's right," Renata said, pretending to remember. How in hell could she learn to set up a quilting frame in a week and a half? "How silly of me to forget."

"It's not like you to be absent-minded."

"It's not?" If that was true, why did Nathan overlook so many of her lapses? "I suppose marriage has affected my brain."

"Callie! The things you say."

She let Lidy Mae ease her into conversation with the woman who had whisked her upstairs and who seemed to be Callie's aunt. Ida joined them and was giving Lidy Mae the recipe for the punch when Renata realized no one but Lidy Mae and Nathan had noticed anything different about her at all. A sadness crept over her. Callie was gone and no one noticed. None of her family seemed to pay her enough attention to tell the difference between Callie and Renata. Had it always been that way? Renata wondered if her own family and friends would react in the same way if someone else were to take her place in the family circle. It was an unsettling feeling.

Chapter Seven

When Molly and Ennis returned from their honeymoon, Renata sent a note inviting them out to supper. She was in no rush to see Ennis again, but she wanted to be sure Molly was all right.

When they arrived, Renata could see Molly wasn't as happy as she had been. She asked her to come with her to the kitchen to help prepare the meal, but her primary interest was a private conversation with her sister.

"Oh, Callie, you were right," Molly whispered. "He isn't the same man who courted me."

Renata glanced at her sharply, then realized this was only a turn of speech as it applied to Ennis. "In what way?"

"He was so thoughtful then. So gentle." Molly turned away. "I hate marriage!"

Renata went to her and put her arms around her. "There, there now. Don't cry. You'll smear your makeup."

Molly laughed through her tears. "What up?

I should hope I haven't sunk to that yet."

Catching her mistake, she said, "Of course, I was teasing. At least you laughed."

"How do you stand it? Being married, I mean? I hate for him to touch me. It . . . it hurts."

"I'm so sorry. It doesn't have to, Molly. Making love can be wonderful."

Molly drew in a deep breath. "Don't let Mama hear you say that. As soon as we came back from the trip, I went to her and asked if I was doing it wrong. You know, maybe I wasn't trying hard enough. She was so upset that I expected to enjoy it, I thought she was going to have one of her spells. I started not to tell you, but since we've always been so close, I thought you might understand."

"I'm glad you told me. You can come to me with anything. Mama is wrong. A man should please his wife as much as she pleases him. Some men are too selfish to care about anything beyond themselves. Does he take the time to be sure you are ready before he begins?" She hoped this was said euphemistically enough for Molly.

"What do you mean?"

"Does he excite you first? Make you want him?"

Molly's cheeks blazed bright pink. "Callie! The things you say these days." She paused. "No, he doesn't."

"Maybe he doesn't know he's supposed to.

Try telling him next time and maybe he will be more romantic."

"I could never do that!"

"Molly, he is your husband." Renata tried to remain patient with the girl. It was hard to remember that Molly's sexual knowledge was less than that of a girl half her age in Renata's time. "You should be able to tell him anything."

"Does Nathan . . . you know?"

Renata nodded and hoped she was right. She couldn't tell Molly she and Nathan had yet to make love. "Of course he does. And because of it, I like to make love with him."

Molly shook her head again. "I don't think I could ever say something like that. Mama says I have to put up with it, though, or I won't have a baby. Maybe after we have a few children, Ennis won't want to do it anymore."

"Maybe." Prior to having lived with Nathan these past three weeks, Renata would have said that was unlikely, but evidently abstinence was the accepted form of birth control these days.

They began putting the final touches on the meal. In the past weeks Renata had learned a great deal about cooking on a wood stove, and even though she still had trouble lighting it and had never mastered the art of banking the fire so it would last from one day to the next, she could turn out passable dishes.

"What's this?" Molly asked as Renata took a broccoli casserole out of the oven. "I've never seen anything like this before."

"It's called a casserole. I'll teach you to cook this way, if you'd like. Casseroles are much easier than cooking meat and vegetables separately."

"Where are the peas?"

"We aren't having any."

"No peas? You haven't run out, have you? The new ones won't be ripe for several weeks yet."

"We don't have peas and beans every meal. Nathan doesn't like beans, and I'm not fond of peas."

"Since when? You've eaten them all your life."

"I guess my tastes have changed. I made three casseroles. Nathan eats more than any man I've ever known. I'll mix the salad."

"What do I do with these? Pour them into a bowl?"

"No, they go to the table in the pan. That's one reason they are so easy to make."

Molly stared at her. "You want me to put the pan on the table? I mean, we're family and all, but Ennis is company in a way."

"Put them on the table and put a spoon in each one. There are hot pads in that drawer." Renata began pulling apart a head of lettuce. She had bought it in town and had been lucky to find it at this time of year. She had made a dressing by mixing catsup and mayonnaise and some of the herbs Callie had dried from the summer before. There were no tomatoes

139

yet, but she had radishes and cheese to cube. She also mixed in a bit of the ham she had cooked the day before. It wasn't a great salad, but it was passable.

She put the salad on the table along with a bowl of the dressing. Molly looked at her as if she had gone out of her mind. "There are biscuits on top of the stove," she said to Molly. "Would you bring them in? I'll go call the men."

"Are you sure this is all of the meal?" Molly asked in an undertone. "There doesn't seem to be much of it, if you don't mind my saying so."

"Casseroles are very filling. We will have plenty."

When Ennis and Nathan came to the table, Renata met them with a smile. She was proud of the meal and knew she had cooked the casseroles to perfection. "Have a seat." She and Nathan had not yet eaten in the dining room, and she wasn't sure which was supposed to be her place. Ennis frowned at the table fare as he took the seat beside Nathan, who had moved to the end of the table. Renata sat opposite Nathan and motioned for Molly to sit across from Ennis.

Ennis stared at her. "Where's the rest of the meal? And why are you sitting down? Molly always waits on the table—especially when we have guests."

"If you need something, I'll get up and go

get it." Renata was trying hard not to show her revulsion. "In my house, women eat with the men, not in the kitchen."

Ennis looked at Nathan. "Looks like I married the right sister." He laughed as if he expected Nathan to laugh with him.

Nathan didn't so much as smile. Ennis turned his laugh into a cough and said to Molly, "Where's the cornbread and peas?"

"Callie didn't cook any tonight. She says she and Nathan don't eat peas or beans every day."

"We have biscuits instead of cornbread, and this is broccoli casserole. I'm sure you'll like it. Nathan does."

Nathan smiled at her. "I've learned to like it. At least it's better than those beans you used to fix."

Renata smiled back at him. He had been brave enough to taste everything she had cooked, and some of it had been pretty bad. She reached for the salad bowl, but Molly caught her eye and bowed her head pointedly. Renata guiltily bent her head. She and Nathan never said grace at a meal in the kitchen, but he was already beginning one now. When he finished, Molly echoed his amen. Renata passed her the salad.

She had to teach them how to put the dressing on the salad. Molly was game to try anything Renata served her, and Nathan was already accustomed to salads. Ennis glared at it suspiciously and after a bite or two ignored it in favor of the casserole.

141

The meal seemed to last forever. Renata knew she should have cooked a more traditional meal, but she was too uncertain in the kitchen. She had seldom cooked at her apartment, and without a microwave she thought she was doing better than could have been expected. Of course none of the others knew that.

For dessert she had baked a pie from dried apples, and while the crust was heavy, it was more of a success than the rest of the meal had been. She hoped Nathan wasn't embarrassed at her lack of expertise as a cook, but she was doing her best. Molly seemed more surprised than any of them, but Molly must know Callie's recipes and the taste of her food. Nathan had accepted the changes in the meals as well as the changes in her personality.

After the pie was eaten, Molly helped Renata clear the meal away. "Where did you learn to make this casserole thing?" she whispered. "I've never tasted anything like it."

"I made it up." Renata knew there was no other way to explain it to Molly. "Didn't you like it?"

"Yes, as a matter of fact I did. It's the first time I've ever eaten broccoli and liked it. I was surprised you cooked it, knowing how I dislike it."

That had never occurred to Renata. "I'm sorry, Molly. I forgot."

"You seem to forget a lot these days. Mama's

birthday was last week and you didn't even go see her."

"It was?" There was so much to trip up Renata. She wished she had had some warning that she would be trapped here so she could have memorized things that would help her pass as Callie. For that matter, she had not even the vaguest idea when her own birthday was—or Nathan's. She didn't even know what year this was. There wasn't even an almanac in the house. She had surmised that Nathan lived such a routine life that there was no reason for him to know the exact date.

"Papa was still upset with you when I returned home from the honeymoon. He says you owe them both an apology."

"He's right. I'll send him a note right away."

"I can take it to them. I'll be over there tomorrow."

"How are they?" Renata asked in hopes of averting some other mistake.

"Well enough. Mama's joints are moving easier now that the weather is warmer. Papa had a touch of gout but it's better now, too. Aunt Eliza has gone back to Shreveport."

Renata wondered if that was the aunt who had escorted her to Molly's room before the wedding. She had met so many people she was beginning to confuse their names. "Have you heard from Alma lately?"

"Yes, she says she enjoyed the wedding and

that she is going to try to be better at answering my letters."

"That's nice."

"I thought you didn't care for Alma. You've always said she was feather-headed and that she wasn't as good a friend to me as I am to her."

"I'm trying to be more forgiving."

"I should be, too. I find I'm collecting grudges these days."

"You? I can't believe it." Renata had rarely met anyone so eager to please everyone.

"It's true. Jemima wrote me a letter the other day, and I just dashed off a short note to her and threw her letter away. Ever since she said she didn't like Ennis, I've had hard feelings toward her."

"I don't like him either, but you still speak to me."

"You're my sister, and you're in a position to know whether you like him or not. Jemima only met him once, and she didn't even come to the wedding."

"Jemima," Renata mumbled as she mentally tried to place the name.

"Nathan's sister." Molly stared at her. "How could you forget that?"

"I didn't forget. I was only saying her name aloud. Jemima. It has a nice ring to it."

"I've always liked the name Priscilla better. Remember how we both named our dolls that?"

"I remember." Renata poured warm water into her dishpan from the large pot she kept heating at all times on the back of the stove and began washing dishes. Molly picked up a cup towel and began drying them. "What do you suppose ever happened to those dolls?"

"Mama packed them in that trunk in the attic."

"I guess someday we can pass them down to our daughters."

"I thought you didn't want to have children. That's what you told me, though I didn't say anything to Mama. You know how upset she would be."

"I may have changed my mind. Molly, do you recall when I miscarried? What happened? Do you think it was because I lifted that heavy load of wash?"

"I'm not sure. That's what you said, but Lidy Mae said she thought it might have been something else. She said she saw you the day before, and that you had been awfully upset about something. She thought maybe it was because Ennis and I had just announced our engagement, but I had told you about it before anyone else knew. It seems odd to me that you would have become upset that day."

"Maybe Nathan and I had had words. I don't remember."

"That doesn't seem likely either. Before you lost the baby, I don't recall you two ever arguing." Molly delicately looked away, and Renata

145

knew it was because Callie and Nathan had argued often since that time.

"If whatever upset me was bad enough to cause the miscarriage, it's important that I figure it out so it doesn't happen again."

"You could go back to see Pete Larsen. Dr. Larsen, I should say. It's so hard to believe Pete made a doctor, isn't it? Anyway, he might be able to tell you something."

"Perhaps." She was reluctant to go to a doctor Callie had been to before because there might be some difference in her that would show up in an examination. Besides, she wasn't all that confident of medical procedures of the nineteenth century.

"I couldn't go to him myself," Molly confided. "I know him too well. I could never let him listen to my heart."

Renata nodded. In these days prior to the routine pap smears of the late twentieth century, baring a woman's chest so the doctor could listen to her heart might be the closest to naked that a woman patient became, short of accidents or pregnancy.

Molly dried the last dish and said, "Cooking that casserole sure uses fewer pots and pans. I wonder if Ennis would let me get by with doing that from time to time."

"It's your kitchen. Unless he wants to do the cooking himself, you should do as you please."

In a shocked voice Molly said, "I couldn't tell him that. And I don't believe you would say that to Nathan either. Even Papa wouldn't stand for his wife telling him what she will or will not cook."

"Mama has a woman to cook for her. There's a difference when you hire someone to do it."

"I suppose. Nevertheless, I'd never dare."

Renata took the cup towel from Molly. "Go in and talk to the men. I'm going to put these last dishes away, and then I'll join you."

Molly left, and as Renata slowly folded the damp cloth, she wondered if it would be safe to write down the names and facts she was learning about people in order to keep them all straight until she was more comfortable here. But what if Nathan found her notes? What if she started keeping a journal and hid it and someone in 1992 found it? What would they make of it?

She heard a sound behind her and turned to find Ennis standing close enough that she could have touched him. "You scared me half to death! I didn't hear you come in."

"I told Nathan and Molly that I was going to the outhouse."

Even though he made her skin crawl, she tried to hide her loathing for him. "So why are you in here?"

"Don't play the innocent with me. Did you really think I would lose interest in you after I married Molly? I told you nothing would change between us."

Renata stared up at him. Surely Callie and

this toad weren't having an affair! "Oh?" she said in hopes he would give her more information.

"I'll be in the woods behind the stream tomorrow. Meet me there."

"I'll do nothing of the kind!"

"Yes, you will, or I'll tell Nathan that you and I are lovers. You know I can prove it."

"You'd never tell him that! What about Molly?"

"What about her? She doesn't have anything to do with this. She will do as she's told, same as you."

"If you say anything like that to Nathan, he'll kill you!"

"Will he? You know I'll say it was all your idea."

Her senses reeled. Did Ennis know something she didn't? She had thought she knew Nathan pretty well, but perhaps she didn't. Or was Callie the one she didn't know well? Perhaps Ennis knew that Callie was so afraid of everything that she wouldn't risk Nathan's rejection by mentioning anything untoward to him. Suspicion crept over her. "Did I see you the day I miscarried my baby?"

"Don't act the fool. You know you did. I met you at the stream where you wash clothes. You were threatening to tell Nathan, until I told you what would happen to you when he abandoned you. You might have been reluctant, but I've never enjoyed it more."

"You were the reason I lost the baby," she whispered. This made sense. Callie must have refused him, and he had raped her. Renata felt sick. How long had this been going on?

"Molly told me you've been acting odd lately. You aren't trying to play sick in order to get away from me, are you? I've told you what happens to girls who get sick in the head. They are chained to a wall in the insane asylum and left to starve."

Renata's stomach knotted with nausea. No wonder he had been able to frighten poor Callie to distraction. She, too, was feeling afraid, even though she knew half of what he said was lies.

"Now come here and give me a kiss," Ennis commanded, roughly pulling her to him and smearing his lips over hers.

As Renata struggled against him, her fingers slipped off his arm and onto the oiled cloth that covered the kitchen table. Her fingers knotted around the table cloth, she jerked as hard as she could. The salt and pepper shakers, the bottle of oil and vinegar and the jar of pickled peppers all crashed to the floor with a resounding clatter. Ennis jumped away from her and glared.

Menacingly, he pointed his finger at her. "You'll regret it if you refuse me. I've had you every time I've wanted you since you was sixteen, and I won't give you up. If you marrying a husband didn't stop me, nothing else will, either." He backed through the door and into the night, disappearing in the direction of the outhouse.

Renata braced herself on the table and let the tears flow. He had used Callie since she was 16! Renata knew Callie had married Nathan when she was 22 and that had been at least a year ago. How had she suffered this brute all these years? Renata felt as if her heart were breaking for Callie.

Nathan and Molly hurried into the room and found her crying. "What's wrong?" he demanded. "Is something wrong?"

Renata nodded. She had to think. She couldn't blurt out that Ennis had been sexually blackmailing Callie for at least seven years. "I was dizzy. I nearly fell." As she heard her words, she realized she was making excuses just as Callie must have. Her tears flowed harder.

"Why are you crying?" Nathan came to her and tenderly put his arms around her.

She held him tightly. She could think of no reason to give him except the truthful one, so she fell back on a ploy women had used for ages. "I don't want to talk about it."

"I think Ennis and I should go," Molly said. "She must be feeling ill." She went to Renata and patted her sister's back. "Whatever it is, she will be herself by morning."

This made Renata cry even harder because she knew it wasn't true. Callie might never be herself again.

*   *   *

Ennis had been filled with anger and frustration as he hurried out of the house, but he had not gone far. About halfway between the kitchen door and the outhouse he had stopped so that if anyone came looking for him, he could make it appear that he been outside taking care of personal matters. As he sucked in a deep breath, he willed himself to be calm. He couldn't believe Callie had done something so foolish as to thwart him and make such a ruckus that was sure to draw attention.

Already relaxing, he leaned against the trunk of a tree and stared back in the direction of the house. By design, there was no direct line of sight from the house to the outhouse, but from his vantage point in between, he could see glimpses of yellow light from the kitchen windows. By now it was likely that Nathan or Molly or both had responded to the commotion and were in the kitchen with Callie. But Ennis wasn't worried. He was sure Callie wouldn't tell either Nathan or Molly that he had kissed her. She wasn't that foolish by a long shot. No, if Callie was going to tell on him, she would have done it years before.

It did bother him, though, that Callie had been acting oddly lately. Molly had not seemed to notice it, but he had. There was a different look in her eye, and she held herself straighter, almost bolder somehow. Callie always had stood or sat as if she were trying to make herself smaller and less noticeable. Ennis didn't like the change.

Feeling completely safe, Ennis took a tobacco paper from his shirt pocket and held it in one hand while he tapped tobacco onto it from a small pouch he kept in the breast pocket of his coat. With his teeth, he closed the drawstring bag and returned it to his pocket. Carefully he rolled the paper around the tobacco, then licked the edge of the paper to seal it. With a practiced twist of his fingers, he closed the ends. As he felt in his pants pocket for his lucifer matches, he stared back at the house.

Callie had always made him want her. She seemed so pure and shy, even after he knew for a fact that she was not, that she constantly enflamed him. Ennis had been sure she would eventually be his wife. When she had married Nathan instead, he had seen to it that she regretted her choice. Ennis's lips pulled back in a smile as he thought how little Nathan must have enjoyed his wedding night. Callie couldn't do anything but cry if a man came anywhere near her. Ennis liked a woman to cower from him, but he knew a lot of men didn't. Nathan probably hated it.

Ennis had married Molly because he thought she would be much like her older sister. But Molly was not. Granted, she had cried and fought against him on their wedding night, but after that, she had put up with him with almost no emotion at all, as if her mind were planning the next day's meals. As a result, Ennis only used her when he couldn't find a more exciting release.

He lit his cigarette and took a deep draw on it. The tip glowed and crackled faintly. As he exhaled a cloud of smoke, he wondered what Callie had told Nathan when he discovered she was not a virgin. He bet old Nathan had been fit to be tied. If the same had happened to Ennis, he was sure he would have felt justified in beating the woman half to death. Ennis took another long, calming drag on his cigarette and smiled.

Since Nathan hadn't come charging out of the house in search of him by now and since he heard no raised voices, Ennis knew Callie had done exactly what he had thought she would. She must have explained the noise as her own clumsiness and left his name entirely out of it. Ennis's smile widened to a grin edged with cruelty. Callie had overstepped the bounds this time, and he was going to teach her that what she had done was a foolish thing, indeed. He knew ways of bringing that home to her, ways that didn't leave a bruise that Nathan would notice.

The sound of the kitchen screened door slamming drew his attention. Molly called out to him and he answered, then he took one final puff on his cigarette and tossed it away in a glowing arc. Assuming an air of innocence, he sauntered back toward the house.

Inside the kitchen, Renata continued to cling to Nathan's powerful body as if he were her lifeline. From outside, she heard Molly suggesting that she and Ennis should go without further good-byes because Callie was not feeling well, and when Ennis agreed, Renata felt a wave of relief that she would not have to face him again that evening. But what about the next time? What could she possibly do to avoid Ennis when he was so bold as to kiss her against her will in her own kitchen with Nathan only two rooms away? She felt a strong measure of Callie's hopelessness. It was evident that Callie felt soiled by Ennis's touch, and thus it was not surprising that she didn't want Nathan to make love with her. Callie must be repulsed by any show of physical affection. Forcing herself to move, she pulled back from Nathan and began cleaning up the mess she had made. Fortunately the bottles had not broken and their tight stoppers had not come loose.

"Let's go upstairs," Nathan suggested. "It's late. There will be time tomorrow to sweep up the salt and pepper."

She nodded. In a farmer's world nine o'clock was like midnight in her own.

As Nathan pulled the kitchen lamp down so he could reach it to blow out the light, Renata went through the dining room and into the parlor. The fire there was out already since the night was warm. She blew out the two china lamps and carried the metal one to the door to light their way upstairs.

Once she was in the bedroom and behind the safety of the folding screen, Renata began to shake. Ennis had made it clear that he wouldn't take no for an answer. Eventually he would find her when Nathan wasn't nearby, and he would try to do with her as he pleased. Renata had never been so frightened. She tried to remember the details of the self-defense course she had taken, but her mind refused to supply any useful information. Wearing Callie's long skirts and petticoats, her ability to run from him or to kick him would be hampered in the extreme.

Hiding behind the safety of the screen, she said, "Nathan, do you trust me?"

"Trust you? Certainly. Why would you ask such a thing?" His tone of voice revealed a hint of suspicion.

"I only wondered. I would never do anything to hurt you."

Nathan came around the corner of the screen as she was pulling her nightgown over her head. "I never thought you might. What are you talking about?"

"Nothing. I guess I'm just edgy."

He looked as if he didn't entirely believe her, but he said, "You let too many things scare you. The world isn't as dangerous as you seem to think. There's nothing here to hurt you. I've never understood why you are so afraid of everything."

"I can't explain it."

"Come to bed." He moved the screen so she could pass him.

She climbed onto bed and slid under the covers. Nathan blew out all but the dim light on his side of the bed. Turning his back to her, he began undressing. Renata couldn't help but watch.

His entire upper torso was as tightly muscled as were his shoulders, which she had seen every night she had shared his bed. He had no hair on his chest or his back, and as he leaned forward to unbutton his pants, the muscles in his back and shoulder flexed in a most provocative manner. She wanted to touch him, to be held and comforted by him. Did Callie have a valid reason not to tell him about Ennis? Perhaps it was because she feared Nathan would actually kill the man, and she didn't want that on her conscience.

Nathan removed his boots and socks, then his trousers and drawers. Renata had never seen a man with a more beautiful body. As he began turning toward her, she closed her eyes. Since he gave her the privacy of undressing away from his view, it seemed likely that Callie would do the same for him.

He came around to his side of the bed and got in beside her after blowing out the light. Renata lay still. She was aching for him to hold her, but he made no move to do so. "Nathan?" she said in the darkness. "Do you love me?"

He paused before answering. "You know I do. Lately you've been different though. I feel as if I don't know you half the time."

"Have I been better or worse?"

"Neither. Just different. Like your crying in the kitchen this evening. That was more like you than you've been in weeks."

A deep sadness swept over Renata. Was it more natural for Callie to cry than to smile? "That doesn't say much for me, does it?"

"It's how you are. You've always cried easily. You used to cry instead of getting mad. Here lately it's been just the opposite. At times I feel as if I'm talking to some stranger. I guess that doesn't make much sense."

"You'd be surprised," she said wryly.

"I know you've been upset about losing the baby, but it seems odd that you'd go on so about it. I don't mean to sound hardhearted, but I can't help but wonder. Other women lose babies or even children, and they manage to get through it. I think you're wrong to insist that we not have a family. Maybe it would even help you to have another baby."

Renata's heart went out to him. He wanted a family, but he seemed to want children more for Callie's sake than for his own. She risked it all and said, "I love you, Nathan."

He was silent for a long time but she knew he was awake. "You haven't said that in the past year or more."

"I should have. I should never have taken you

157

for granted. Not many women ever meet a man like you, and no one else I know has as good a husband."

Through the darkness she could hear Nathan turning over so he could look at her. "Why are you telling me this?"

"I think you should know. I want our marriage to be better."

"You should get some sleep," he said gruffly. "I don't want to do something that you will hold against me in the morning. You haven't let me touch you in months. You said you never would again. I want you to think on this so you don't blame me for forcing you into doing something you dislike so much."

Renata eyes filled with tears again. Nathan knew Callie hated for him to touch her, but he had no idea what the reason was. She was tempted to tell him, but she was afraid. Callie might know him better and have a reason to remain silent other than her fear of Ennis. Renata decided it would be wiser to bide her time a little longer.

Nathan stared at the ceiling as he lay still in the darkness listening to his wife's breathing. After a long time the sound became softer and rhythmic in sleep. Nathan rolled over and raised up on one elbow to look at her.

He had loved Callie for a long time, but he had never understood her. Tonight, for instance, he and Molly had heard a loud crashing noise from the kitchen and had rushed in thinking Callie had fallen or hurt herself only to find her standing there crying with the tablecloth and condiments about her feet. It seemed unlikely to him that an accident would have pulled the cloth and relish jars so completely off the table, and he could only assume that Callie had done this on purpose. He knew Callie usually crept about making as little noise as possible, and it was completely unlike her to make such a mess. It made no sense—but then what about her ever had?

In the dim moonlight that made its way through the windows, he could see her pale, oval face. Her hair, which she no longer braided at night for some unknown reason, was tumbled over the pillow. As he gazed upon the lovely woman next to him, his love for her tightened in his chest until he felt as if his heart might burst. He deeply loved her, and he had always wanted to protect her, even before his love for her had begun to grow. She was so fragile and easily broken, like the tender shoot of a plant in early spring.

Lately he had seen changes in her, and while he was not sure why she was different, he was certainly intrigued. He could tell by the way Molly and her parents spoke to her that they were unaware of any change in her, but Nathan knew it was there. Even though he always ached when she cried, he had been almost glad to see her tears this evening. She had looked more like the Callie he was accustomed to than she had in quite a while.

He touched a tendril of her hair, moving gently so he would not awaken her. When they were first married, he had often watched her sleep. It was as close as he was able to come to her and not see fear in her eyes. He had spent more than one night puzzling over what he had done to frighten her so and over the other inconsistencies in his wife. He knew that her parents were and always had been strict, but that in itself should not have made her so vulnerable. More than once he had asked her why she jumped if he moved suddenly and why she hated for him to walk up behind her in a room. Callie had had no answer.

Now, much to his amazement, she said she loved him and wanted to know if he loved her in return. They had talked more tonight—really talked as husband and wife—than they had in months, maybe even in years. Too numerous to count were the times Nathan had talked and Callie had only cried. Tonight, in bed, she had talked of love. It was still hard for him to believe he had heard her correctly.

He had not thought she loved him. At first he had, or at least he had assumed she was beginning to love him, but that seemed like a long time ago. It upset her for him to say he loved her, so he had finally stopped telling her. Now that he thought about it, he wasn't sure she had ever come right out and said she loved him—not like she had tonight, just out-right and without any qualifications.

He supposed he would never understand her, but he wasn't too sure any man ever really understood women. That was part of their mystery. All the other men he knew seemed content to have it that way, so he never told anyone how Callie fascinated him and how much he wanted to know how she felt and what she thought.

For a minute, he considered waking her and asking her why she had talked about love in the one room where she never wanted to talk at all. But he knew he would see the all-too-familiar fear leap into her eyes and that she would draw away from him as if he were a snake.

With a sigh, Nathan lay back on his pillow and closed his eyes. He couldn't bear to see her flinch away from him, and she would be certain to do that if she caught him looking at her in their bed at night; she had become hysterical over less than that in the past. Nathan tried to will himself to sleep and to conquer once again the love for her that had become a physical need.

Chapter Eight

Renata was on her hands and knees on the kitchen floor, scrubbing at the baseboards with a brush. She had never been fond of housework, and she had never dreamed it could be so difficult. Each thrust of the scrub brush was punctuated with a muttered oath that Callie would never have used. Every drop of water she used had to be drawn from the well on the porch, and every household tool was powered by muscle rather than by electricity. She was glad she was in Callie's seasoned body rather her own pampered one.

Outside, she heard Nathan speak to the dog as he came up the kitchen steps. When he saw what she was doing, he paused in the doorway. "I'm going into town. Do you need anything?"

"Not unless electricity and indoor plumbing have been invented," she muttered under her breath.

"What? I didn't hear what you said."

"I said 'no, thank you.' " She sat back on her heels and rested her aching arms. "How long will you be gone?"

"Only long enough to pick up a block of salt for the cows and some feed. Aren't we running low on flour by now?"

"We still have a ten pound bag."

"That won't last long. I'd better get some more."

"I suppose." She thought how long ten pounds of flour would have lasted with the little cooking she used to do and shook her head. "You'd better get some sugar, too. You wouldn't believe the lumps that are in that sack. Maybe if we try a different brand."

"Sugar is sugar. I don't think the store has more than one kind. All sugar is lumpy. That wooden mallet of yours does a pretty good job of making small lumps out of the big ones."

"Mallet? Oh, yes, the mallet. Of course it does. I just get tired of having to do it, I suppose." She brushed a damp tendril of hair off her forehead.

Nathan squatted down on his heels so they were the same height. "Callie, are you sure you are feeling well? Sometimes it's as if you don't remember the simplest things, like what kind of sugar the store stocks. How can you forget something like that?"

Renata put down her scrub brush and wished she could be honest with him. It wasn't fair for Nathan to be deprived of his wife, even if she suspected their marriage was an unhappy one. He must have loved Callie to have married her, and he deserved more than lies from a stranger. What would he say if she told him the truth?

"I know you must be lonely out here, even if you don't admit it. Why don't I go by Lidy Mae's house and ask her to come out for a visit?"

"That would be nice." Renata didn't know what else to say. Lidy Mae and Callie were best friends, and Nathan would have thought it odd for her to have refused. Besides, Renata *was* lonely. "Do you think she could come out tomorrow?"

"I'll be in the back field all day. Tomorrow would be perfect." He stood up to leave.

"Nathan?" she said uncertainly.

He looked at her.

"Never mind." Honest or not, she didn't want to risk losing him. If she told him she wasn't Callie, he might not allow her to remain here. Although she wasn't sure it would make a difference in her getting back to her own time, she thought it might be better to stay near the place where she had arrived. She refused to let herself consider that she also didn't want to leave Nathan.

As he walked back down the steps and across the yard, she watched him from the kitchen window. The sight of his broad back and narrow hips did things to her libido that still surprised her. At times she still felt as if she were a mix of herself and Callie, but her desire for Nathan was entirely her own. Callie was too afraid of men to allow herself to want even her own husband. Nathan deserved better than that, Renata told herself. She might do most things wrong and appear to have lost her senses to a person who didn't know how she had ended up here, but she was positive she could be a better wife to Nathan than Callie could.

In a way it was like saying, "If only I had known then what I know now." Through all this, was she being given an opportunity to correct an error in her own past? If so, she was determined to correct it. Perhaps Lidy Mae's visit would cast some light on the puzzle of Callie's marriage.

As Nathan drove away in the wagon, Renata stepped out onto the porch. Their life together was far from idyllic, but it wasn't unpleasant. She detested housework as much as she ever had, but she knew it would be no different whether she lived in town or on the farm. Nathan had to work hard too, but he seemed to enjoy it.

As Renata listened, the noisy rumble of the wagon faded into the distance and again she could hear the subtle sounds of the woods and creek. The country was never quiet. It was as if life bubbled all around her. Renata had never thought she would make a good farmer's wife, but now she found she wanted to do that quite badly.

A movement at the edge of the woods by the stream drew her attention, and as she watched,

Ennis stepped out from behind one of the trees. Renata drew back, and her eyes darted after Nathan. He was too far away for her to be able to call him back. She edged closer to the door.

Ennis had apparently been watching her and was fully aware that Nathan had left. Her heart thudded painfully in her chest. How had he known Nathan would go into town today?

When Ennis started up the hill toward her, Renata rushed back into the house and locked the door behind her. But due to the warm weather, the other doors and all the windows were wide open. Ennis could get into the house a dozen ways.

Hurriedly, she began slamming the windows, but she was trembling so hard she was having difficult latching them. Although she could not see him, she knew Ennis was still coming, and he didn't yet realize she was locking him out. As she was leaving the front parlor, she remembered to lock the seldom used front door, but the key that always stayed in the lock proved hard to turn. Precious moments later the lock turned, securing the door, and she ran to shut the other windows.

As she latched the last of the front parlor windows, she heard Ennis' steps on the front porch, then heard the doorknob jiggle as he tried to come in without waiting to be invited. She stifled a scream, thankful that she had gotten to this room before him, but wasted no time going to the next room. The windows there were already secured, and a chill went through her as she realized she couldn't remember for sure which rooms she had already done.

He was beginning to circle the house, checking both doors and windows, and he was starting to call out her name. At first he sounded amused, as if he enjoyed her fear of him, but when he discovered how thorough her efforts to keep him out had been, he became angry.

Renata reached the kitchen as Ennis came off the porch. She could see him now, and that made it even more frightening. All her instincts as Callie rose and threatened to paralyse her with fear. She slammed the kitchen door and threw the bolt with a click. Her fingers fumbled at the windows on either side and then with the back one that faced the smokehouse. Ennis was trying each window, only moments behind her.

Finally, satisfied the house was secure, she backed into the middle of the kitchen. He was glaring at her through one of the windows, and she was afraid he might break the panes and come in despite her efforts. She knew if he did, she would be in danger. The kitchen table touched her hips and she felt her way around it, never taking her eyes off Ennis.

He grinned malevolently, then disappeared from sight. Renata looked about frantically. He must have remembered another way into the house, but where?

She ran back to the front rooms and looked out the windows, but she couldn't see him. She hurried back to the kitchen. She could hear the sounds of his activity, but she couldn't tell where they were coming from. She forced herself to stand still and concentrate. Her eyes fell on the door to the root cellar.

She rarely went into the root cellar because she was convinced that snakes and spiders congregated there. It was a dark, unpleasant place for the storage of canned goods that wouldn't fit into the pantry and for food that was best stored at a cool temperature. Nathan had once said something that suggested it also doubled as a storm cellar when tornadoes were in the area. As a safety precaution in case the house should be blown down over the cellar, he had put in a door for a second exit. Renata had seen it, but she had assumed it was kept locked.

Putting her ear to the door, she listened frantically. The sounds had grown faint, as if Ennis knew she might be listening. She didn't dare open the door to see if she was right. A muffled creak verified her assumption had been correct. He was opening the outside door of the root cellar and soon would be inside. Somehow she had to prevent him from coming into the house through the inside cellar door which had neither bolt nor lock.

Renata unlocked the kitchen door, but only long enough to dash out onto the service porch. She knew Ennis could easily outrun her, so she didn't attempt to leave the house. Instead, she grabbed a hammer and a tin can of nails which Nathan kept there for quick repairs and ran back into the house, leaving the kitchen door open behind her.

She put a nail to the cellar door and drove it in with sure blows. When the third nail was in place she hurried back to lock the kitchen door. Ennis was at the cellar door, bellowing in his frustrated rage. Renata clutched the hammer to her breast, hoping it would be weapon enough if he managed to get in.

Suddenly it occurred to her that there must be a gun in the house somewhere, but she was so frightened she couldn't think. Drawing a calming breath, she reminded herself that Ennis couldn't get in, and that when he realized he couldn't, he would have no choice but to go away and leave her alone. Unless, of course, he decided to break a window.

Nathan's dresser! There was a pistol in Nathan's dresser! She had seen it one day when she was putting his clothes away. At the time it had repulsed her because she had always had an aversion to guns.

She ran upstairs and jerked the drawer open. Rifling through his shirts and socks, she came across the cold steel of the gun barrel. She took the weapon out and held it gingerly. Was it loaded? Even if it were, she wasn't sure how to shoot it.

She went back to the stairs and sat down on the top step. This way Ennis couldn't slip up behind her if he managed to get in. Holding the gun on her lap, she waited. She tried to recall all she had ever heard about how to fire a pistol. Did she have to cock it or would it fire if she simply pulled the trigger? It looked large and deadly, like the guns she had seen in western movies. She struggled to remember what the actors had done to fire the prop pistols and hoped her recollections were accurate.

Minutes passed, each one seeming like an hour. Her muscles grew stiff from being tensed for so long, but she was afraid to relax. Was there another way into the house? She knew she would hear it, if Ennis broke a window. Why hadn't she gone to town with Nathan? She could have scrubbed that floor anytime. Because Ennis hadn't been out to their farm since the night he and Molly had come for a visit, she had assumed that she was safe from him. Had he watched the house from time to time, or was it simply coincidence that he was in the woods when Nathan was leaving for town?

She heard a noise from the yard, and her eyes darted from the front door in the foyer below to the windows she could see in the front parlor. Her mouth was dry and tasted of copper.

"Callie? Callie, why is the door locked?"

Relief swept over her. The voice was Nathan's. He was back. Still clutching the heavy pistol, she scurried down the stairs, barely keeping her balance, then hurriedly unlocked the door and fell into Nathan's arms.

"What's wrong? Is that my pistol?" He held her tightly. "What happened?"

"A . . . a prowler. There was a prowler. He tried to get into the house." She was afraid to tell him it had been Ennis. What if he didn't believe her? How could he believe Ennis would try to attack his new bride's sister? "Hold me, Nathan. I was so afraid."

He chuckled softly. "You must be. You've always been scared to even look at my pistol. Why didn't you get the rifle from behind the door?"

"Rifle?"

Nathan pointed at the door that led from the back parlor into the dining room. Because there had never been a reason to close that door, Renata had never looked behind it.

"It's loaded. This pistol isn't."

"I didn't remember the rifle."

"This pistol would have knocked you flat. The rifle is easier to shoot."

"Will you show me how?" She didn't care if Callie would have known this. She had to take the chance.

"Sure. What did this prowler look like? Have you ever seen him around town?"

"No. No, I don't know who he is." She put her face on Nathan's chest so he wouldn't see she was lying.

"Has he been here before? Is that why you are afraid to be here alone?"

She nodded. It felt so safe to be held by Nathan. Nothing and no one could harm her when he had his arms around her. Renata had never put so much stock in being protected before, but then she had never met a man who seemed so capable of it.

"Let's open the windows. It's awfully hot in here." He gently unwrapped her arms from around him and stepped away.

Renata watched as he opened the windows. A cooling breeze wafted through, lifting the white cotton curtains. Why had he been so eager to release her? Renata felt like crying. Was he so distant in his feelings for Callie that he couldn't bear to touch her? What if he never changed? She would be stuck in the wrong century in a bad marriage that wasn't her fault at all.

When Nathan went into the kitchen and saw the nails in the door to the cellar, he looked at her questioningly.

"He tried to come through that door. There's no lock."

Without comment he began pulling out the nails and put them into his pocket so he could later hammer them straight and reuse them. Still feeling uneasy, Renata looked out one of the windows. By the length of the shadows, she knew it was past mid-afternoon. "I'll start dinner," she said.

"Supper," he corrected. His voice was distracted as if he was thinking. "It's funny a tramp would try to get in this way. How would he know the cellar opened into the house? Most of them don't."

"I guess he stumbled onto it by accident. How should I know?"

Nathan glanced at her. "Are you sure you never saw him before?"

"What are you suggesting?" she snapped. "Of course, I never saw him before." Her nerves were still on edge. What if Nathan opened the door and Ennis was still in the cellar? Images of all the slasher movies she had ever seen came to mind and refused to leave.

Nathan opened the door to the cellar and the room at the bottom of the wooden steps yawned as empty as ever. The outside door was fastened again. "Why would he bother to close the outside door when he left?"

"How should I know?" she answered, her voice rising in frustration. "Maybe he was a neat prowler," she quipped with growing sarcasm. "Maybe he was afraid of drafts. Maybe his mother taught him always to close doors when he finished plundering the neighborhood." She leaned forward and looked down the steps for herself to be sure the cellar was empty.

"There's no need for you to lose your temper. That's not like you."

"No? Maybe it should be. I'm still afraid and you act as if nothing important has happened."

"You've imagined things before, Callie," he said softly.

Renata glared at him. "I didn't imagine this!" She took him by the arm and pulled him toward the window where Ennis had pressed his palm against the glass. "Look! Did I imagine it so well as to leave a hand print on the glass?"

Nathan leaned closer to inspect the glass and discovered there was indeed a hand print on its surface. He frowned and straightened. "I guess I owe you an apology. Someone was here."

"I wouldn't lie about something like that. Why would I?"

"I thought you were after attention from me."

Renata lifted her chin. "If that were the case, which it wasn't, I should think you would make an effort to correct the situation. Why would you ignore your wife until she went to such lengths to get you to notice her?"

"I must have been wrong. You spend most of your time trying to convince me that you don't want my attention at all."

The barb struck home. Renata knew he was right. Callie wouldn't want any man's attention. She would have preferred to be invisible, if possible. Once again she wished Callie could have had the services of a good psychiatrist. Maybe if Callie had resolved some of her problems with the opposite sex, Renata wouldn't have been so reluctant to marry and wouldn't have chosen a boring man like Bob Symons as a fiancé. Not boring, she tried to correct herself. Civilized. Bob was civilized—so civilized he wouldn't cause a wave if he were drowning.

She turned away from Nathan and began preparing their supper. This meal was fairly easy, as she had only to warm what was left from dinner. As she worked, Nathan went out to his workshop. When he returned, he had a bolt lock in his hand. Without a word he attached the bolt lock to the cellar door.

Renata was nervous the next day from the time Nathan went out to the back field until she saw Lidy Mae's buggy rolling down the drive. She went out to welcome her, and Lidy Mae waved when she saw her.

"I'm so glad you could come," Renata said when Lidy Mae stepped onto the porch.

"I miss getting to see you every day. I was beginning to wonder if we weren't friends anymore." Lidy Mae preceded Renata into the foyer where she removed her driving gloves and hat and hung them on the hall tree. "Why is it you never come into town these days?"

So that was how Callie avoided being alone in the house when Nathan was out all day. She had gone into town to visit Lidy Mae. Renata told herself she would have to learn to drive the horse and buggy one way or another. "I've been doing my spring cleaning," she lied as they walked back to the back parlor, "and then there was Molly's wedding."

"Yes. I still can't abide that she married Ennis Hite."

"You don't like him either?"

"You know I detest the man." Lidy Mae frowned at Renata for forgetting. "He makes me think of snakes and grub worms."

"Exactly." Renata offered Lidy Mae a seat, then took one herself. "Molly should never have married him. Why do you suppose she did?"

"I guess she must love him. Molly certainly wasn't lacking for lovers."

Renata started to object to Lidy Mae's statement, then realized "lovers" was the current term for boyfriends. "I'm sure you're right." She decided it would be safer to fish for information from Callie's friend than from her husband or family. "It seems as if we have been friends for ever. How long has it really been? Do you remember?"

"No, we've known each other all our lives, I guess. Remember that summer we went wading and your aunt was so upset over us showing our pantalettes in front of those boys?"

"Yes," Renata said with a smile to encourage Lidy Mae in more memories. "It was so hot that summer."

"That was the same year I was determined to learn how to swim. I made you stand guard while I stripped down to my unmentionables and went into the pond behind my house."

"I remember."

"Imagine me wanting to learn to swim. It's a wonder I didn't drown. And the time we tried to teach Mama's old milk cow to take us for a ride?"

Renata laughed, even though the memories weren't hers. She was glad to see Callie hadn't been afraid of her shadow all her life. "And when we started dating boys?"

"You mean when we started walking out with them? Yes, I do. You had been to several church outings before my parents would let a boy walk me there and back. It seemed so daring at the time. I was afraid I would never know what to say to them."

"I suppose all girls feel that way when boys first enter their lives."

"I can't imagine our parents ever feeling awkward with each other. It's like they were born married."

Renata smiled. "When exactly did I start walking out with Nathan? Do you recall?"

Lidy Mae thought for a minute. "Was it the spring Papa bought that roan colt that kicked a hole in the barn? Yes, I think it was. I know you were already being paired with Ennis." She paused. "What did you ever see in him?"

"I can't recall. I must have been out of my mind," Renata said with conviction.

"Of course, your parents encouraged it, so there wasn't any way to politely refuse, I suppose. Maybe that's why Molly fell in love with him."

"You can't fall in love on demand."

"Your families have been friends forever. Don't you even have a few cousins in common? I think so. Anyway, Ennis isn't bad looking, though I would never call him handsome. Not like Nathan."

"Nathan is, isn't he?" Renata smiled. She loved to talk about him. "I still can't believe I'm here with him."

"Neither can I, in a way. I never expected you to marry a farmer. I'd have said you would be miserable way out here in the country."

Renata laughed. By automobile, the farm would have been a mere ten minute drive from town. "I like it here."

"And you were so afraid of him, at first. You told me you were terrified of being alone with him."

"Nathan?" She couldn't imagine being afraid of such a gentle man, but then Renata had never been subjected to sexual blackmail as had Callie. By her calculations, she must have started seeing him when she was about 20 or 21 years old. Ennis had first molested her at 16. Renata felt sick to think of it.

"I couldn't see why. He's always been such a gentleman. I was curious why your father agreed to the marriage."

178

"He must have known I didn't want Ennis for a husband."

"That is probably true. Also, he did loan Nathan the money for this farm and livestock. He must have believed Nathan would be in the family for him to have done that."

"Yes." Renata wondered why William Graham had done that. He seemed to her to be the image of a stern patriarch, an absolute ruler in his home. Perhaps William had greater affection for his daughter than Renata had assumed, as well as greater insight.

"Of course it was easy to see why you wanted to marry Nathan. Even if you were afraid of him, you worshiped the ground he walked on."

"I still do."

"But you were so shy. Don't you remember? You stopped walking out altogether for months at a time. Molly teased you about becoming an old maid. You said you thought you'd accept Nathan if he asked you to marry him because that was better than having to settle for Ennis."

Renata understood. If Callie was trying to find protection from Ennis, who would be better for the job than Nathan? She must have thought she would be safer out here in the country, too, although that had proven to be false. Rather than being safer, it made it easier for Ennis to molest her without witnesses. Therefore, Callie might not have loved Nathan at all. She might have been merely seeking a protector. Renata's heart went out to Nathan. He must have been bitterly disappointed and hurt when Callie proved not to love him or even to want to be touched by him. No wonder she was having so much trouble breaking through his emotional shell.

Lidy Mae was off on another memory. "Do you recall that old Rhode Island Red hen that we had? Mama would send us out to gather the eggs, and we always saved that old bird for last because we knew she would peck us. I was so glad when she finally ended up in the stew pot. I swear she was as tough as saddle leather."

Renata nodded. She wished she had a memory to add to the conversation, but she didn't dare make anything up.

"Pete is asking me to set the date," Lidy Mae said with a blush and a smile. "I told him I thought November 20th would be a nice date. It's right before Thanksgiving and . . ." Lidy Mae's voice trailed off and her eyes grew wide. "You don't suppose folks will read anything into that, do you? I mean, I am older than most brides."

"Nonsense. A fall wedding will be perfect."

Lidy Mae frowned as she reconsidered. "I was trying to pick a time when Pete would be less busy. People are generally healthier when the weather first starts to cool and before the winter sets in. Maybe I ought to move the date. No, I can't do that. To change a wedding date is terrible luck."

"I think a Thanksgiving wedding will be perfect. You can do little pumpkin centerpieces for the reception tables and maybe some out of that colored corn."

"Where on earth would I get colored corn? I never heard of that. And nobody grows pumpkins around here."

Renata sighed. Everything was so much simpler with supermarkets on hand. "We'll think of something better. Dried flowers, for instance, or mums."

"Like tussy-mussies you mean? That could be pretty. And we can use flowers that have certain meanings, like purple lilacs to show he was my first love, lamb's ears for gentleness and peppermint leaves for warmth of feeling." She searched Renata's face. "Is that too forward, to indicate warmth of feeling?"

Renata laughed and shook her head. "You're marrying him. One would hope and assume you have warm feelings for each other."

Lidy Mae blushed again. "I must confess that it's true. Now don't think I'm wanton, Callie, but I have to admit that I'm looking forward to being a married woman."

"Good. I'm glad to hear it. Pete must be glad of it, too."

"Well, I haven't told him, for goodness' sake!" But Renata could tell by the rosy glow on Lidy

Mae's cheeks that a verbal statement had probably been unnecessary.

"Just be happy and make Pete happy. My grandmother used to say that to me whenever the subject of marriage came up."

"She did? I can't imagine her saying such a thing. Now, you will stand up for me, won't you? Otherwise Mama will want me to ask my cousin Sarah, and she's such a lump."

Renata wasn't sure what the term meant, but she didn't think anyone would want a bridesmaid of that description. "Of course I will."

"We can make the dresses together. You are so good at needlework."

"Sure." Renata wondered how hard it would be to learn to sew and whether she could accomplish it before the wedding. "I'm honored that you want me."

"Silly! We've always said that we would stand witness for each other. Did you think I'd forget after you asked me to stand by you in your wedding?"

Renata was confused. She was certain that Molly had been her bridesmaid.

Lidy Mae sighed. "I'm still fretting over my having the fever then. Were you terribly disappointed?"

Relieved that she hadn't remembered wrong, Renata said, "I understood that you were sick." Renata felt a special warmth for Lidy Mae, and it occurred to her that she had never had a lifelong friend as had Callie. She wondered if perhaps Ennis' treatment of Callie might not be to blame for that as well as for her reluctance to marry Bob.

Chapter Nine

Renata asked Lidy Mae to extend her visit until it was almost time for Nathan to come in from the fields. She remembered all too well the scare Ennis had given her the day before, and she knew he would never dare come near the house if he saw Lidy Mae's buggy hitched to the post out front. Lidy Mae was more than willing. She had missed Callie's company and was eager to catch up on all the news.

It bothered Renata that even Callie's best friend now didn't seem to notice the difference in her. Did that mean Callie had so little assertiveness that no one expected much from her, or did it mean Renata was that much like her? Since Renata was making no effort to disguise her likes and dislikes, she had to believe it was because in this past life she had been, and therefore still was in a sense, Callie Blue. The notion fascinated her. She had always believed the soul survived after death, but she had never considered that part of the soul might be the personality. If reincarnation were indeed a fact—and she was no longer in a position to dispute it—a person might be easily recognizable in spite of their current life's changes to the personality. Perhaps death had even less reality than she had assumed.

She wanted to discuss this with Lidy Mae, but as soon as the word "reincarnation" came up, Lidy Mae looked blank. Renata tried to explain the concept of a soul having more than one life on earth, but the other woman shook her head.

"I could never believe that, and I don't believe you do, either. Why, that's scandalous! It's not mentioned anywhere in the Bible."

Renata wasn't entirely convinced of that, but she let the subject go. Arguing with Callie's friends wasn't the best way to spend the afternoon. "Will you help me start supper? Since Nathan has been away from the house all day, I should fix him a hot meal."

"Of course." Lidy Mae smiled shyly. "It won't be so very long before I'll be fixing supper for Pete. Won't that be something? Both of us old married women." She laughed at the idea.

Renata wondered again what year it was. She knew Callie never reached old age—or even middle age, for that matter. What would happen to her if she was still here when Callie died? An icy cold washed over her.

"Did a goose walk across your grave?" Lidy Mae teased.

"What?"

"I saw you shiver, and you were looking as if your thoughts were a long way off."

"I just had a bad thought. That's all." She knew Lidy Mae would never let her off without an explanation. "Yesterday a tramp tried to break into the house while Nathan was in town. Whenever I think of it, I'm afraid again."

"That's terrible! Didn't your dog bark or anything?"

Renata shook her head. If it had been a real prowler the dog would have chased him away. She wondered if that had occurred to Nathan. "I guess he was in the barn or something."

"How horrible. You need another dog. I've always said that one is next to useless. He doesn't even come see what buggy is arriving."

Renata nodded. On her first day here the dog had sniffed her but had accepted her almost at once. If Nathan had had a better watch dog, she might not have been able to pass as Callie. Now that she was here, she should do something about that. "Where can I get one?"

"I'll ask Pete. He knows everyone in town and may know of a dog that needs a good home."

They went to the kitchen where Renata took down the copy of Mrs. Butler's home companion and turned to the section on recipes. Lidy Mae moved about the kitchen as if she were accustomed to being there. She took one apron out of the drawer and tied it about her waist and handed another to Renata. Renata had discovered how handy an apron could be now that her clothes were so difficult to wash.

"This sounds good. Hopping John. It's made of red beans and rice."

Lidy Mae laughed. "Of course it is. Everybody knows that. I thought for a minute there you were serious." A look of puzzlement replaced her smile as she watched Renata open the cupboard and take out two plates. "What was that you cooked when Molly and Ennis were over?"

"Molly told you about it?" Renata was instantly on her guard. "It was broccoli casserole."

"I never heard of it before. She and I went through my *Home Companion* and we couldn't find a recipe for anything at all like that. I thought we both used the same book." She picked up the book from the countertop and read the title. "We do. Where did you get the idea to make it?"

"I guess I heard it somewhere. It doesn't matter."

"You never heard of it in Lorain or it would have been the talk of the town. Molly said there were almost no dishes to wash and that it was really good."

"That was nice of her. Ennis was less pleased."

"Pooh. Ennis is never pleased about anything a woman does."

Renata wondered if Lidy Mae had any idea how revealing that statement was. Ennis had also struck her as a man with a deep psychological problem, and she had reason to know he was dangerous. "Nathan likes my casseroles so I assumed Molly and Ennis would, too. I suppose you must be right. I evidently heard of casseroles somewhere other than in Lorain."

Lidy Mae stared at her. "You've never been more than twenty miles from here in your life. What are you talking about?"

"Let's see if the beans are done," Renata said evasively. She had put the beans in the pot before Lidy Mae had come, and they had been cooking slowly all day.

Maintaining her questioning tone, Lidy Mae said, "For dinner today you made an egg pie with ham in it. I had never heard of that either."

"I guess I've started dreaming recipes in my sleep. Didn't you like it?"

"Yes, but it struck me as odd. You never seemed that fond of cooking before."

"I'm still not. I've been trying to find new things to cook that take less time." She used a wooden spoon to press a bean against the pot's side to test it. "They're done." She lifted the heavy pot away from the fire and set it on the ledge above the stove. "I'll put the rice on. Nathan really dislikes beans, but for some reason that's all I seemed to put up last year. Thank goodness we are almost out of them."

"You put up beans because you like them. You said Nathan would have to learn to eat them."

Renata looked at her friend. "I said that?"

"I've worried that you might not be happy. Is something bothering you that you're not telling anyone?"

"Not really. I guess you could say I've just had a change of heart." She measured water into a pan and set aside a third as much rice. Callie might have been about to ruin the remainder of her life and Nathan's happiness, but now Renata was in charge.

After supper, Renata and Nathan retired to the back parlor as usual. She sat in the rocker, curling her legs under her, and Nathan glanced at her but made no comment. She pretended to be reading a Dickens novel, but her thoughts were on Nathan. He saw a difference in Callie that he couldn't understand—she was sure of that—yet he never commented on it anymore.

Did he find her attractive? Renata thought he must. She was more objective about Callie's features than she had been about her own, and she knew Callie was beautiful. Had he preferred Callie's more submissive nature? If he found Renata too assertive, he never mentioned it.

She shifted in her chair and turned a page so it would appear to him that she was reading.

Nathan was an enigma. He held himself so aloof and never let a hint of vulnerability show. Lidy Mae had said he loved Callie, but Renata wasn't positive that Lidy Mae knew more than Callie had seen fit to tell her. Nathan seemed to confide in no one.

Sleeping next to him had been more than difficult. Renata had a woman's desires and responses, and when she lay next to this man she loved, she wanted to touch him. So far she hadn't dared. Her few advances had been rebuffed politely but firmly. Did he no longer desire his wife? Renata knew he had no other woman on the side; he worked such long hours on the farm, he had no time for anyone else.

Never having felt love toward any man, Renata was at a loss. In her own time period, she would have let him know how she felt, and if he felt the same, they would have let nature take its course. It wasn't that simple now. It was as if she were trapped in the intricate steps of a dance she only half-knew. If she made the wrong move, his rejection might be final and complete.

When at last he rose and started upstairs to bed, Renata was more than ready. She had made a decision. Since she might never return to her own time, she wasn't going to be caught up in a lifelong bad marriage without trying to do something to revive it.

Reflections in Time

As always, Nathan went to his side of the bed and turned his back to her as he began removing his clothing. Renata lifted her head and watched. He thought she had retreated behind the dressing screen as usual so his movements were natural and unhurried. Her heart beat faster as she watched him removing his clothing. Nathan never went without a shirt in her presence and the sight of his bare skin awakened her desire. His back was paler than his arms, and the way his muscles knotted and corded beneath his smooth skin reminded her of the marble sculpture of David by Michelangelo. But Nathan looked much warmer and infinitely more tempting. His hips were narrow and his buttocks lean and firm. The more of him she saw, the more she wanted him.

When he turned to pull down the cover, he noticed she was watching him. Nathan stood perfectly still. Renata knew she had at last broken through his shell. Slowly he pulled the covers back from the sheets and straightened up, making no move to cover himself from her gaze.

"I like to look at you," she said softly.

"That's news to me. It was your idea to put that screen up so you wouldn't have to see me or me you."

"That was then and this is now." She smiled at the confusion she saw on his face, and without taking her eyes off his, she removed the pins from her hair and let her hair billow about her shoulders and cascade down her back like pale fire. Renata enjoyed the sensuous feel of its weight. Her hands moved to the buttons on her dress.

Nathan stood as if he had been turned to stone. Renata was enjoying his surprise, and she used the element of uncertainty to her advantage. Continuing to gaze into his eyes, she removed her dress and let it float to the floor.

Placing one foot on the frame of the bed, she began untying her shoes. When she had removed them, she rolled her stockings down, taking all the time she wanted. Knowing Nathan was watching her every move was exciting her beyond all reason. With deliberate slowness she untied the pink ribbon that secured the neck of her chemise. The fabric was thin and almost sheer. She knew he could see the outline of her nipples against it and the shadow of her breasts.

When the ribbon was loose, she lifted the chemise over her head. She heard him catch his breath and knew he had expected her to become shy at the last moment. Had Callie never undressed in front of him before? Apparently not. The cool air of the room touched her breasts and made her nipples bead into tight buds.

A moment later, she stepped out of her bloomers and stood naked before him. Seductively, she lifted her arms and ran her fingers through her hair so that it swept around her hips and shoulders. If she had known how sexy long hair felt against bare skin, she would have let her own hair grow.

As if she didn't know he was still watching her, Renata went to the lamp that had lit their way up the stairs and blew it out. The room was now illumined only by the paler glow of the small one on Nathan's side of the bed. Renata went to her side of the bed and drew down the covers. Nathan hadn't moved. As if he were awakening from a dream, he blinked and shifted uncertainly. Renata lay down, her hair making a cape about her, and pulled the covers back on his side of the bed in obvious invitation.

Nathan lowered himself to the bed. "Callie?" he said uncertainly.

"I love you, Nathan." She was almost afraid to say the words because she knew Callie must not have said them often or with any conviction. Callie had been a fool not to realize what a jewel she had in Nathan.

He bent to blow out the lamp, but she put her hand on his arm.

"Leave it on," she said.

He looked back at her, and his eyes were full of wary hope. "Do you know what you're doing?"

"Yes, Nathan. I do."

He lay beside her and she slipped nearer until their bare flesh met down the length of their bodies. Renata felt dizzy with the sensation. Her body molded against his in a perfect fit. She laid her head on his pillow and smiled at him. Slowly, as if he still expected her to change her mind, he lowered his head and kissed her.

Renata had never experienced the depth of sensation Nathan's kiss awoke in her. His lips were soft but firm, tasting hers hesitantly at first, then with greater assurance. Renata returned his kiss and slipped her arm around his shoulders. He was so close and so accessible, and his skin was warm to her touch. Excitement rushed through her. For weeks she had wanted to do this, and it was even better than she had hoped it might be. Nathan knew exactly how to kiss her to fan the flames of passion that she had never known existed.

Her hand explored his body, caressing the muscles of his back and the ridges of his rib cage. His waist was lean and his hips narrow, but his buttocks were rounded with more muscle. When he pulled away with a questioning look, she laced her fingers in his hair and brought his lips back to hers. His hair was thick and clean. It had occurred to Renata before that he bathed more often than she had thought any Victorian man did, and his hair, like his body, was always clean when he came to bed.

"You smell good," she whispered. "Like that yellow soap in the barn and like the meadow when a breeze is blowing."

He looked at her sharply, and for a moment she wondered what she had done wrong now but decided not to care. She only wanted to feel his hands on her. Taking his hand, she put it over her breast, and when his fingers moved over her nipple, she caught her breath in ecstasy. "Yes," she murmured. "Touch me."

Nathan brought his lips down on hers again with greater urgency, and Renata opened her lips and touched his tongue with her own. When he groaned as if he hadn't expected this but was thoroughly enjoying it, she ran her tongue over the velvety smoothness of his inner lips.

His hands became more insistent as if he were a starving man who had been seated unexpectedly at a banquet. He lifted his head and gazed down at her body as his hands stroked her flesh. His eyes, always a warm brown, had darkened to black, and she could see his barely leashed desire in the tenseness of the muscles of his chest and arms. With her hand, Renata caressed the hard wall of his chest and down the ridged muscles of his belly. His manhood was pressed against her abdomen in such a way that she couldn't reach it, and she thought it was probably fortunate or she would have shocked him even more.

"You're so beautiful," he said. "I had forgotten how beautiful you are."

How long, she wondered, had it been since Callie had let him make love with her? Her heart went out to Nathan. "I enjoy looking at you, too. I've never seen anyone as perfect as you are. Never."

His eyes studied hers. "You always wanted the light out before."

"I can't see you in the dark and you can't see me. Isn't this better?" She drew his lips down to hers and kissed him with all the love and longing in her heart.

His hand was large and warm on her skin. It was rough from hard work out of doors and this excited her as a soft hand never would have. She could feel his body trembling with his effort to hold himself in check. It was exciting, even heady, to know he desired her so much. This time there was no question of him retreating into his shell of aloofness. Tonight he was hers.

When he touched her hips she moved to offer herself to him. Nathan paused as if he hadn't expected this, so she slipped her leg over his thigh and drew him closer. He rolled her onto her back, supporting his weight over her. For a long time he gazed down at her, but he didn't ask the questions that were in his eyes.

Renata met his gaze and her lips parted in invitation. Her breath was coming quickly as if she had been running, and she thought he must surely be able to hear the hammering of her pulse.

"I want to please you," he said softly, his voice deep with emotion. "I want to show you how good it can be, if you'll only let me."

She nodded. "I want to make love with you all night. I want to lie in your arms all day tomorrow and kiss you and hold you until you know how much I love you."

His lips turned up in a smile. "I love you, Callie. God, how I love you."

The sound of another woman's name on his lips gave Renata a bit of a start, but she knew this had to be. What else would he call her except the name he knew her by? "Touch me, Nathan. Teach me how to please you."

He bent his head to her breast and lightly kissed her nipple before closing his mouth over it. Suckling gently, he drew the turgid bud into his mouth, and Renata arched her back to give herself to him more fully. His tongue urged her body to responses that Renata had never experienced before. It was as if their souls touched and entwined, as if he knew exactly what she would like and was ready to give that to her and more. As Renata resumed her exploration of his body, her excitement grew. Nathan was eager for her and no longer seemed shocked by what she was doing. Renata allowed herself to be swept up in his passion and matched his with her own.

When at last Nathan came into her, Renata felt as if she would explode. With the second stroke of his body, her desire flamed into a bonfire and she spiraled up the heights of ecstasy. Wave after wave of love filled her, and she cried out and held to him tightly. For what seemed to be an eternity, her soul and body was one with his. Slowly her senses returned to her, and she opened her eyes to see him smiling down at her.

"You see?" he asked. "It can be beautiful for you, too."

"Nathan," she said his name as if it were a caress. If she had loved him before, she loved him all the more now.

He began moving again, and she was surprised to find her body responding at once. This had never happened to her, and wonder filled her eyes. Nathan shifted so that she lay half-beneath him and so that he had one hand free to fondle her. Through the roaring in her veins, she could hear his voice, and it sped her back up the heights of bliss. This time when she reached her peak, she felt him reach his own pinnacle. He moaned and held her so close she thought she would be unable to breathe, but the feeling was so good that she had no intention of moving away.

For a long time he lay within her, his shoulder cradling her head while he stroked the cool skin on her back and hip. Renata had never been so happy and so satisfied. She rubbed her hand over his shoulder and upper arm and smiled to feel him so warm and close, so entirely hers. For the first time since she had come here, she felt entirely safe. Nathan loved her and she loved him. What could mar her happiness? Then she remembered it wasn't that simple in her situation, and she clung to the softness of afterglow, made more poignant by the knowledge that it might not last.

"Are you cold?" he asked.

She shook her head. "I couldn't be cold when I'm so close to you." She smiled and traced her finger over the curve of his jaw and across his lips. "How about if I burn all my nightgowns? I like this much better."

Nathan caught her hand in his and examined her fingers as if he had never seen them before. He placed a kiss on them and said, "Who are you?"

Renata started. "What? What did you say?"

"I asked who you are."

"I'm Callie Blue, of course." She gave a shaky laugh. "Who else would I be?"

"You look like Callie, you sound like her, but you aren't her. I know for a fact Callie isn't a twin, and I know her body well enough that her twin couldn't fool me, if there were one. But you're different. You have been for several weeks."

Renata hesitated. If she was ever going to tell him, this was the time. "I don't know how to explain it. I am Callie—in a way. At least I was. My name is Renata O'Neal."

Nathan moved away from her. "Then I'm right?"

199

"Don't pull away. You are, but then again, you aren't. Nathan, I was born in the year 1962."

He frowned and sat up. "What?"

"I was having trouble sleeping so I went to a psychologist—that's what you might call a mind doctor—to have him hypnotize me. Something went wrong. I found myself down by the stream washing clothes. I had no idea how I got there or how to get back."

"You expect me to believe this? Do you take me for a fool or have you lost your mind?"

"Neither. You said I'm different. You're right. All I can figure out is that I was Callie Blue, your wife, in a past life. This life, I mean. It's so confusing, Nathan. Don't frown at me like that."

"I think you and Lidy Mae got into the cooking sherry."

"If you hadn't asked me, I would never have told you."

Nathan was silent.

"I didn't come here on purpose." This was partly false. She had wanted to see Nathan again after the glimpse of him at his wedding to Callie. "That's not entirely true. I had been here before. It was the day you married Callie." She found it hard to continue.

His eyes snapped to hers. "Tell me about it."

"I was upstairs and Mrs. Graham, Callie's mother, was giving me the most useless piece of advice I had ever heard and Molly was helping me arrange the ruffles on my dress. I was so shocked at being there that I couldn't speak and tell them who I was. Then we went into the hall and down the stairs. I was starting to worry since it all seemed so real, and yet I knew it couldn't be. I came into the room and saw you. Something happened, Nathan. I fell in love with you. Just like that, before we had exchanged so much as a word. That's why I know I was once Callie and that I was feeling what she must have felt."

He put his legs over the edge of the bed and reached for his pants. "That's how I knew you weren't Callie. She never said she loved me. Not once. And she would never have done what you did tonight."

She caught his arm. "Don't leave me. Please."

"How can I stay? I've already done too much. I don't understand all this, but if you didn't look so much like her, I would never have been fooled. You're nothing alike."

"But I *am* her. That's what I'm trying to say. This is Callie's body. I'm your wife." When he hesitated, she repeated, "Please don't leave me."

He let the pants drop to the floor. "I must be crazy myself to be listening to all this. You can't be anyone but Callie. Anything else is impossible."

"But at the same time, I'm not. I look like Callie, but I feel like Renata." She gave him a wry smile. "It's funny, isn't it, that my mother named me Renata. It means 'born again.' I don't think this was what she had in mind."

He frowned at her. "If indeed you are this Renata person, where is Callie?"

"I'm her, too. I can't explain it. I don't have any of Callie's memories, but it's as if I have her emotions. I fear what she fears, I love what she loves."

"I told you that she doesn't love me."

"I think you're wrong. It may have been true at first, but she fell in love with you, or I wouldn't have loved you so quickly and so completely. After I saw you at the wedding, I had to see you again. I had Dr. McIntyre hypnotize me and send me back again. This time, I lost touch with him somehow and here I am."

"Are you here to stay?"

Renata swallowed and tried to keep the fear out of her voice. "Maybe. I don't know. Would it be all bad if I am?"

"I can't answer that." He reached again for his pants. "I have to think." He stood and pulled them on and buttoned the fly before he turned. For a minute he frowned down at her, then he turned and left the room.

Renata lay back on the pillow and wished with all her heart that she could recant her confession. Would he believe it if she said she had been teasing or pretending? No, he would certainly think she had lost her mind if she did that. She reached out and touched the sheets

where he had lain beside her. She loved him—
and he would never believe it.

Nathan went downstairs and felt about in
the dark for a lamp. Finding one, he lit it
and carried it out onto the porch. Beyond the
rail the night was deep, and he could hear the
sounds of insects and in the distance an owl.
She wasn't Callie? Impossible. But in his heart
he knew it was true. Callie would never have
let him touch her, let alone to love him back
in such a way that he still felt shaken to
the core.

Was her story possible? Who knew what mar-
vels the future might bring. True, 1962 wasn't all
that far into the future, only 80 years, but why
would she have made up such an unbelievable
story unless it was true?

He could see the difference in her in other
ways, too. She was less likely to jump if he
moved suddenly, and she no longer asked that
he not leave her alone when she knew as well as
he did that he had work to do. And then there
was what had happened at the wedding.

When he had seen Callie come in the door to
her parents' front parlor, it was as if he were
seeing her for the first time. Her eyes weren't
lowered as they usually were and she didn't look
as if she were being led to the slaughter as she
had for the several weeks before the wedding.
At times he had been afraid she would call off
the wedding altogether. But that day she had

looked straight at him, and he had seen love spring into her eyes. He had been sure of it. That was why he had been so hurt when the ceremony was over and she was again acting as if she expected him to attack her on the spot. In the years since, he had managed to put a wall between his emotions and his life, but it hadn't been easy and he had thought it would never be any better.

Tonight it had been. It had been so much better that he had made love with her even though he knew that somehow, impossible as it seemed, she wasn't Callie. He had never been unfaithful to his wife until tonight. But did this count? Only if he believed her story. And it had been so much better than he had ever expected it to be that he actually found himself hoping that the change would be permanent.

Nathan put his head in his hands and wondered what to do. When he heard the door beside him open, he looked up.

"I can't let you sit out here all alone," Renata said softly. "Not tonight."

"Let's go back to bed," he said after a moment.

When he stood up she preceded him into the house.

Chapter Ten

The closer it got to dawn the more foolish Nathan felt for having given Renata's far-
fetched explanation any credence. Someone
else in Callie's body? Ridiculous!

He lay in the double bed and listened to
Callie's soft breathing. Something was defi-
nitely changed about his wife, but not this,
not something impossible. Had Callie's mind
snapped?

Being careful not to awaken her, Nathan
rolled over so he could look at her. She was
as beautiful in sleep as she was when she
was awake. Her glorious hair was tumbled
around her face and over the pillow, and her
long eyelashes made a dark lace design on her
cheek. He had always been struck by Callie's
beauty.

At first when she had agreed to walk out with
him, he had been as tongue-tied as a young
boy. He had known her in school, but she had
been so popular he had never risked rejection
by trying to become her friend. As far back as

he could remember, he had known Callie and had loved her. He had known she didn't love him when they married, though she had tried not to let him know. He had never been able to figure out why she had wanted to marry him, but then, he also didn't know why she had become so shy and reclusive about the time she turned 16. It had been far better to accept the miracle and her hand in marriage and ask no questions.

Their marriage hadn't been very happy. Callie had detested making love from the very beginning, and he had been hurt and angry to find he wasn't her first lover. He still couldn't believe a woman who so disliked being touched would have gone to bed with a man who wasn't her husband. It hadn't made sense.

Now Callie had veered off in a different direction. The woman he had made love with last night was the one he had expected the young Callie to grow to be. For her to become the frightened, timid woman he had married was less likely than for her to become the person he had known the past month or so. The question was, what had made the difference?

Callie stirred in her sleep and her left hand came up to rest on the pillow. Nathan looked at the wide gold band that marked her as his wife. He wore a band exactly like it on his left hand. He recalled the day of their marriage and the momentary difference he had seen in Callie. At the time he told himself he had imagined it, but the woman he had married was the one who lay here beside him.

He had heard of a woman near Baton Rouge who seemed at times to be a different person, as if she had two personalities. He had never met her, however, and he only half-believed the stories. Now he wondered if Callie might not be like her. He shook his head. The other woman swung from one personality to the other. Callie seemed to settle in one and stay there for weeks, except for that brief glimpse at the wedding. It really was as if another woman was in her body. Nathan would be more concerned if he didn't love the new woman best.

Careful not to disturb her, Nathan got out of bed. This sort of thinking was ridiculous. Callie was Callie, not this Renata as she claimed to be. One person didn't land in another's body from a different time. No one had ever heard of such a thing.

He took clean clothes from the drawer and quietly dressed. She needed to sleep. They had spent the night making love. It had been a night such as he had hoped would brighten his marriage from the very first. Callie sighed in her sleep, and her lips curved up in a smile as if her thoughts were also on their night of love. The cover had slipped down, exposing her bare arm and shoulder. Love and desire rose in him despite the hours they had already spent in each other's arms. He knew people who claimed it was sinful to love anyone, even one's wife, with such intensity. But these people didn't know Callie.

Nathan went downstairs and made himself a breakfast of cold biscuits and molasses. He had a lot to think about, and he couldn't think with Callie around. After last night, he wouldn't be able to concentrate on anything but her, if she were near. The memories put a smile on his face. He didn't know where she had suddenly gained so much knowledge about how to please a man or why she had suddenly let him touch her and please her as he had always wanted to, but this morning he was a happy man.

For a moment he even let himself hope that they might now have a baby. Callie would be a wonderful mother, and he had always liked and wanted children. Not just because a man needed to have children to help with farm work, but because he genuinely wanted them. He knew most of his male friends would tease him about it, so he had never told them. Callie had known, but it hadn't been enough to convince her to let him touch her—not until last night.

He drank a glass of milk and stared sightlessly at the barn past the kitchen windows. If Callie wasn't making all this up about being someone named Renata, why was there such a drastic change in her?

Renata awoke to find Nathan gone. At first she was disappointed. She would have liked to make love with him in the morning light so she could see every inch of his body. She almost laughed aloud. Never had she dreamed of a night like the one before. All she had read of Victorian sexual taboos had been exaggerated; the Victorian age had also been the age of the greatest erotica ever written. She was thoroughly grateful that Nathan fell into the latter category.

She dressed quickly and hurried downstairs. By now Nathan would be at work, and she had wanted to make him a huge breakfast. He ate more than any man she had ever known, and it all seemed to go to muscle rather than to fat. She knew it must be due to the long hours he labored plowing fields, building fences and repairing the house and outbuildings. She had never known a man who was so active.

As she had thought, Nathan was already in the barn. He had already finished the milking for her—a chore she detested—and was carrying the pail of frothy milk back toward the house. The barn cat and her half-grown kittens were trailing him expectantly. When he saw her, he grinned and Renata's heart did a flip-flop.

"I had wanted to make you breakfast," she said. "Are you still hungry?"

"I had the rest of the biscuits and syrup. I'll stop early for dinner." He stopped walking and merely looked at her.

Renata felt a most pleasant blush rising and

she smiled. She knew he was thinking about the night before. "I was hoping you would wake me up," she said gently. "That we might get a later start today."

"I was tempted. Unfortunately Beulah wouldn't have understood." He lifted the milk pail. "She was complaining as it was."

Renata took the milk pail. "Thank you, Nathan."

"For what?"

"For being who you are. For being so wonderful."

He laughed. "You sure have a strange way of putting things, Callie."

Renata sighed. She had hoped after her explanation the night before that he would call her Renata, at least when they were alone. Now that she thought about it, he hadn't called her by either name after they went back to bed. Maybe he didn't believe her after all. If someone had told her the same story, she wouldn't have believed it either.

"Do you remember Molly is coming today?"

"Molly? Alone?" Renata couldn't keep the panic from her voice. She was terrified of seeing Ennis again.

"I assume she will be. You were to go shopping."

"I remember now. Yes. For a minute it had slipped my mind."

Nathan tilted his head to one side as he did when he was puzzling over something. "Have you and Ennis had hard words?"

"Why do you ask?"

"I saw him in town the other day and he crossed the street to keep from passing by me."

She considered telling him but couldn't, not when she had lied to him about it being a stranger who had tried to break into the house that day. Was this how Callie had originally slipped into Ennis' blackmail noose? "I have to get to work if I'm to finish before Molly arrives."

"You didn't answer my question."

"No. Ennis and I didn't have an argument." She couldn't meet his eyes. Taking the pail of milk, she hurried back into the house.

Renata put a ham along with plenty of water in the pot to boil for dinner and cleaned the house. She had only been to town a few times since coming here and always with Nathan. He was no more eager to shop than most men, and she was looking forward to the outing with Molly.

While she waited for Molly, Renata went out onto the porch to think about some of the changes she planned to make in the yard. Unlike Callie, Renata could not manage to get time to rake a pretty design on the packed dirt, so she had decided that when late fall came, assuming she would still be here, she would plant bulbs. Where Callie's swirls had been, she would plant circles of jonquils and narcissus in as many varieties as Lorain had to offer. And she thought some of those yellow blossoms, the tiny variety that grew wild near older homesteads, would look nice along the walk. She could see already that keeping the weedy runners of grass plucked so the grass would not get a foothold in the yard was going to be a challenge, but the time that chore would take was far less than the frequent raking Callie must have done. As yet, Nathan had not asked why she had stopped raking designs in the dirt, but when he did she was prepared to tell him about the plans she had for the beautiful flowers. Her biggest challenge was going to be learning how to plant the bulbs and care for the flowers as they grew, but she was sure the finished result would be beautiful and that Nathan would like it. Whether Callie would have thought it was a good idea, she supposed, would always remain a mystery to her.

The thought of Callie renewed the speculation she often had had about what had happened to her. In one sense, Callie Blue had never left since Callie was an earlier part of herself. But the Callie everyone had known before had been a person in her own right, and at times Renata was concerned that the original Callie might not get to finish out her own life. Why had she landed here in Callie's life? Was there something she was to do that Callie could not?

She also was curious about her own body that had been left behind when she came here.

On her earlier visit, time had been telescoped in such a way that what took a seemingly long time here had been only a few minutes in Dr. McIntyre's office. Was it possible that all this had happened and her body was still under McIntyre's hypnosis? That no one there realized she was here?

Renata shook her head. There was no way of knowing what was going on in the office of a man who wouldn't be born for decades. She had to assume this was all being taken care of on some cosmic scale far beyond her own grasp. She had to take each day as it came and hope that someday she would somehow receive reassurance that she could stay with Nathan forever. But, she mused, did anyone ever have reassurance like that?

When her sister arrived, Renata was ready to go. Molly waited for her to climb in beside her on the buggy seat. "You have to get over this fear of driving," Molly said good-naturedly. "We would have an extra thirty minutes to shop if you would come into town."

Renata was relieved to see Callie had provided her with an excuse not to drive. She had wondered how long she would be able to avoid it. "I'm trying to overcome it." She pointed at the barn. "I want to tell Nathan I'm gone."

Molly obligingly drove to the barn where Renata saw Nathan fitting a salt block to a post in the lot. "We're leaving," she called. "I won't be late."

He waved and smiled.

Molly tapped the reins against the horse's rump. Renata settled back to enjoy the ride. Spring was fading into summer and the fruit trees now had more green leaves than blossoms. The ground in the orchard was pink and white and more petals floated in the breeze. She had planted the vegetable garden because Nathan had plowed it for her, but she had little hope the plants would thrive. She had never had a green thumb. "I love spring," she said. "Everything looks so clean."

"I know. It's my favorite, too. Look, there's a new calf."

Renata nodded. "Nathan said it was born yesterday. Isn't it sweet?"

"Remember the time you made a pet of the yearling Papa was fattening to kill? Mama had to tell you it ran away from home."

Renata tried to smile. Some things in this day and age were more harsh than comfortable. She made a mental note not to befriend anything that might be destined to end up on the table.

Lorain was much smaller than the town Renata knew, but some of the buildings were strangely familiar. She was positive the dry goods store was the computer store in her own day, even if it had donned a facade of pastel aluminum. The hotel was larger than she would have expected, but there were no major towns within an easy driving distance. She saw only white people coming and going through the doors. Smyth's Drugstore was now Petersons's Emporium, but it was relatively unchanged. Two small shops stood where she was accustomed to seeing a paved parking lot.

Molly stopped at the dry goods store, and Renata climbed down. "Mr. Downs has put his gingham on sale. I thought this would be a good time to get material for summer dresses."

Renata had figured out how to work Callie's pedal-driven sewing machine so she nodded. At least she knew how to sew on a machine. Was it possible to buy a book that would teach her how to do embroidery stitches? These days every woman seemed to grow up knowing such things.

The store was laid out in neat aisles, and Renata could smell the fabric dye and cardboard scent that seemed to accompany it. Her shoes made a clicking sound on the oak flooring. The ceilings were high and of a pressed tin. One wall held shelves of what Molly called "notions."

"Good afternoon, Mr. Downs," Molly said. "How are Mrs. Downs and Barbara?"

"Fine, thanks. What can I do for you ladies today?" He rubbed his hands together and bowed slightly as he spoke to them.

"We want to see the gingham," Molly said.

"It's right over here." He led the way even though Molly probably knew where it was as well as he did. When they reached the row of bolts he made an expansive gesture. "Here they are. This blue would look mighty pretty with your eyes, if you don't mind my saying so."

Renata smiled. She had never received so much personal attention in a fabric store before. She finally recalled where she had heard his name before. Barbara Downs was the girl with the reputation for being "loose."

Molly asked for ten yards of the blue checked gingham, an amount Renata thought was excessive until she recalled the long gathered skirts and rows of obligatory ruffles that seemed to be necessary for even a housedress.

On a nearby counter she saw a wire contraption that she finally figured out must be a bustle. Displayed along with these were corsets and whalebone petticoats. Renata was glad Callie had been too slim to need cinching and that a bustle and full petticoat would be too bothersome on a farm. She was having enough trouble adjusting to long skirts and high-topped shoes and to having no bra.

"Aren't you going to get any gingham?" Molly asked. "This pink would be pretty on you."

Renata wasn't so sure pink was a wise choice with her hair. She put her hand on the bolt of green sprinkled with a design of peach-hued rosebuds. "I'll take this one."

Molly gave her a curious look as Mr. Downs lifted the two bolts and took them to the cutting table. "I've never known you to wear green before. I thought you didn't like that color."

"I guess it's because of springtime and all the new leaves," Renata said lightly. "Besides, change is good for a person."

"Look. The new hats are out." Molly led her to a showcase where several hats were displayed. Most of them sported feathers or flowers or paste fruit. "Aren't they lovely? Mrs. Downs does such good work."

"His wife makes them?"

"She always has. Don't you remember how Mama used to order special trim and how we would go back there to her workshop and watch her put the hat together?"

"Of course I remember. I only meant she has made unusually pretty ones this year." She really did like the hats. They were so unabashedly feminine that she longed to try one on. A plumed hat, however, would be even less logical on a farm than would a bustle.

She and Molly let Mr. Downs help them choose thread and buttons for the material. Renata thought she could do as well without his help, but this service seemed to be the rule. While Molly tried to decide between two types of pearl buttons, Renata wandered away to explore the store.

As Molly had said, a woman who appeared to be about Mr. Downs' age sat stitching a brown velvet bow to a hat in the back room. When she smiled and waved, Renata returned the gesture. Nearer the hats she found a display of hat pins of various lengths and design. She knew someone in modern Lorain who collected them, and she wished she could buy one for her. For a while she toyed with the idea of buying something and putting it in a secret place where she could retrieve it if she ever returned to her own time. It might prove this was really happening. She took a hat pin with a red ladybug and added it to the material she was purchasing.

When Molly was ready to leave, she told Mr. Downs to put the purchases on her account. Renata felt a moment of panic. For some reason it had never occurred to her to wonder how she would pay for her purchases.

Mr. Downs smiled and bobbed at her. "Shall I put yours on Mr. Blue's book?"

"Please," Renata said with relief.

She and Molly left with their parcels wrapped in brown paper and tied with string. "Let's go to the Emporium. I'd love a cherry phosphate."

Renata had no idea what that was, but it sounded cool. The day was already turning hot, and her long sleeves were sweltering. Did women wear long sleeves all year around? She knew next to nothing about Victorian Fashion.

Molly pushed open the door to the Emporium, and the delicious aromas of lavender and roses poured out to meet them. "I always love to come here and just breathe," Molly said with a laugh. "Wouldn't it be nice if our houses smelled like this?"

"This would be a pleasant place to work."

"A woman work in the Emporium?"

"Maybe some day." She found the lack of equality hard to handle. "Haven't you ever considered women's rights?"

"Suffragists, you mean? Ennis would be fit to be tied if I mentioned such a thing in front of him. He thinks Susan B. Anthony is unnatural and determined to destroy the American home."

"Somehow I'm not all that surprised he would have that attitude."

Molly leaned closer and whispered, "But I hear talk that some of them are planning to form an Association of Women."

"If it happens, they can count of me. Maybe I'll even help start it."

Molly sat on one of the stools at the counter and ordered two cherry phosphates. When they were delivered, Renata sipped on the straw and found it was as cooling as she had hoped it would be. The soda fountain was made of white marble, and the spigots were of polished brass. The man who served them had a handlebar moustache that made Renata stare before she could stop herself.

"Are you making a new Easter dress this year?" Molly asked. "I think I may wear my old one. Mama is scandalized, of course, but I don't need a new one and Ennis likes me to be frugal."

Renata made no comment. "I think I'll wear my old one, too. Do you remember it?"

219

"You wore the brown checked taffeta, didn't you? The one trimmed in snuff-colored velvet?"

"Yes." Renata smiled. That had been easy. She was beginning to learn how to get information without asking directly.

"While I'm here, I think I'll get some of the lavender powder that Alma uses. I love lavender. Maybe now that I have a place of my own, I'll plant some for myself." She smiled. "Does it still seem odd to you that you're a housewife and can plant your own lavender if you please?"

"Yes, it does." Renata thought that was the largest understatement she had ever made.

They finished the phosphates and Molly paid for them both. Renata followed her to a counter where powders and fragrances were sold. She didn't recognize a single brand name, and flower scents seemed to be the only ones offered. She lifted a bottle of rose water and smiled. "This is nice."

Molly nodded. "That's the kind I gave you last Christmas, isn't it?" To the clerk, a young man who seemed barely old enough to be out of school, she said, "Lavender powder, please. The kind in the box with the picture of the blond lady. I forget the name."

He brought a box and put it on the counter. "Is this the kind?"

"Exactly." Molly beamed at Renata as she opened the lid. "Smell. Isn't it wonderful?"

"Beautiful." Renata looked at the sentimental portrait of a woman with plump arms and face, a tightly laced middle, and a come-hither expression. Advertising hadn't changed all that much. Sex was still a selling tool, even if the customers would be shocked to hear it.

Molly was searching in her reticule. "Oh, dear, I forgot to bring enough money and Ennis doesn't have an account here. I guess I'll have to buy it another time."

Renata opened her own bag. "Maybe I have some." She had glanced in the bag but hadn't had time to thoroughly explore it before Molly had come to pick her up. She found the change purse and opened it. "I have money. How much is it?"

The clerk gave her a bored look and named the price.

Renata handed over the money and waited for her change while Molly wandered down the aisle to examine a jar of bath crystals. The clerk handed her the change and began wrapping the powder in brown paper.

Renata automatically counted the coins. "I'm short by a quarter."

"I beg your pardon?" The clerk drew back as if this were a personal affront.

"You miscounted the change. You still owe me a quarter."

Molly came back. "Is something wrong?"

"Only the change." She waited for the clerk to rectify his mistake.

221

"I'm sure I counted it correctly. I suggest you count it again," he said coldly.

Molly looked at the coins. "I believe my sister is right."

The clerk frowned. "I've already closed the cash register drawer."

"Then you'll just have to open it again." Renata wasn't going to allow him to get away with this, not when a quarter went so far these days.

"I'll do no such thing. I'm positive I gave it to you. I think you dropped it into your bag. By mistake," he added.

Renata's temper flared. "I don't like your attitude."

"My what?"

"I'd like to see the manager."

By now a man with gray hair was coming toward them. "Is there a problem?"

Renata upended her reticule and let all its contents spill out onto the counter. "Your clerk has made a mistake in giving me change and has accused me of putting it in my purse and lying about it."

The older man frowned at his employee. "You did that?"

The younger man sputtered. "I only said I thought it had happened. By accident, I said."

Renata spread the contents of her purse. There was a lace handkerchief, a button from a blouse, a comb and assorted hair pins, a vial marked "Mother McGrew's Smelling Salts" and what appeared to be small harness brass, but no quarter. She glared challengingly at the clerk.

"I must have made a mistake," he stammered. "I'm sorry." He opened the cash register and handed Renata a quarter.

"I'm sorry this happened, Mrs. Blue," the older man said. "He's new at the job."

"That's quite all right," she said coolly. "Everyone makes a mistake from time to time."

When she and Molly were in the buggy and heading home, Molly said, "I was amazed to see you stand up for yourself like that. I would never have had the nerve, and I would have said you would have died first. As shy as you usually are, how did you have the courage to face him down like that?"

"I knew he was wrong. Courage had nothing to do with it." She knew, however, that Molly was right and that Callie would never have been so assertive.

Molly was still marveling over the way Renata had called the clerk to task when they reached the farm. Nathan came out to meet them as he wiped his hands on a rag stained with grease.

"You ladies are home early. Did you run out of money?" He grinned at them teasingly.

"Just the opposite. You should have seen Callie. That new clerk in the Emporium gave her the wrong change and she made him do it right. She even called over Mr. Fisher, and you know how intimidating he can be. He frightens me sometimes. Callie stood right up to them

223

both and insisted that she get her change."

Nathan was still smiling but it no longer reached his eyes. "You did that, Callie?"

"It was nothing, really. Just a simple mistake." She wished Molly wasn't making such a mountain out of it.

"I'm proud of you," Nathan said. "Mr. Fisher gets by with that all too often. You saved me a trip into town."

Renata held out her hand to let him help her out of the buggy. "I don't think he will short-change me in the future." She felt good for having finally asserted herself. In the past weeks she had been so afraid of making mistakes that she had sometimes felt as shy as Callie.

Nathan was still studying her as Molly repeated exactly what had happened in the store. Renata hoped he wouldn't ask her any embarrassing questions in front of Molly. She had confided in him, but she didn't think it was wise for anyone else to know her secret—especially not Ennis' wife.

Nathan took her parcel of fabric out of the buggy's box and put it under his arm. "Won't you stay for supper, Molly?"

"No, I have to be getting on home. I have to cook for Ennis." She didn't sound as if the prospect was pleasing, and Renata wondered if that meant Molly was no better at cooking than Callie appeared to be.

"Give him a casserole," she teased with a

smile. "That should make him appreciate your cooking."

Molly rolled her eyes. "That would be the day." She waved and tapped the reins.

When she was out of earshot, Nathan said. "You really confronted Mr. Fisher?" Renata could see the puzzlement in his eyes.

"He was wrong and I was right." She waited for him to make a comment, but he only handed her the parcel and went back toward the workshop.

Chapter Eleven

Renata knew Nathan was concerned and confused about her. Since the night they spent making love, he had avoided her whenever possible and she wasn't sure why. He had enjoyed making love with her; she was positive of that. But Nathan was a private sort of man who didn't make his thoughts known.

Since that night she had been thoroughly and undeniably in love with him. She often found herself smiling for no reason other than that, and she had trouble keeping her mind on her work. At times she would find herself gazing dreamily into the distance while she thought of something he had said or done. Renata had never before been a romantic, but she was enjoying this new aspect of herself. She only wished Nathan was enjoying it, too.

The days had turned hotter, and the sky was a brassy blue. Nathan had said they needed rain, and she agreed. Her vegetable crop was wilting, and without the convenience of a hose and sprinkler, she had no easy way to water the seedlings. If the oppressive heat continued, she would have no choice but to haul water in buckets from the well to the vegetable patch.

She had learned how to keep the house clean, though she wished she had some of Callie's secrets as to how to do it more efficiently. Even the simplest jobs required much physical exertion. At night she found herself dreaming of vacuum cleaners and clothes washers.

Occasionally she thought about Bob and wondered how he was doing and whether he had found someone new, but such thoughts were surprisingly infrequent. He paled so in contrast with Nathan that she found him easy to forget, and that made her feel guilty because Bob wasn't a bad person and deserved better than her indifference. She was sure his mother didn't miss her, however. When she thought of the house Bob wanted to buy with its off-white walls, fake paneling and plastic smell, she didn't miss him much at all.

Thinking about her previous life reminded her of the hat pin she had bought. The idea of having her own private time capsule intrigued her. If she ever returned to her own time, the pin would serve as proof of her having been here, but where she would hide it was still an open question.

She had thought herself to be thoroughly familiar with the town of Lorain, but now that she considered it, she realized she had never paid much attention to the different houses on her drives around town. She couldn't remember which ones had survived the passage of time and the changes made in the name of progress. Her present house was so dear to her that she couldn't bear the idea of its being demolished. It was possible that it would still be standing, but if so, another family would be living there. Getting inside to retrieve her hidden hat pin might be difficult, if not impossible.

The barn and outbuildings were possible choices, but it seemed likely that they would be torn down before the house. There were stores in town that she knew would survive, but she had no way of hiding the pin in one of them. No, her house was the best place.

As she turned the hat pin in her fingers, looking at the bright red ladybug, an inspiration came to her. Quickly gathering paper and pen and guessing at the date, she wrote, "Renata O'Neal, 1885, I was here." With a smile, she tore the excess off the paper so the note would be as small as possible and pierced it with the hat pin. She didn't want to leave too large a clue or someone would find it before her time.

The attic was on the same level with the bedrooms and occupied the space over the kitchen where the roof sloped too low for the area to be useful as a room. She didn't especially like going in there because it was always dark and mysterious and was a haven for spiders. Yet, it was for that very reason she decided the attic was ideal for the pin and note. No one was likely to spend much time rummaging around there, and it would be unlikely that the pin and note would be found by someone else. Retrieving it later might be difficult, but she decided she would have to cross that obstacle when she came to it.

She went to the attic, opened the door and was greeted by the musty air. Stepping just inside, she turned and pushed the hat pin firmly into the wood above the door. It was practically invisible because of the angle of wall studs and the poor lighting. Satisfied, she went back into the well-lit house.

The sun was heating up the east side of the house so she closed those windows and opened the others wider. The house had been built to take advantage of breezes, and situated on the hill as it was, there was almost always a breeze to be found. Renata was learning by trial and error how to shut out the heat and cool the house, and her efforts were proving effective— at least according to Nathan who had complimented her on how much better she was managing this summer. Nonetheless, she missed air conditioning and suspected she would miss it even more before the summer was over.

Sooner than usual, she finished her cleaning chores, and since Nathan was working in the corn field today and wouldn't be back to the house until late, she decided she would have time to cook Nathan something special for supper. This time she thought it would be better to prepare something that was more familiar to him so she got *Mrs. Butler's Home Companion* off the shelf and began leafing through it. The book was informative, and from the worn, dog-eared pages she could see that Callie must have referred to it often. Renata herself already had found the book useful.

The section in the book on how to do housework had taught Renata the best way to use the primitive cleaning tools in the house, as well as how to be thrifty in the trimming of lamp wicks and candles. Another section advised women on how to be proper wives. Renata had laughed at the outdated suggestions until she remembered that women of this time were generally expected to be as subservient and menial as Mrs. Butler advised. After that it hadn't seemed so humorous.

A recipe for fried pies caught her eye and she nodded. Callie had put up a large quantity of dried fruit, thanks to the bountiful orchard, and she knew Nathan liked desserts.

As usual, making the pastry dough was tedious. Renata thought this must be one of those chores that probably had a few shortcuts that were too common for Mrs. Butler to have mentioned in her book, but nevertheless, she managed. The finished product was thick but serviceable.

Next she put dried apples into a pan and began stewing them. By this time she realized she should have reversed the order of these tasks. With a pencil, she made a note to that effect in the margin. Eventually, she told herself, she would learn.

When the apples were done and cool enough to handle, she cut the dough into small circles using a saucer from the cupboard. Then, while a generous dollop of lard was heating in a black skillet, she put a spoonful of sweetened fruit on the dough, folded it over and crimped the edges. The entire process was taking longer than she had expected, but she could see no way of speeding it up.

Finally, she eased one of the hand-sized pies into the hot lard, and when they began frying, the kitchen soon filled with a delicious aroma that reminded her of her grandmother's kitchen and of her childhood. She was so busy with her cooking and her memories that she didn't hear Ennis until he was right behind her.

"Hello, Callie."

She jumped and whirled to face him. "How did you get in here?"

He grinned mirthlessly. "You forgot to lock the screen door. You knew I wouldn't give up easy." He reached out to touch her face, but Renata slapped his hand away.

"Get out of here," she demanded in a threatening voice. "Nathan will be home soon."

Elizabeth Crane

"No, he won't. I happened to see him in the corn field on my way out here. It's real handy having your fields so close to the road. I can pretty well keep up with what you're doing without having to ride all the way to the house."

"You have a nerve taking such a chance on coming here," she said, trying to stall for time. She was so frightened her heart was pounding, and she was having trouble thinking coherently. "Where does Molly think you are?"

"I told her I was going to look at a horse. She never asks many questions. Your Mama taught her to keep her mouth shut real good. Too bad she didn't do as well with you."

Renata wasn't sure what he was talking about. The reports she had of Callie hadn't led her to think Callie was particularly talkative.

Ennis took another step closer. She could smell tobacco on his clothes and breath. Renata backed away until she could feel the heat of the stove on her arm.

"There's no point trying to avoid me. You know I always get my way." His expression became more threatening. "And I have a score to settle with you for locking me out last time."

"You wouldn't dare hit me," she said with more assurance than she felt. "Nathan would know something was going on if you did that."

"I never leave bruises. At least not where they will show." He leered at her. "I don't know why you're putting up such a fuss. Let's go upstairs and get it over with."

Renata glanced at the door that led to the stairs. Ennis had forced Callie to submit in her own bedroom? No wonder she was so sexually repressed. "Hell will freeze over before I let you get anywhere near me," she assured him.

His expressionless green eyes widened. She could tell he wasn't accustomed to having Callie refuse him. As quick as a striking snake, he grabbed her wrist and twisted it, and Renata cried out at the unexpected pain.

As Ennis started dragging her across the floor, Renata impulsively grabbed the skillet of hot grease and dumped it, pie and all, over his other arm.

Ennis shrieked in pain as he turned her loose. Renata dropped the hot pan back onto the stove, but only long enough to grab a hot pad. When she turned back to him, she again held the pan threateningly. "Get out of here, Ennis, or next time it goes in your face."

He gripped his arm and was bent over with pain, but she could see most of the grease had missed him. He was hurting but not seriously injured.

"You heard me. Get the hell out of my house."

Ennis slowly backed away. "You'll be sorry for this, Callie. Mark my words. You're going to regret having done this. So will Molly," he added.

Renata felt her stomach turn with fear. Would he hurt Molly? Was this only a threat to frighten her? "If you hurt my sister, I'll shoot you." At that instant, she meant every word she said, and Ennis knew it. She watched him back out the kitchen door and down the steps, still holding his left hand to his body.

She waited until he was across the yard before she went out onto the porch. He untied his horse from the hitching post, then awkwardly mounted. For a brief moment, he glared back at her, then rode away.

Renata felt a wave of weakness wash over her. Now that he was gone, she realized she had taken a terrible chance. What if she had been unable to grab the pan? Not only would she have been raped, but the hot grease could easily have caught on fire and the house could have burned to the ground. She leaned weakly against the kitchen door. Somehow she had to put an end to Ennis' threats against her, but she didn't know how.

Once sure that Ennis was gone, she went back inside. The kitchen was a mess. Grease was spattered over the floor, and the half-cooked pie was under the table. At the moment, she didn't feel like even trying to clean up. Let Nathan come home and find it like this. At least it would give her a reason to tell him what Ennis had done.

Nathan should be told. She knew that as surely as she knew anything. Yet she was afraid to do so, not only because she hadn't gone to him from the first, but because she knew him well enough to know he would kill Ennis. She didn't want Nathan having to stand trial as a murderer and having to face the publicity that would follow. Also, if Molly knew what Ennis was up to, how could she continue to be close to Callie? Renata had heard enough about rape victims in her own time to know the victim was often ostracized as much as the rapist, sometimes even more. Victorian victims must have an even more difficult time.

With a trembling hand and a scoop she used for flour, she got some dirt from outside and scattered it over the grease to make it easier to clean up, then she picked up the pie and tossed it out the door for the chickens.

An hour later the kitchen was clean, but she was still shaky. Ennis had managed to get into her house without her hearing him at all. He could do it again just as easily, and next time he would know she would try to defend herself. The element of surprise would no longer work for her.

Renata sat on the porch steps out back trying to decide what she should do. Telling Nathan was out. So was telling her parents or Molly. There was no way she could get help from Lorain's law enforcement officers since she couldn't have Ennis arrested without her family and Nathan knowing why. She doubted there were such things as restraining orders these days, and she knew they did little good anyway since they were practically impossible to enforce. She felt as helpless as Callie must have felt.

Until now Renata had privately thought Callie was weak to allow Ennis's abuse. Now she understood more fully. Callie had done what she had to do in order to survive and to keep her family intact. The fact that Ennis had misused her for years must have made it even more difficult for Callie to find a way out, especially given the fact that Callie was subject to what a modern doctor would call panic attacks and probably an assortment of neuroses as well.

"I've walked a mile in her moccasins," Renata said to the chickens who were pecking at the ill-fated fried pie. "I see her point of view, and it's worse than I had thought."

Unless she wanted Nathan to ask unpleasant questions, she had work to do, so she rose and went back inside. As she fried the rest of the small pies, she tried to think of some way out of this situation. Nothing came to mind, but she was positive that Ennis wouldn't stop even after this.

By the time Nathan was through with his day's work, the skies were darkening with storm clouds and Renata had to light a lamp in order to cook supper. Her mind, however, was on far more weighty subjects than storms. She knew she should tell Nathan. To do otherwise would be to continue playing into Ennis's hands. She should have told him as soon as she realized she had a problem, but she couldn't let the fact that she hadn't done so dictate her actions for the rest of her life.

After they ate, Nathan left the kitchen and Renata cleaned up the dishes. She had been quieter than usual, and she knew he had noticed her silence and probably wondered why, but he hadn't asked, and she hadn't volunteered. Telling him over dinner wouldn't have been right. She smiled sadly when she recalled how he had enjoyed the fried pies. After her horrifying experience while cooking them, she wasn't likely to want to cook them again in the near future.

When the dishes were washed and put away, Renata busied herself straightening the kitchen. She knew she was doing unnecessary work to avoid what she felt she must do, but she was nervous. How could she bring up the subject?

She found Nathan out on the porch. There was no breeze, and it was as if nature were holding its breath in the face of the approaching storm. In the distance lightning flashed and moments later thunder snarled. Nathan looked back in surprise when he heard Renata come onto the porch.

"It's going to be a bad one," he commented. "Those clouds have been building all afternoon."

"Maybe it will cool the air."

He looked at her in the dim light that filtered through the windows. Her face was flushed and damp from the heat in the kitchen, and a loose strand of curling hair lay on her cheek. He had seldom seen her look so beautiful. "We need the rain. Your garden is in sad shape."

"I know." She went to the rail and leaned against it as if in search of a breeze.

"I liked those fried pies. You haven't cooked them in a long time."

She was silent for a moment. "Good. I'm glad you like them."

"Is something wrong?"

She glanced at him, then back at the flashing clouds. She opened her lips as if she was going to say something, then closed them again.

To make it easier for her, Nathan said, "I was thinking about this place today—how you've done so much to make it a home. I know it wasn't much when I bought it, but you've worked as hard as I have. I was afraid you would regret moving to the country. I appreciate all you've done."

"Do you?" she asked.

"I think my life is just about perfect these days." He put his arm across her shoulders and felt the warmth from her skin through the thin cloth of her dress. "For a while I thought we wouldn't learn to pull together."

"Pull together?" she said as if she had never heard the phrase before.

"Like two mules. If you put a couple of mules in harness that aren't used to working together, one may want to pull one way and one the other. Until they both lean into the harness together, you don't get much accomplished. I think marriage is like that. Some couples start off working and living together as if they have been doing it all their lives. Others are like us. One mule goes one way and one the other."

Renata put her arms around his waist and rested her head on his shoulder.

Nathan could smell the soap-clean scent of her hair, and her curves fit exactly to his body. "Not that I'm calling you a mule. Up until lately, I'd have said you didn't have a stubborn bone in your body. These days you're more bullheaded than you ever were, but I find that for some reason, we're getting along better."

"Maybe you don't like submissive women," she said.

He mulled over that notion before answering. "You could be right. There have been times when I wanted to argue with you—to clear the air, I mean—and you would give in. I can't argue with someone who won't fight back. Sometimes I wondered if you cared enough about anything to get riled up."

"Did you ever think something might be bothering me? That it might be something so big that it took all my energy?"

"The baby, you mean." He had hoped she had finally put that in perspective. Although she didn't move, he could feel her body tense. He hoped she wasn't going to move away from him. He enjoyed being close to her like this.

"The baby," she repeated after him. "It might have been . . . maybe . . ." She sounded breathless, as if something had just occurred to her. "Do you recall if I ever said anything about, well, who it might look like, for instance?"

"You said once that you hoped it looked like me. Then you turned pale and stopped talking like you used to do at times. That was something I never figured out. After we lost it, you said you didn't ever want to have another one, that you were too broken-hearted over losing it. But before that, you didn't seem all that happy to be having one. Not after the first excitement was over. Which was it?"

She seemed to be picking her words carefully. "I wanted to have your baby, Nathan. I was only . . . afraid. I think I was afraid that it might not look like you."

"Your mother is to blame for that," Nathan declared as he frowned out at the night. "She was always filling your mind with all that folderol. There's no way a farm wife can keep from looking at a dog or from seeing a frog from time to time. I don't think she believes that herself, no matter what she said." He added, "I never saw a baby that looked like a dog or any other animal, and I'll bet you never did, either. That's just a silly superstition."

"Maybe I meant something else."

"Oh? What was that?"

She was silent again. Thunder filled the air and the windowpanes rattled. Something was tugging at his memory, but he couldn't quite bring it in.

"Nathan, there is something that Callie was afraid to tell you," she said tentatively.

"Don't start that again."

"What? Start what?"

"Telling me that you're not Callie. Honey, if you were to say that to most people, they would think you were out of your mind."

"Do you?"

"No, I don't." He scowled and moved away from her, taking a position at the corner of the porch. "I don't understand you, but I have no doubt that you're in your right mind." He didn't want to think about her being some stranger as she claimed to be. It was impossible, or so he had first thought, but now somehow it seemed too likely.

She was different, and she was different in ways that a person wouldn't think to change. If for some reason she was pretending to be someone else, she might change the way she spoke, which she had, or the way she wore her hair, which she had tried to do. Or what she cooked. But how could she change the way she slept? Callie had always slept on her left side with her back to him and with her body curled into a ball. Now she slept on her back and often snuggled next to him.

Then there was the way she carried herself. Often she sat with her legs tucked under her, and at times she stood with one hip cocked to the side instead of with both feet flat on the floor. She might have pretended she no longer knew how to cook a meal, but what woman didn't know how to start a fire in a fireplace? Or how to plant a garden? When he saw how she was putting the seeds in the ground, he had thought none of them would sprout, though he had said nothing.

And the way she had made love with him that night. He had not touched her again, though he had ached to do just that. He had enjoyed it too much. Callie might have changed her mind about a lot of things, but it was unlikely that she could change it about that, not when she had always detested being touched. Callie had remained virginal, in a way, even though they had been married several years. But that night she had known ways to make love that had amazed him. He had not been with another woman since they had been married, but he was no virgin before that time. None of the women he had known had ever been as skilled at lovemaking as Callie had been that night.

No, he didn't want to consider that she might be someone other than Callie. If she was, there was no guarantee that she would stay. If she was someone else, had he been unfaithful to his wife by making love with her? He had loved Callie all his life, and even though he loved her now with a depth and passion he had never expected, he wanted to be true to Callie.

"What was that you said the other night? Reincarnation? What is that?"

"It means a person has more than one life. That they are reborn after they die."

"They don't go to heaven?"

"Most believe people continue to grow spiritually, life after life, until they are worthy of going to heaven, as I understand it. I don't know much about it myself."

"I can't see why you know about it at all. I'm not sure I ever heard the word before."

"It's not that uncommon a belief where I come from."

"There you go again." He moved farther down the porch.

"You brought it up. You asked me." She followed him.

"I thought you would say Lidy Mae told you about it or maybe Molly." Even as he said it, he knew that would have been almost impossible. They had no more access to that sort of knowledge than Callie did.

"No, you didn't. You know I'm right."

"I don't know any such a thing." As he watched the storm roaring across the sky, fat raindrops started to fall. Although they were invisible in the darkness, he could hear them splattering onto the dirt.

She came to him and drew him around to face her. "What if I'm telling the truth? Could you still live with me? You haven't touched me since that night."

He gazed down at her. She looked the same as always. Her face was still shaped like a heart and was delicate in its features, her hair still that unusual shade of red. She *had* to be Callie. "I've wanted to touch you. There have been times when I thought I might die from wanting you. Today I almost came home from the fields just to look at you."

She turned away. "I wish you had. Nathan, do you ever wonder if I'm safe here when you're away?"

"Safe? In your own house? Of course you are. I've told you that for years."

"Oh? How many?"

"Ever since we were married. I don't know why you're so afraid of being alone, but it's something a person has to learn to do. I would have thought by now you would think nothing about it."

"What would you do if you found out someone had . . . touched me?"

He frowned down at her as jealousy and doubt leaped into his heart. "Someone touched you?" he demanded. "Who? When?"

She backed away. "I didn't say it happened, exactly. I only wanted to know what you would do."

"I'd kill him." He said the words simply because to him they were that simple. "You're my world, my life. If anyone ever lays a finger on you, I'll tear him apart."

"You say that so easily."

244

"That's because it's true. A man could do a lot to me or to my belongings, but not to you. You know what a problem I've always had with jealousy. I'm surprised you would even bring it up."

A flash of lightning rimmed her in ghostly yellow. Her eyes were frightened and her face was drawn. That was it, he suddenly realized. Callie was terrified of storms. Always before, if one was brewing, she wouldn't budge from the house and would call to him until he came inside with her. Now she was out here on the porch in one of the worst storms he had seen in years, and she seemed to be completely ignoring it. The fear he had seen in her eyes was because of the expression she had seen on his face.

"Forget I said anything. I was only wondering." She turned and hurried into the house, thunder marking her departure.

Nathan frowned after her. Her fear of storms had begun early in her life. She had once told him it went back to the time lightning had struck an elm tree next to her house, causing it to fall onto the kitchen, demolishing it as well as killing the maid who was in the kitchen at the time. Callie had been standing next to the maid only minutes before, and the tragedy had scarred her for life. Now she was able to stand unprotected in a storm so wild it was lashing the huge trees in their yard as if they were saplings.

Nathan followed Renata into the house and stood across the room looking at her. She was the same, but then again, she wasn't.

"Will you make love with me?" she asked. "I need you to hold me."

"The storm isn't bothering you?"

She shook her head. "I only want you. I love you, Nathan, and I don't know how much time I have to be with you."

He didn't ask what she meant. If she was someone else, she might be whisked away again as quickly as she had arrived. He might never see her again. "Bring the lamp," he said as he blew out the lamp next to him. He would be a fool not to enjoy her for as long as he could, loving her the way he did.

"Nathan," she said as they went up stairs, "Next time you feel as if you ought to come home and see if I'm all right, maybe you should do it."

He wondered what she meant by that.

Chapter Twelve

"Nathan, I want to go into town today." Renata had decided to take matters into her own hands and learn to use the buggy. She couldn't continue to wait until he happened to be going that way to buy the things she needed, and it hampered her need to be independent. "We're out of corn meal and baking soda."

"I'll saddle a horse for you before I go to the fields."

She hadn't expected this. Of course! That was how Callie managed when she wouldn't drive the buggy. The day she had arrived Nathan had mentioned she had a horse named Janie. The mare had foaled that day, and Renata had often gone down to the barn to watch the antics of the colt. Surely Janie couldn't be gone from her colt for several hours.

As if he were reading her mind, Nathan said, "I'll saddle Red. He's getting up in years, but he's reliable."

Renata was glad to hear it. She had ridden often when she was a child, but that had been years ago. "Thank you," she said. "Can I get you anything from the store?"

"There's nothing I need. You'll find money in the top drawer in our room."

Renata went up to get the money and the riding hat that appeared to be indispensable for a woman who was venturing out into the sun.

By the time she got to the barn, Nathan had a sorrel horse saddled and waiting for her. The animal regarded her with bored eyes. She liked him already. Nathan held his head while she went to the left side to mount from the wooden block. She put her foot in the stirrup, grasped the saddle horn and swung onto the saddle. Her right leg dangled where she had expected the other stirrup to be. It was then she noticed the curving protrusion beside the horn. This was a sidesaddle. Her eyes met Nathan's.

For a minute he was silent. Then he came around to her and said, "Get off and I'll show you how to do it."

Renata dismounted, and Nathan demonstrated how to loop her leg around the saddle. Renata was embarrassed that she had made so obvious a mistake. Then she realized that Nathan was explaining it to her as if he knew she had never ridden this way before. He believed her!

"Are you sure you want to do this?" he asked. "I can take you into town in the buggy and work that field tomorrow."

"I have to learn how to get around. And I want

you to teach me how to drive the buggy. Sometimes I just need to do something for myself, and I've always enjoyed shopping alone."

Nathan gazed down at her. After a while he said, "You really aren't Callie, are you? She would never say anything like that. She's afraid to go half a mile away from the house alone, and she has ridden sidesaddle all her life."

"No, I'm not Callie. At least not entirely. She's part of me, but I'm Renata."

"Renata." He spoke the word experimentally. "It's an unusual name. It sounds Spanish."

"My mother read it in a book. Nathan, do you mind very much that you appear to be stuck with me?" She was afraid of his answer, because she knew it would be completely honest.

"No, I don't mind it at all. Do you object to being here?"

She shook her head. "I meant it when I said I love you. In some ways I feel as if I belong here more than I belong in my own time."

"If anybody heard us, they would think we had both lost our senses."

"I know. It has to be our secret." She turned her eyes from his to say, "Nathan, sometimes, like when we're making love, for instance, could you call me 'Renata?' "

He reached out and touched her cheek. "I could do that . . . Renata."

Her heart skipped at his caress, and she smiled up at him. "I would have traveled to the ends of the earth to find you. I think that's why I was able to come here. It's as if you're a part of me."

"Is that why it happened?"

"I guess we'll never know. Maybe it's partly that and also because I had a part of myself that needed mending. Callie's fears were well-founded, but they didn't belong in my life."

"What do you mean by that?"

This was the perfect time, but she couldn't tell him. She had to handle it on her own. "I love you, Nathan, and I'm taking care of it. It's something I have to do."

"If you say so." He handed her into the saddle and made sure she had wrapped her leg securely in place. "Try riding him around here a bit before you leave. I want to be sure you won't fall off."

Renata touched her heel to the horse's side and reined him down the drive and across the grassy area in front of the fenced yard. Red obeyed her commands as obediently as if she had ridden him for years. She discovered that it wasn't nearly as precarious to ride sidesaddle as she had always assumed. With her knee around the brace and her foot in the stirrup, she was firmly anchored in the saddle. She cantered back to Nathan. "I'm fine. I won't be gone too long."

He waved, and she turned Red and began riding away. Calling after her, he said, "I love you, Renata."

She looked back with a grin and waved back. Hearing her name come from his lips made her glow all over.

She enjoyed the ride into town. The day was warm but not as hot as it would be in the weeks to come, and the sky was the shade of blue that brought forth nostalgic memories of her childhood. While she was alone, she took the opportunity to see more of town. When she came across the small chapel that in modern times had led her to Nathan, she stopped for a closer look. Its graveyard out back was much smaller, and looking at the lot surrounding it, with its yet undisturbed grass, made her feel odd because she was accustomed to seeing it filled with headstones. It was especially eerie that the black wrought-iron fence she had become accustomed to seeing, the one that would someday surround the graves of Callie and Nathan, was not there. Knowing their fate made Renata's eyes fill with tears. Impatiently, she brushed them away. She had never liked to cry.

Turning the horse down the street and around the next corner, Renata rode to the site where her apartment building would someday be built. Staring into the air over the existing buildings, she imagined that her particular apartment would be situated approximately over the current owners' henhouse. Renata had no desire to see where Bob would live, so she headed for the store. It was unsettling, she thought, to find how easily she was able to forget the man she had considered marrying. On the way to the store she passed a house under construction and realized she was seeing the birth of the house that in her time was owned by Lorain's Historical Society and was considered to be an historical treasure.

She bought the sack of corn meal and the baking powder which the grocer's boy tied behind her saddle. She thought this would be a good time to return Lidy Mae's visit, but she was confused by the streets that were similar to the ones she knew but not exactly the same. She turned to the boy. "Excuse me. Do you know who I am?"

The boy gave her a suspicious glance. "No, ma'am, I'm new to town."

Renata smiled in relief. It wouldn't do to ask someone who knew her. "Could you tell me how to find North High Street?"

"Yes, ma'am. Go down to the feed store and turn north. Go to the house with the magnolia tree in front and the blue shutters. Turn right and the next street over is North High."

"Thank you." She didn't know if it was proper to tip him for carrying out her package, but before she could decide, the boy had already started back into the store. Renata used the mounting block out front of the store to get back on her horse. She had never been one to casually drop in on friends unannounced, but without a telephone, it was more difficult to arrange social calls.

Lidy Mae was at home and pleased to see Renata on her porch. "Come in, come in. I was just thinking of you. Isn't it funny how that happens sometimes?" She called toward the back of the house, "Hattie, will you bring us some iced lemonade?"

They sat by the open windows, and Lidy Mae picked up her embroidery work. "I hope I finish this in time for the wedding. It's to go on my nightgown." Lidy Mae blushed. "I know it's daring, but I wanted a really pretty one."

Renata examined the handiwork. "It's beautiful," she said honestly.

"Mama is upset with me. She says it's too bare. What do you think?"

"I think it's quite proper. After all, you'll be a bride and you should wear something like this." The few open areas would still be unrevealing by Renata's standards. "Will you teach me to do this?"

"You silly girl—you taught me. Mama had given up on me ever learning to do needlework." Lidy Mae gave Renata a piercing glance. "You sounded serious just then."

"You know me, always kidding," Renata said lightly to cover her mistake. She was becoming tired of having to watch her every word. If she couldn't admit she needed to know, how would she ever be able to learn the skills necessary to Callie's life?

253

Hattie brought the glasses of lemonade and left as silently as she had come. Lidy Mae leaned forward and whispered, "Hattie's young man told her yesterday that he is going to marry the girl who works for the Fishers. She has cried all morning. Mama told her to stop, but I told Mama that I was sure Hattie can't help it and that I would cry, too, if Pete decided to marry someone else. Mama is angry with me for that as well."

"I agree with you. Is there anything we can do to help Hattie?"

Lidy Mae shook her head. "He wouldn't have been good for her anyway. I hear he lost his job at the feed store and that he isn't even looking for another one. And you know what Jemima said she caught him doing that time."

Renata nodded and tried to look as if she knew what Lidy Mae was talking about. She wondered if she might dare tell Callie's best friend that she was really Renata. However, reason prevailed and she decided not to chance it.

As they drank their lemonade, Lidy Mae said, "Mama would be even more upset with me if she knew I wrote that article for the newspaper in Shreveport." Her eyes sparkled with eagerness as she continued. "You were right about having me use Pete's return address. Papa would have wondered why someone was sending me money." Her face sobered. "But Pete says I mustn't do it again. He said once for a lark was fine, but that it's not ladylike to earn money."

"That's ridiculous," Renata said before she thought. "I earn money and I'm a lady." She realized what she had said and avoided her friend's eyes.

"You? When have you earned money? Doing what?"

"I meant that if I wanted to earn money, say by selling articles to a newspaper, I wouldn't compromise myself. I'm glad you tried. A lot of people wouldn't be so daring."

"It's not as if I were writing about some risqué subject. After all, it was only about planting roses. I signed it Anthony Edmund, just as we decided. Pete wasn't too pleased about that, either, but if they saw a woman's name on the article, they probably wouldn't have printed it. I was even asked to do another one."

"That's wonderful! You'll write it, won't you?"

"I don't know. I want to, but everyone except us seems to think a woman shouldn't want to earn money. Even you have expressed some doubts."

"I was wrong. Now I think it's a great idea. Maybe you should try to write a book."

"I could never do that. If I did, though, it would be for children. Remember how we used to make up stories about fairies living in the woods?"

"It seems to me, you've at least considered doing a book. You already know what it will be about. What could possibly be wrong in writing

255

stories for children? All mothers tell stories to their children, and this isn't any different."

"When you put it that way, I guess it isn't." Lidy Mae looked thoughtful. "I suppose I could try."

"Good for you." Renata looked out the window and saw a young man coming up the walk. "You have more company."

Lidy Mae leaned forward to see the porch. "It's Pete. Let's sit on the porch. Mama isn't receiving guests today. It's one of her headaches." Lidy Mae laughed. "She really *would* be upset if I let Pete come in when she isn't downstairs. Besides, I don't want him to see me sewing on a nightgown."

They went out to greet Pete. Immediately, Renata could see what Lidy Mae found desirable in him. Pete wasn't what she would call handsome, but he had kind eyes, and it was easy to tell he was thoroughly in love with Lidy Mae. They sat on the white wicker furniture on the wide porch, and as if Hattie had radar, she reappeared with three more glasses of lemonade.

"Your brother-in-law is mending nicely," Pete said to Renata.

"Ennis, you mean?"

Pete nodded. "That was a nasty burn. He was lucky it's not any worse than it is."

"Did he say how it happened?" Renata asked carefully.

"He said it happened at the blacksmith's shop.

I still don't see how a coal could have hit him like that. It looked more like a burn from a hot liquid to me. He'll carry a scar for a while."

Renata made no comment. She hadn't expected Ennis to tell anyone the truth.

"Molly was simply beside herself," Lidy Mae said. "She came over that afternoon and was practically distraught."

"Wouldn't you be if I was badly burned?" Pete asked with a smile.

"Of course I would, but Molly was rather too upset. I mean, it's not as if Ennis is in any danger. It was only a burn, after all."

Pete nodded. "Sometimes the family takes it harder than the patient. I don't know why that is. Another thing I've noticed is that widows and widowers seem angry after they lose their mates. I wouldn't have expected that. Sorrow, yes, but anger? I had a woman come in today to pay her bill, and she came right out and told me that she is mad at her husband for dying and leaving her all alone. Can you imagine? I wish I knew if other doctors have noticed this."

"Why don't you ask and find out?" Renata asked. "Maybe you'll find out it's universal."

"I would feel like a fool. No, I'm sure it's just that some people show grief in different ways. So, Callie, how are you today?"

"I'm fine. I came to town for corn meal and thought I'd drop by and visit with Lidy Mae before going home."

"You have a glow about you," Pete said. "I

wish all my patients looked so healthy."

"I'm happy these days."

"And Nathan? Is he doing all right?"

"Yes, thank you."

Pete gazed at her as if he were thinking something that he had no intention of voicing. Renata wondered if she had made some slip or if Ennis had been more honest to his doctor than she had expected.

"I was glad to hear you are standing up for Lidy Mae in our wedding. I intend to ask Nathan to be my best man."

"He will be pleased, I'm sure."

"Well, after all, he is my favorite cousin."

Renata managed not to show her surprise. She hadn't realized that Nathan and Pete were kin. That would make Lidy Mae her cousin by marriage. In a town as small as Lorain and with travel so difficult, it made sense that almost everyone had some connection with everyone else. "Would the two of you like to come out for supper some night? I'm not the best cook in the world, but I would love to have you."

"I'd like that," Lidy Mae said eagerly. "Pete's patients couldn't find him out there, and we would have an entire evening all to ourselves."

"Now, Lidy Mae, you have to get used to the idea of me being called out for sickness. If someone is bad off, they can't wait for me to keep regular office hours."

"I know, but it seems as if everyone gets sick right at suppertime."

Pete smiled at her and patted her hand. "When we are married we will live so close to the hospital I can be there and back before you know it."

"That will be an advantage," she admitted. "You were lucky to find a house that's so convenient."

"The time alone will give you a chance to write," Renata said.

"Write?" Pete asked with a raised eyebrow.

"Lidy Mae is considering doing some children's stories. I've told her that I think it's a wonderful idea."

Pete turned to Lidy Mae, who was frowning at Renata and shaking her head. "I thought we agreed that you won't do that again."

"Why shouldn't she?" Renata countered. "She must be able to write well or the Shreveport paper wouldn't have published her article. I think it's a good thing for her to be able to support herself."

"Support herself?" Pete was frowning in earnest now. "Why on earth would she ever need to do that?"

"What if something happens to you? How would she live?"

"She would come back to her parents."

"What if her parents are gone by then?"

"Then our children will care for her."

"What if . . ."

"Callie," Lidy Mae burst out. "Please!"

Renata sat back in her chair. "I only meant

that it would make you more secure to be able to earn your own living."

Both Lidy Mae and Pete were frankly staring at her. She shifted uneasily. "Well, wouldn't it?"

Cautiously Pete said, "Lidy Mae has told me you've been saying some things lately that don't make sense. Not lunatic ramblings, of course. I don't mean that. Now that I've heard you, I believe she's right. Maybe you should come to the office tomorrow and let me take a look at you."

"You can see me just fine right here. There is nothing wrong with me." She added with sudden inspiration, "I've become a suffragette."

Lidy Mae relaxed visibly and Pete blinked. "A suffragette? Since when? I've heard you say they must all be unnatural and misled."

"I said that? Surely not!" Callie might be more shy than Renata, but surely she wasn't that close-minded.

"I heard you, too," Lidy Mae said. "So did Molly."

"Well, I was wrong." Understanding came to her. Callie had been brought up believing in blind obedience. It was partly this unquestioning obedience that had made her such an easy target for Ennis. "I've changed my mind, and I intend to help start a local chapter."

"You're full of surprises today," Pete said slowly. "Are you sure you're feeling well?"

It occurred to Renata that it was paradoxical

that no one in her family except Nathan seemed to question the difference in her, nor did Callie's best friend. Yet Pete, who must know Callie less intimately than the others, saw a change. Perhaps, Renata thought, it was because the others were too close. "Can't see the forest for the trees," she said.

"Pardon?" Lidy Mae asked in confusion. "What did you say?"

"Nothing. I was merely thinking aloud. I ought to be going." She stood, and Pete hastily got to his feet out of politeness. To Pete she said, "I hope you'll reconsider Lidy Mae's wish to write. If she can adjust to your seeing patients whenever they send for you, surely you can bend a little for her."

"I'll consider it."

Renata bade them good-bye and left. She knew they were both watching as she awkwardly mounted her horse, but she was too unfamiliar with the saddle to do it gracefully. Without looking back, she rode away.

Pete was an enigma, she thought as she trotted through town toward her home. On the one hand he seemed to be introspective and aware, if only vaguely, of the psychological effects problems could have on people. In her own time, he might have become a psychiatrist. On the other hand, he could be as close-minded as anyone she had ever met. She doubted that he would give Lidy Mae's writing career another thought, but she expected that she had given Lidy Mae enough to think about that she might pursue it anyway.

Renata wondered if Lidy Mae would become a successful writer, and if, under some other pen name as unlikely as Anthony Edmund, she had read one of her books. The complexities of having gone back in time were mind-boggling at times. Renata often felt as if she were living with a foot in each world.

When she reached home, she saw Nathan coming down the fence line toward the house. She waved and he waved back. Riding to the barn, she dismounted and tied Red to the fence. After some struggle, she managed to remove the saddle, carried it into the tack room and put it over the saw horse like the others in the room. She was currying Red when Nathan came into the barn.

"I'd have done that for you," he said.

"I know. I like doing for myself." She turned to him. "Lidy Mae had an article printed in the Shreveport paper. Did you know she wants to write?"

"That's news to me. Pete won't be too pleased about it."

"Why not?"

"You know how he is." Nathan stopped and said in a softer tone, "He thinks women belong in the home."

"She can write at home."

"You know what I mean."

"I do, and I think it's ridiculous. I told him so, too."

"You did? You said that to Pete?"

"Is there some reason why I shouldn't have?"

"Not really. He must have thought it strange, though. He has been concerned about how frightened you are of men. I mean Callie," he amended. "He has asked me if something has happened to you to make you so afraid."

"He said that?" She had to give Pete credit. He was certainly ahead of his time when it came to psychology.

"He's said it more than once. I told him that nothing has happened." He looked directly at Renata. "Was I right?"

Renata felt her mouth go dry. She opened her mouth to tell him the truth, but couldn't speak. In her mind she could see him on the porch a few nights ago saying in a deadly calm voice that he would kill any man who dared to lay a hand on her. "Yes, you were right. Nothing has happened to me." At least that part was true.

Nathan nodded, but he didn't look convinced. "Pete gets some odd ideas at times. When you were so melancholy over losing our baby, he said he thought it would be good for you to have another baby as soon as possible. I couldn't tell him that we had stopped making love. That would have been too personal."

"It's no longer true, either." She coaxed a

smile out of him. "Maybe I'll surprise us both some day."

"You've already surprised me more than I ever thought possible." He finished brushing the horse and took him to the gate at the back of the barn where he unbridled him and let him into the lot. "You don't have any more surprises in stock for me, do you?"

Renata pretended not to hear. Directness had always been her way and tact wasn't her strong point.

Nathan walked with her toward the house. "If you really did come from the future, you must know a lot of things I can't imagine."

Renata had dreaded this subject. She wasn't sure she should tell Nathan what the future held, especially as it applied to him personally.

"I was wondering if farming ever gets any easier," he said.

She laughed with relief. "Easier than you would ever imagine. It's never become a completely easy job, but wait until tractors are invented and electricity."

As they walked to the house she tried to explain how houses would be cool in the summer and warm in the winter. He completely rejected the idea of computers and microwaves as being tall tales, but he listened avidly to how tractors would do the work of several teams and drivers. "I could plow a field as big as the back forty in a day?"

"It probably wouldn't take that long. I don't know much about farming and next to nothing about tractors, but it seems to me that it would be possible."

Nathan shook his head. "I can't imagine such a thing. It won't happen in my lifetime."

"Yes, it will," she said without thinking. "Tractors will be invented long before your death."

He glanced at her sharply. "Do you know my future?"

"I only meant that you're still young. These inventions aren't that far away. There are already motors in factories, and the automobile will come along in less than twenty years, as well as I remember."

"So you don't know what will happen to me?" He put out his hand and made her stop walking.

She couldn't lie to him. Not when he was looking at her like that. "I know that you will live a long life. Please, Nathan, don't ask me any more."

He wanted to ask her a great deal more. She could tell that. Who wouldn't? But he finally released her arm and walked by her side again. "Tell me about these automobiles."

As she explained what little she knew about cars, Renata gave thanks he had not pressed her for details about herself or whether they would have the children he so wanted. She couldn't let herself tell him something that would make him so unhappy. Besides, she thought, that might be changed now that she was here. Callie was afraid to have a child and afraid to protect herself from Ennis, but Renata wasn't. Maybe she would be able to stay long enough to change these things for Callie. Wasn't it possible that she could change the future by changing the past?

As they walked up the porch steps, she asked as casually as she could, "What year is this?"

He smiled and glanced at her as if he found it amusing that she wouldn't know that by now. "It's 1887."

Renata felt as if someone had pumped ice water into her veins. "1887?" she asked.

"Yes. Why?"

"No reason. I'm just surprised, that's all." She felt so numb from shock she couldn't feel her feet. She made herself smile to reassure him.

Nathan went into the house to wash up for supper, but Renata couldn't move yet. Callie had died in 1887. But Renata didn't know the month or day. Feeling sick to her stomach, she went into the house and pretended as if nothing were wrong, for Nathan's sake.

Chapter Thirteen

Of all her chores, washing clothes was undoubt-edly the most difficult, and Renata always put it off until it was a necessity. Nathan helped her load the basket of clothes into the wheel-barrow, and she pushed it down the hill. Callie had always carried it by hand, but Renata wasn't that fond of lifting heavy loads and carrying them up and down hills. At first Nathan had teased her about using the wheelbarrow, but later he had agreed that it seemed to be a good idea.

At the side of the stream, Renata set up the black iron pot and lit a fire beneath it. Using a pail that was always left hanging on a limb of a nearby tree, she bailed water from the stream into the pot. When the almost full pot had heat-ed to a simmer, Renata tossed in the first batch of their dirty clothes, her light-colored dresses and their undergarments. Later she would do the brighter clothes, and last of all, Nathan's soiled work clothes would go into the pot by themselves.

With her battling board, she stirred the clothes until the water came to a boil, then she began removing them, one garment at a time. The first out was one of her favorite dresses. She spread the dress out on a flat trough-like apparatus that stood at the edge of the water, and with the cake of yellow soap she kept in a canvas bag in the clothes hamper, she began scrubbing the dress and remembering the day she had come. By her calculations that had probably been in March since the redbuds were beginning to lose their blossoms and the dogwoods were starting to show theirs. Now it was early July. She still couldn't believe she was here or that she could trust herself to be able to stay here. As she had so often, she tried to remember exactly what Dr. McIntyre had said to bring her back to the present the first time—not that she wanted to return to Lorain of the 1990's. Far from it. She wanted to find out all she could in order to avoid her return.

Once the dress was clean, she bent and rinsed it in the stream. She put the wet dress back into the basket in the wheelbarrow and fished another out of the pot. Ennis hadn't been around since she poured the hot grease on him. That was reassuring. She hoped he had decided to go after easier game, though she sensed he wouldn't give up so easily. For a long time she had been afraid to come to wash clothes alone, but for some reason he never showed up on wash days.

Her thoughts shifted to her primary concern these days. Six weeks had passed since she had learned what year she was in. So far she had no symptoms of ill health, and she was careful not to take physical chances, but the clock ticked on.

Would Callie's death be altered now that she was here? Renata knew she had effected some changes, but she didn't know if her presence alone would be enough to prevent Callie's death. At least, she thought, she knew Callie had died from a fall off a horse while on an outing with Molly and Ennis. She told herself that she would be safe if she avoided any such outing, but she wasn't certain.

Since she had burned Ennis, it seemed unlikely he would want her to go for a ride. She had made it clear that she wasn't going to be as compliant as Callie had been. Maybe that had been enough. Or was it somehow ordained that she must die this year in order to fit some cosmic plan? Renata shivered. She had never believed in predestination, but now she was having to bet her life on it.

She had given a great deal of thought to Callie's death, and she had decided that it was at least possible that if it did indeed happen, she might find herself back in Dr. McIntyre's office. At least she hoped it would work that way.

When Renata was at last finished with the washing, she pushed the handle of the battling board through the iron loop on the side of the pot, causing the pot to tip over, pouring out the dirty water and dousing the fire at the same time. It had taken her a number of times to figure out how to do this correctly, but the great sense of accomplishment she felt made all the effort worth it. She kicked the embers apart to be positive the fire was out, then lifted the handles of the wheelbarrow and headed home.

Practice had helped her manage most of her chores, and it wasn't long before she had finished hanging the clothes on the line to dry. With the day hot and without a cloud in the sky, she was sure they would dry fast, and with luck, she thought she might finish the ironing before bedtime.

When she went inside, she found Nathan pouring over some papers scattered all over the kitchen table. She peered over his shoulder. "What are you doing?"

He rubbed his chin and said, "Bookkeeping. I'll be out of your way in a minute."

"Bookkeeping?" She looked with greater interest at the papers.

"I'm trying to work out my yearly budget. These are receipts from last year and the year before, and I'm trying to figure out if I'll have enough money to put in all my crops and still have extra to live on." He gave her a sad grin. "We won't ever be rich, Callie. Not the way I am at arithmetic."

Renata's face brightened. "Nathan, are you in luck! I may not be able to make decent cornbread, but when I do math, birds sing in the trees."

"Pardon?"

"Move over."

Renata hadn't realized how much she had missed working with numbers. Her job as an accountant had become mundane to her, but after months of not balancing so much as her own checkbook, she enjoyed the challenge of a math problem. Only a few minutes later she declared, "We'll have enough and then some, unless prices go up at the feedstore next year."

Nathan was looking on in amazement. "Where did you learn to do that? It would have taken me several hours to do what you just did."

"I majored in math in college. I'm a Certified Public Accountant."

"I never heard of that."

"It means I do things like this for a living where I come from."

"You work?" Nathan seemed shocked. "Your parents allow that?"

"I was thirty years old. My parents had finished raising me long ago. I was on my own."

"An old maid?" he asked empathetically. "I can't imagine you having to live alone."

"I didn't have to," she said rather defensively. "I chose to do it."

Nathan smiled but didn't look convinced.

"I was, in fact, engaged to be married. His name is Bob Symons—or at least it will be when he's born."

"You were in love with someone else?" Nathan's eyes darkened. "You never told me about him."

"It's odd, but I sometimes forget about him myself. I know now it would have been a mistake to marry him. It would never have worked out." She laughed. "He wanted his mother to live with us."

"Is there something wrong with that? I think that shows he's a man of character. Don't sons take care of their elderly mothers where you come from?"

"Certainly. But his mother isn't infirm. She is barely sixty. Don't look at me like that. That may seem old now, but in my time it's barely past middle age."

"People live to be one hundred and twenty years-old?"

"You needn't be so literal. We do, however, stay active much longer—probably because we have time-and labor-saving devices and don't work ourselves half to death the way you do." She added, "And men don't buy houses their mothers like that don't suit their fiancées."

"I can agree with that. I thought of you first and would have even if my parents were still alive. Someday, however, Jemima may have to move in with us. Her husband is considerably older than she is, and she will almost certainly be a widow. So far they have no children to take care of her." He looked at her searchingly. "Do you love Symons?"

"Bob? No, I thought I did, but I know better now. I had never been in love before I met you. Now I can see it would have been a mistake."

"And a costly one."

She nodded. "Divorce isn't cheap."

"Divorce? I meant you would be stuck with him for the rest of your life. You would have actually *divorced* him?"

"It's not scandalous in my time. Certainly it's not something to be considered lightly, but society no longer ostracizes people who divorce."

"Are you making all this up?" he asked suspiciously. Then another thought struck him. "If you were not yet married, you were a virgin when you came here. Since Callie and I had been married for years, I must not have hurt you the first time we made love, but you must have been confused and frightened."

Renata gazed up at him. She knew Nathan wasn't ready to hear about twentieth century morals as opposed to Victorian ones. "I wasn't afraid of you. I already loved you."

He looked relieved. "If only you could have told me. I never intended to hurt or to alarm you."

"You didn't."

He was thoughtful for a minute. "If you were

a virgin, how do you know so much about love-making?"

"I'm inventive," she said lightly. To change to a safer subject she said, "Would you like for me to take over all the paperwork for you? I enjoy it, and I believe I can find ways to make our money grow."

He laughed. "You sound as if money is a crop. Why not? I would rather you grow money than those red beans you planted."

"Is that what those vines are? I was hoping they were peas."

"No, Callie, to grow peas, you have to plant peas, not beans. Didn't you look at what you were doing?"

"I didn't pay much attention, to tell you the truth. I never planted a garden in my life. I lived in an apartment and didn't have a yard. As a child I wasn't interested in growing things. I have a few pots of ivy in my apartment, but that's altogether different."

"Is an apartment like the rooms Widow Parmelee rents out in the boarding house?"

"It's similar, but an apartment almost always has at least a bedroom, a living room, a kitchen and a bath. Some have two or three bedrooms."

"All inside someone else's house? How can that be?"

"Apartment houses are built differently from regular houses." On the back of one of the previous year's receipts, she drew a floor plan. "See? They all fit together and stack side by side and on top of each other. The building is never intended for only one family's use."

He shook his head. "I would rather have my own place."

"I felt the same. I wanted a house built at about this time, as a matter of fact. Do you suppose I was subconsciously looking for you even then?"

"Subconscious?"

"I'll explain that one another time," she said hastily. "It can get confusing." She begin gathering up the papers so she could file them in the boot box Nathan used for this purpose.

"You amaze me. I've never known anyone who thinks and acts the way you do. Are all women brought up the way you were?"

"More or less. People and places are different, but we almost always have at least a high school education, if not a college degree."

"You've been to college?"

She nodded. "I have two degrees."

Nathan frowned. "I never went to college. I must seem stupid to you."

"You're not any such thing, and I won't have you say it. We're from different cultures. If the tables were reversed, you would understand if I had stopped after high school."

"Callie never got that far. That's why I was so surprised when you started reading Dickens and Radcliff in the evenings. She could read, but not well enough to do it for enjoyment."

"I still can't get over how I was able to pass as Callie at all. As far as I know, her parents still don't suspect a thing, and neither does Molly. Lidy Mae and Pete were suspicious, but they have accepted me."

"What else can they do? You look and sound like Callie."

"Please, tell me about Callie. Didn't anyone think it was odd that she became so depressed after her miscarriage?"

"We all did, but there wasn't anything we could do about it. She was more melancholy than any of us had ever seen her before. This wasn't the only baby we lost." A muscle tightened in his jaw. "The others were barely more than an idea. I was sure that this last time she would be able to carry it to birth." He glanced at her. "Am I speaking too frankly?"

Renata smiled. "No, you aren't shocking me. Tell me more."

"I know I shouldn't say this, but I was starting to wonder if she was causing herself to lose them."

"What? Why would you think that? Is it possible?"

"There are plants down in the woods that would cause a miscarriage. I wouldn't have thought she would do such a thing, but more than once I've found some cotton root bark and squaw vine in the kitchen. There isn't much else she could have been using them for in the same potion." He leaned his forearms on the table and sadly poked at the salt and pepper shakers. "Why would she do a thing like that, do you suppose?"

"Maybe you're wrong." Renata wanted to comfort him, but she suspected he was right. If Callie couldn't be sure the baby wouldn't look like Ennis instead of Nathan, she might go to such drastic measures. "Surely she wouldn't do that."

"I wish I was sure of that. Before we were married, Callie said she wanted children, but she always sounded reluctant. I thought it was because that was a subject that really wasn't proper for us to be discussing, but once she started having so much trouble, I didn't know what to think. Then, after that last one, she said we wouldn't . . . sleep together again. I guess she didn't want children after all."

Renata's heart went out to Callie and her secret pain. How terrible it must have been for her to have to drink the tea made of squaw vine and cotton root because she knew she didn't dare give birth to a child that might not be her husband's. Renata had always liked children, but she, too, had known a reluctance to bear them. Callie's fear had been transmitted to her next life.

That brought something else to mind. In her head, Renata again began counting the months. Without a calendar, she found it difficult to keep track of the weeks, but now that she thought about it, her last period had been over a month ago. Was it possible? She added it up again. Yes, even counting conservatively it had to have been over a month ago.

Excitement laced with fear leaped within her. She might be carrying Nathan's child! She couldn't be certain yet since Callie's body didn't seem to be as regular as Renata's own. Certainly she couldn't tell Nathan until she was sure.

"What are you thinking?" he asked. "You're smiling."

"Nothing really. I was just wondering if I might some day be able to give you a child." She wondered if he was right about Callie or if her body simply wasn't capable of childbearing.

Nathan covered her hand with his own. "Nothing would make me happier. I've wanted children all my life. I like children and enjoy being around them. Not just boys to help with the fields, either, but girls as well." He smiled shyly. "Maybe we could even manage to send them to college. There I go, building castles in the air again. Callie always got upset whenever I did that. She said it wasn't logical."

"I don't agree. I love to hear you dream aloud."

"I had such fine hopes," he said, gazing out the window. "I was going to raise horses—not just ordinary ones, but the kind a man may not own but one of in his entire life."

"Why don't you?"

"I don't have the time. It takes all my time looking after the crops and harvesting them. The money hasn't come in as easily as I had thought it would. I have to work hard just to make ends meet, let alone to have enough to buy the type horse I would need to get started."

"Maybe I could help in some way. If Lidy Mae can earn money by writing articles, maybe I could earn some by writing explanations of how to invest money and keep books."

Nathan looked uncertain. "I never heard of a woman doing that."

"I could use a pen name." Renata leaned forward eagerly. "No one would have to know I'm a woman. And I could mail my articles to cities far from here. I think I'll try it."

"You'd do that for me?"

"Nathan, you would never believe all I'm willing to do for you. I've never cared more for someone else than I did for myself—until now. It's a wonderful feeling. And I would love to try writing the articles. It'll be our secret. I can't tell Lidy Mae or Molly."

He shook his head. "They know Callie wouldn't know the first thing about writing, let alone about bookkeeping."

"Then you don't object?"

Nathan smiled at her. "I'm not Pete. I know it won't lower me a single notch to have a wife that can do more than cook and clean."

Elizabeth Crane

"I think you'd fit into my time," she said teasingly. "You are remarkably unchauvinistic."

"If you say so. You know more fifty' cent words than I ever heard." He added softly. "I'm proud of you, Renata."

She was touched as she always was when he called her by her real name, and his compliments were better than gold to her. "I love you, Nathan."

To her surprise, she saw his eyes grow moist, and he looked away. "I never thought I would hear those words from your lips, and everytime you say them, I feel as if I could fight tigers for you. It touches me."

Renata had never felt so happy. Her own vision was blurring from the tears welling in her eyes as she helped Nathan put the receipts in the box.

Renata wasn't at all sure how to write an article on money management using nineteenth century terms, but she was determined to try, even without aid of a typewriter, much less the computer she was accustomed to using. Using Nathan's notebook, she sat in the porch swing and started to write.

The words came easier than she had expected once she got past the first few sentences. She aimed her article at the men who were starting out on their own, the kind of men she thought would be more likely to heed her advice. When that one was finished she wrote one aimed toward the female population. Regardless of everyone's assumption that women were cared for by husbands, parents or other family members, Renata knew there must be others who, for one reason or another, had no one to advise them. She suspected there were even more who thought they could do a better job themselves than their respective families and who could benefit from the article.

When it was finished, she carefully copied it onto the white paper Nathan used for important correspondence. Her handwriting would never be as graceful as the hand in which Callie had written recipes and household notes, but she hoped the editors of the papers would overlook that. She had decided to send the article to as many papers as she could find that would be likely to print it. Nathan had rarely spoken to her of his dreams and hopes, and she was determined to see him get his horse farm.

For the next two weeks Renata waited impatiently. Then one day two letters arrived addressed to Nathan with return addresses of cities she had sent the article to. Her fingers trembled as she opened the envelopes. Nathan knelt by her chair, almost as nervous as she was.

Inside the first letter Renata found a bank draft. For a moment she could only stare at it. Nathan took the letter from her and read it. "They want you to write more articles for them. How large is the check?"

She handed it to him as tears of happiness rolled down her cheek. She had made less on this sale than she made in an hour as a CPA, but she had never been happier. "They really bought it," she whispered.

"This man thinks I wrote it," Nathan said with a frown.

"I used your name. I didn't think you would mind. I couldn't use my name or Callie's and expect it to be published. Lidy Mae taught me that. It had to be a man's name. I should have asked you first. Do you mind?"

"Not at all." He read the letter again as she opened the other envelope.

"It's another sale," she said with wonder in her voice, "to *The Housewife's Friend*."

"That's a woman's magazine."

"I know. I took the address from that copy Molly had loaned me. I thought women might want to know something about balancing books and how to stretch their household allowances—as much as I dislike that word," she couldn't refrain from adding. "The idea of a grown woman needing an 'allowance' from her husband, as if she were a child."

Nathan grinned at her and waved the two checks. "I may become a suffragette myself."

With the checks in hand, Renata hurried over to the oak secretary in the corner, pulled down the front and opened the small drawer above the pigeonholes. Placing the checks inside, Renata announced, "This will go toward our first horse. If the others sell, we may be able to start looking for one by next month."

"You're really doing this for me," he marveled.

"I'm doing it for us both. I enjoy using my brain and doing something more useful than washing clothes and scrubbing floors. That's important, too, but it doesn't help you get your horses."

"Callie said I was wrong to want to raise horses. She said it was worse than farming to breed animals."

"Yes, well, Callie had a few more mental quirks than I do. If I were you, I'd start keeping an eye open for a suitable horse."

"I'll do that. Together we'll make it work."

Renata smiled and hugged him, but in the back of her mind she heard over and over as if it were a litany, *Callie died from a fall off a horse.* "You will have to train them to ride," she said. "I'm not up to handling anything more spirited than Red or Janie."

"That's fine with me. I wouldn't expect you to do that. Besides, most of the colts will be sold green broke." When she looked confused, he explained, "We will teach them to lead with a halter and whoever buys them will train them to the saddle."

"I can do that if you'll show me how."

"We're going to be a team," he said, lifting her up and swinging her around in the air.

Renata laughed with him and hugged him back. Never in her wildest dreams had she envisioned this chapter in her life.

Chapter Fourteen

Callie's parents were coming for Sunday dinner, and naturally Renata was nervous. She tried baking a cake, but the result was disastrous. The pigs, however, enjoyed it. At times she thought more of the food that she cooked ended up in the pig trough than on the table, but she was not discouraged. Trying again, with success this time, she baked two peach pies to take the cake's place and put them in the pie safe to cool.

No casserole would do for this meal. Instead, she had cooked a roast with potatoes and carrots and had made the seemingly indispensable red beans and cornbread. Finally she was satisfied with her efforts. Leaving the roast simmering and the cornbread on the warming shelf, she hurried upstairs to put on a clean dress.

As she was fastening the mother-of-pearl buttons on her dress, she heard a buggy arriving and looked out the window to see not only Callie's parents, Ida and William Graham, but

Molly and Ennis as well. "Damn," she muttered as she bent over and brushed her hair smooth so she could coil it into a bun. It hadn't occurred to her that Molly and Ennis were also coming. Fortunately, she had learned to cook far more than was necessary for a meal and wouldn't be embarrassed at not having enough food to serve them.

By the time they reached the door, Renata was crossing the foyer. She glanced around the spotless house. Had she forgotten to do anything? When William rapped on the door, she hurried forward to open it. "Come in, come in. I didn't expect you so early."

"It's never too early for family to visit, I should hope," William said pedantically.

"I didn't mean . . . Come in and make yourselves comfortable. Would you like some iced lemonade while we wait for Nathan to come in from the barn?" She smiled at everyone but Ennis.

Ida turned toward the front parlor, and Renata realized this visit would be more formal than if Molly were here alone. Ida turned about in the center of the room as if she were inspecting it. "Beautiful. Simply beautiful. You've done wonders in here, Callie."

"Thank you. Please, sit down. Lemonade?" she asked again.

"Yes, please," Ida said. "The ride out was so uncomfortable. I wonder if it will ever rain again."

"It has been dry," Renata agreed as she went to get the lemonade.

With an ice pick, Renata began to chip ice from the large block of her icebox until she had enough for the glasses. Molly came in to help her and held the glasses while Renata filled them.

"You're really taking a chance," Molly whispered.

"What?" Renata dropped a precious chip of ice on the floor. "What do you mean?"

"Having Mrs. Blue's picture on the mantel instead of Mama's. You know how much Mama disliked Mrs. Blue."

So the stern-faced woman in the picture was Nathan's mother; therefore Nathan must have taken after his father's looks. "Mr. and Mrs. Blue are both dead now, and Mama will just have to learn to bury the hatchet. Besides, I don't have a good daguerreotype of Mama and Papa." She hoped this was true and was proud that she had remembered the term.

"Why on earth would you want one of those old things? Photographs are so much better."

Renata sighed, wishing she had paid closer attention to history and antiques when she had had the chance.

Molly continued. "I wish Mama would sit for a photograph, but she refuses to even consider it. She says it feeds the sin of pride. Alma has sketched her and Mama says that is good enough, but as much as I like Alma, she isn't

287

all that good at portraits. Don't you tell her I said so."

"I won't." Renata poured the lemonade and put the glasses on a painted tray to carry them into the front parlor.

When they entered the room, Renata saw Ida turn from the photo on the mantel, her lips set in an uncompromising line. Renata wondered what the two women had quarrelled over that was of so solemn a nature as to cause Ida to resent Mrs. Blue's image even after the woman was dead. She was likely never to know, unless Nathan had the answer. There were so many things that she might never learn since she could ask so few questions.

She handed the glasses around, still refusing to make eye contact with Ennis. Knowing he was in the room was bad enough. She didn't think she could bear to make polite conversation with him. When he took the glass she noticed the fresh, pink scar on his hand. She wondered if anyone believed a popping coal from a blacksmith's furnace could have caused a scar of that shape. Evidently Molly believed it.

Renata took one of the upholstered chairs by the window. It, like the other three "ladies" chairs, had wooden trim on the sides of the seat at the back to prevent a woman from sitting too far back into it and to provide room for bustles. Renata noticed that Molly and Ida, neither of whom happened to be wearing a dress with a bustle, seemed quite comfortable sitting on the front half of the seat with their backs straight and a precise six inches from the back cushions. Renata straightened her posture and reminded herself to keep both her feet on the floor.

"Your Papa sold his dun mare," Ida said to Molly. "I was glad to see her go. It's so hard to get rid of a horse once they start to age."

"That's so true," Molly said. "I don't plan to keep my horse more than another year."

Renata opened her mouth to tell about the progress of her horse's colt, but Ida shifted the conversation before she could speak.

"I saw Mrs. Fisher the other day. She said her eldest daughter now has a son. Do you remember her?"

Molly nodded. Renata pretended to be engrossed in her lemonade.

"One can only hope the child resembles his father. That Fisher girl was never a beauty." Ida sipped her drink. "This is good, Callie. I always like a cold glass of iced lemonade in the summer."

"I'm glad you like it. I—"

Ida interrupted smoothly, saying, "Molly, did you try that fish recipe I sent you?"

As Molly nodded, William and Ennis stood up. "We'll go down to the barn and see what's keeping Nathan," William said. "This talk of recipes and babies is no place for us. Am I right, Ennis?"

"I couldn't agree more." Ennis said.

Renata felt Ennis's eyes on her, but she refused to look his way as the two men left.

"I guess I cooked the fish too long," Molly said. "It seemed dry to me."

"I only cook it the shortest time," Ida said. "It's hard to get my woman to do it properly, but it's of prime importance."

Again Renata opened her mouth to join in the conversation, but again Ida surged on without her.

"I've heard Barbara Downs has taken to drink!" Ida said in a conspiratorial whisper to Molly. "I'd never mention her name in front of our husbands, but I have it on good authority that she was seen drunk on the street last week."

"Maybe she had good reason," Renata said.

"What reason could she possibly have to drink alcohol?" Ida demanded.

"Maybe she's lonely. I never hear any good about her."

"Posh! That sort never get lonely. They don't have keen sensibilities like the rest of us." Ida drew herself up so haughtily that the plumes on her hat quivered.

"Everybody gets lonely. Why is everyone so determined to keep her beyond the pale?" Renata risked asking. "What exactly has she done?"

Molly whispered, "You know as well as I do that she had a baby out of wedlock." The expression on her face was as scandalized as was Ida's. "No one knows who the father was,

290

and she has always refused to say."

Renata was silent. This was almost exactly what Callie had feared would happen to her. She had been lucky that she either never became pregnant before Nathan married her, or that she was able to keep anyone from knowing. Renata now knew, more clearly than ever, why Callie was so afraid of having a baby that didn't look like Nathan. She wondered if Barbara Downs was no more guilty than Callie.

"Whenever she is asked about it, she sulks and won't say anything. I should have known she would come to no good the way she was always flaunting herself in front of people."

"Isn't it possible she was raped?" Renata asked.

Both Molly and Ida gasped and stared at Renata.

"Well, it does happen," she defended herself. "Maybe Barbara had no say in the matter at all."

"I've heard that she was, but if so, it was her own fault. Traipsing around smiling at men and wearing her hair down long after she was of an age when it should have been up."

"Her own fault if she was raped!" Renata was so outraged she forgot to be careful. "That's the most ridiculous thing I ever heard in my life. Rape is a terrible crime. It's a crime of violence, not passion."

Ida glared at her. "Callie, I'll thank you not to speak to me in that manner. As for your subject matter, I can only say I'm appalled. You were brought up to be better than this."

"But if she was attacked, it wasn't her fault. Can't you see that? She would have been forced." Her own near-miss at Ennis's hands fortified her already strong feelings about the issue. "How can any woman say such a thing?"

"Callie, that's quite enough. I'll thank you to keep a civil tongue in your head."

"Please, Callie," Molly said, "let's not talk about it anymore."

"Sure. Great. Let's just sweep injustice under the rug and not look at it," Renata snapped. "That way we can pretend it never happened and go on our way without having to do anything about it."

"What has gotten into her?" Ida demanded of Molly. "She never used to be this way."

"Maybe it's because you talk around me as if I'm not here," Renata retorted. "Hasn't it ever occurred to you that I may have something to add to the conversation? You talk to Molly and not to me almost all the time."

"That's nonsense."

"No, it's not. And I find Barbara's predicament, if indeed she is in one, of far greater importance than how to cook a fish!"

"I think we had better be going." Ida stood and said, "Molly, be a good girl and run get the men." She and Renata glared at each other.

"Mama, we can't do that. What would Nathan think? What would Papa say?" Molly went to her mother and pressed her back into the chair. "Please, Mama. Callie is just upset about something. Isn't that right, Callie?" She gazed imploringly at Renata.

Renata realized she had allowed her tongue to overrun her reasoning and forced herself to say, "Yes, that's it. I'm sorry I spoke to you that way."

Ida huffed and her hat feathers continued to tremble, but she nodded and said, "I accept your apology."

Although it was difficult for her, Renata sat quietly as Molly and Ida resumed their discussion of tepid topics and household hints. She could see why Callie had been so depressed. She knew by Barbara's example that she would be ostracized by everyone if the truth about Callie and Ennis ever came to light. Renata's heart went out to Callie, and she wondered how Callie had managed to do as well as she had.

A few minutes later the men returned, and Nathan went straight upstairs to wash up and change into clean clothes for the meal. Renata was now even more ill-at-ease in the same room with Ennis. Making an excuse of needing to see about the food, she retreated into the kitchen. Soon Molly was beside her.

"What on earth were you thinking of to upset Mama like that?" she demanded as she poured the red beans into a bowl. "You know not to say that word."

"Rape?"

"I'm surprised you even know what it means. I would certainly never say it out loud and never would I say it to Mama."

"But I had a good point, didn't I? What if Barbara Downs was raped and that's why she had a child? She shouldn't be shunned because of that."

"I didn't make the rules," Molly snapped as she stuck a serving spoon into the bowl of beans and stomped away with the bowl to the dining room table. Moments later she returned with a frown still on her face. "It's a good thing Papa won't hear of it."

"Mama won't tell him?"

"Of course not. She would never say that word to a man. Callie, sometimes I don't understand you at all."

Renata sighed and dumped the square pan of cornbread upside down on a platter. After turning it right side up, she cut it into serving-sized portions. "I just don't think a person should be blamed for something they couldn't prevent."

"Neither do I, but that's just the way it is." Molly carried the cornbread in to the table.

When she returned Renata said, "Would you blame me? If I were forced like that?"

Molly frowned. "I don't know. Why do you ask me things like that?"

"I've asked you that before?"

"Several times. Nothing like that is ever going to happen to either one of us. We have husbands to protect us."

Renata turned away, unable to meet Molly's eyes. So Callie had tried to bring up the subject on more than one occasion. Renata knew she had been right not to tell anyone.

All during the meal the air was strained between Renata and both Ida and Ennis, but no one seemed to notice. She was beginning to see another facet of Callie's emotional problems. Everyone but Nathan and Molly seemed to look right through her. Was it because they were so accustomed to Callie's shyness, or was it because they simply didn't care that much for her? In the months she had been here, this was the first visit Callie's parents had paid to the farm, and they had seen fit to bring Molly and Ennis with them without mentioning it to Callie beforehand.

Renata put her hand under the table and lay it on Nathan's leg, feeling the need to rely on his strength and know he was being protective of her. Yet all her life Renata had prided herself on being able to take care of herself. With determination, she removed her hand. She had never needed anyone to protect her, and she wasn't going to weaken now.

When Nathan smiled at her, she returned his smile. At least he was spared the misery of knowing Callie's secrets. Renata made firm her decision not to confide in him about Ennis and to handle the problem with Ennis on her own.

Each time during the meal when Ennis tried to speak directly to Renata, she ignored him, pretending to be deeply interested in the conversation on her other side. And the one time he asked her to pass a dish, she shoved it at him as hard as she dared without drawing attention to what she was doing. Maybe Callie could stand to play by Ennis's rules, but Renata had no intention of doing so.

William was saying to Nathan, "I still say those suffragettes are out of their minds. Now I hear Miss Anthony's second book is being sent to libraries. Next thing you know, she and her cohorts will be storming Washington."

"Susan B. Anthony?" Renata asked. It still amazed her to hear of historical figures spoken of so matter-of-factly.

"Who else?" William said. "What woman would ever listen to such goings on?"

"I would." Renata nodded decisively. "I hear there's a Women's Suffrage group forming in town, and I intend to belong to it. Molly, would you like to go?"

Molly, her eyes wide, shook her head slowly.

"Well, I'll go alone, then."

William frowned at his suddenly outspoken daughter. "You're certainly getting high-and-mighty these days. I'd say you have enough to do around here to keep you busy. Wouldn't you, Nathan?"

Nathan smiled at Renata. "Callie can go if she pleases. I'm glad to see her taking an interest in things again."

"All women have melancholia from time to time," William protested. "It's part of their nature. You shouldn't humor her like that."

Nathan drew a deep breath as if he was stepping over a boundary he had always avoided before. "I'm interested in it myself. It's only right that a woman be able to own property and testify in court. Sometimes it's downright necessary."

"No lady would ever speak in public at a place like that," Ida put in. "Next thing you know, they'll be wanting divorces from their husbands."

"I doubt any woman will want a divorce on the grounds of being able to testify in court or because she can buy her own property," Renata said. She was still angry at the woman. Narrow-mindedness had always made her angry. Now she knew why it was so instinctive with her.

"Or because they can be educated or possess their own children," Nathan added.

"They can't do that either?" Renata exclaimed.

"I had a feeling you didn't know that," Nathan said, humor shining in his dark eyes.

"Of course she knows that," William said. "Callie may be a bit slow, but she hasn't lived in a cave all her life."

Renata's mouth dropped open, and she was about to tell him what she thought about being described as "a bit slow" when Nathan's hand clamped down on her leg, causing her to bite back her words.

"Callie has been acting very peculiar lately," Ida said to the others as if her daughter was nowhere near. "I'm beginning to wonder about her."

"So am I," Ennis said.

Renata wanted nothing more than to run from the table or to dump a bowl or two of her food over her guests' heads, yet she refused to let herself move.

"I've noticed that, too," Nathan said. "I like it."

Renata was so touched she felt like crying. Nathan was risking his in-laws' disapproval by standing up for her, and she knew how difficult this must be for him since they evidently didn't have all that good a relationship to begin with. "Thank you, Nathan," she whispered.

"Don't mention it," he said with a grin.

"You had better be sure you wear the pants in your family," William counseled Nathan. "You could live to regret giving her too much freedom to say and do as she pleases."

Nathan's eyes gazed into Renata's. "No, I won't regret it."

Renata thought the visit would never end, but at last Callie's parents climbed into the buggy along with Molly and Ennis and waved good-bye. As they pulled away, Molly was still giving Renata curious glances as if she were dying to ask questions, but didn't dare. Renata felt as if she had been holding her breath during the entire visit.

As she finished straightening the kitchen—Molly had insisted on helping her with the dishes and Ida had come in to leave the men to their conversation—Renata heard Nathan go upstairs to change back into his work clothes then go out to the barn. From her kitchen window she could see him walking past the yard fence and across the grass to the barn and feed lot. The mere sight of him warmed her heart.

She wiped the countertop dry and stepped out onto the kitchen porch and shook the crumbs from the tablecloth. Instantly the chickens scrambled after the leavings. Renata watched them for a moment, scurrying about as though they hadn't eaten in days, which she knew wasn't true because she had fed them herself only that morning. Their odd behavior usually held her attention, but today she had other things on her mind, so she went back inside. Methodically, she folded the cloth and put it on the kitchen table. Whether or not this was a good time, she needed to talk to Nathan.

Not bothering to put on a bonnet, she went out to the barn. Sunlight slanted through the rough planks that formed the stalls and through the door at the far end. "Nathan?" she called out.

"Up here."

After gathering up her skirt, she climbed the narrow steps that led to the hayloft. Nathan was moving bales of hay from the dark end of the loft to the end closer to the square of sunlight. Soon he would bale this year's crop of hay, and the new bales would go to the dark end so the old would be used first. Wearing work gloves, he lifted the heavy bales as if they weighed nothing at all. She watched him for a minute, enjoying the way his lithe body moved. "I wanted to thank you for taking my part in the argument at dinner."

"I really do feel the suffragettes have a point." He stopped stacking the bales and kicked at the loose hay on the floor. "I think women ought to be able to buy property. What if I died and we didn't have this place? Without your family to take you in, you would have nowhere else to go."

Renata grimaced. "I wouldn't go to them. I don't like your in-laws."

Nathan laughed but made no comment.

"I don't think you like them either."

"Molly is a fine person."

Renata smiled. She liked the way he had of getting across the point that he disliked a person without saying something bad about them. "Maybe you should have been a politician."

"Not me. I just want to stay on my farm and raise horses someday."

"We will." She crossed the rough-hewn floor and gazed out the window. "You're good to me.

I'm not sure I've ever told you that."

"I love you. Of course I want to be good to you. Until today I wouldn't have crossed your father like that, but lately you've made me think about some things. Before a few months ago, you would have been mad if I expressed a difference of opinion to him. Lately I've decided some ideas are worth fighting for."

"Was I that bad?" Renata and Nathan had fallen into the habit of referring to her arrival as being "before" or "after" and of assuming she and Callie were one person.

"Not bad. Just different. I loved you then, too." He pulled the gloves off and tossed them onto the nearest bale, then sat on the loose hay and looked with her out the open doorway. "I guess I've always loved you and that I always will."

"Sometimes in the middle of the night I lie awake and wonder if you are somewhere in the world I left and whether I ever would have found you."

"That's occurred to me, too. I wonder why we didn't end up together then."

"Maybe we would have, eventually. I was only a little older than I am now. If we met, we would have still have had a long life together."

"Not if you were married to that Bob person."

Renata smiled at the hint of jealousy in his voice. "I doubt I would have married Bob anyway. I was already getting cold feet."

"Good."

She sat beside him and hugged her knees to her chest. "Maybe you weren't looking for me then. Maybe you were so unhappy in your marriage to Callie you didn't want to take a chance on repeating it."

"I said I've always loved you." He didn't meet her eyes.

"I know," she replied gently as she put her hand on his arm. "I remember how it was when I first came here, though. You and Callie were living under the same roof, but not together. You never smiled at first, and every time I said anything to you, it was as if you expected me to attack you verbally."

Nathan was quiet for a moment. "I guess you could say matters were tense between us."

Renata rested her cheek on his shoulder and ran her hand down the length of his arm and back. "I'm so glad I was able to come and make some changes. Who knows? We may be born again two hundred years from now and this time we will be determined to find each other."

"You think it works that way? That I might remember you and know you when I find you again?" He studied her face and reached up to smooth a loose curl back into her hair.

"I would bet everything I have on it. After all, I came all the way back here to find you, and as soon as I saw you, I fell in love with you. I know you think Callie didn't love you the same way, but I think you're wrong. I think Callie loved you as much as she could. There may have been reasons why she couldn't show you the way I can."

"I can't see what they could be. A wife ought to be able to tell her husband anything. She sure ought to be able to let him touch her."

"I don't understand that part myself." Renata thought it would have made more sense for Callie to welcome Nathan's lovemaking in spite of her fear of men just to insure that if she had a child, he would accept it as his own. Or was she determined that the opposite be true? That if she became pregnant her secret would finally be out in the open and someone would have to act on it? Renata knew she would probably never know.

Renata lay back on the hay and gazed up at the cobwebs laced beneath the barn roof. "At least it's cool up here."

"There's always a breeze. In the winter it's not a blessing."

She put out her hand and rubbed Nathan's back. "I love to touch you. Sometimes I wish I could just follow you around and watch you move and listen to you talk and touch you. If I had my way, neither or us would ever get anything done."

"That sounds good to me." He leaned back beside her, his body propped up on his elbow. He took a straw and tickled her neck. "As soon as we get rich, let's do that."

"Why wait?" Her eyes dared him to match her teasing.

"I need to get you a clock. Don't you know it's broad daylight? You know what happens when you look at me like that."

"The dishes are washed and this hay will still be waiting for you an hour from now. Neither of us has a bus to catch."

Nathan lifted an eyebrow, then relaxed. "I'm not even going to ask what that means." His eyes were sweeping over her face as if he were memorizing her features. "You're so beautiful. Sometimes when I look at you I'm reminded of a porcelain doll my sister had. It was so dainty and delicate, and it looked as if it would break if you breathed on it hard."

"I won't break. I promise." Her voice was throaty with her desire for him. "You can touch me all you please."

"Renata," he murmured. "You could drive a man wild with wanting you."

"Kiss me," she whispered. "I want you, too."

Nathan bent over her, his body pressing against hers. His lips coaxed hers open, and she met his tongue passionately. When he opened the buttons of her dress, the cool breeze made her flesh tingle, but her trembling was due to what his fingers were doing to her.

His hand covered her breast and his fingers teased her nipple until it swelled and throbbed at his touch. Renata moaned as desire swept through her. She fumbled at his clothing in her eagerness. When his shirt was open, she pulled it from him and covered his warm flesh with kisses. "You taste so good." She ran her tongue over his skin and left butterfly kisses along his shoulder. "I can't get enough of you."

He laughed and helped her loosen his belt. "I'm glad to hear it. I never knew any man who couldn't stand to wait until nighttime to make love with his wife. And I sure never heard of any wife who followed her husband to the hayloft with this on her mind. I like your century better than I do mine."

"I'd like any time, any place, if you were there."

He sobered and looked deep into her eyes. "Never leave me, Renata. I don't think I could stand it."

She couldn't answer because she wasn't sure she could make that promise.

Chapter Fifteen

When the nausea first hit her, Renata was gathering eggs from the row of hen nests along the back of the smokehouse. She was so rarely sick that she felt a surge of panic as the first waves struck her. She leaned against the building and clutched the egg basket so tightly that her knuckles turned white. Gradually the feeling subsided, and with quivering hands she went back to the nests and her chore.

The hen sitting on the nest at the end watched her balefully. Renata had been pecked by this chicken more than once, and she was also keeping an eye on her. None of the other nests were occupied, and all but one had a white or brown egg on the hay inside. It had taken Renata a while to learn she was supposed to search for the eggs and to figure out where to look. The chicken on the end with the vile temper had taught her about nesting hens and not to disturb one that was determined to raise chicks.

She picked up one of the brown eggs and found it was still warm. She smiled when she remembered that she had never hunted eggs before she had come here. Not all the hens preferred the man-built nests so she had found nests in several unlikely places. It gave her a sense of being one with nature to gather eggs and make bread and hang clothes out to dry on the line. Renata had never considered that any of these chores might be fulfilling in any way before they had become part of her life. But that was before she met Nathan.

Seeing him smile, hearing him speak, watching the way he moved had become important parts of her daily life. Often she caught herself pausing in her work as she recalled the way he had looked when he had touched her hair or bent to kiss her. When she realized she was again smiling, happiness buoyed up in her.

Almost at once the nausea struck again, this time with a wave of dizziness and a trembling weakness that she had never experienced before.

Renata hurriedly gathered the last of the eggs and went back to the house. Her thoughts rushed in all directions as she tried to determine what might be wrong with her. Had the meat she cooked at noon been bad? Was something wrong with the water supply or the cow's milk? She sat on the steps to the side porch and let a breeze cool her face as she tried to breathe deeply and not panic any more than she already was.

She saw Nathan coming up the path from

the toolshed, a bucket of nails and a hammer in one hand. When he saw her sitting on the steps, clutching the basket of eggs to her, his steps faltered. He changed direction and came toward her.

"Are you all right?" he asked. "Your face is as pale as those eggs."

She managed to nod, but she knew her smile must be weak and unconvincing because he put the bucket of nails on the top step and sat down beside her. "I feel funny."

"Funny?"

"Odd. Sick to my stomach." She studied his face. They had eaten the same food and had drunk the same water. "How do you feel?"

"I'm fine." He put his hand to her forehead and added. "You don't have fever. Do you hurt anywhere?"

She shook her head. "No, I don't hurt anywhere." The nausea returned, and she bent over the basket and tried not to be sick.

Nathan took the basket and drew her to him. "You'll feel better soon," he promised.

"I can't imagine what is wrong with me."

"The last time you said you felt like this, you were carrying a baby."

Renata lifted her head. She had never considered it might be morning sickness—not in the afternoon. "It's not morning. Do you think that's what it is?"

Nathan smiled and nodded. "It's been two months since you wore a nightgown to bed."

She knew what he meant. Quickly she counted for herself. He was right. "Then I really might be pregnant? I really might?" The thought that she might become pregnant had occurred to her, but until now she hadn't really believed it would happen. She put her hand on her waist.

Nathan covered her hand with his. "Do you mind if you are?"

"I might be carrying your baby?" Thoughts rushed at her. This time there was no doubt who had fathered the baby. It had to be Nathan's child. Happiness flooded over her. "Oh, Nathan, I really could be!" She threw her arms around his neck and held him close.

Nathan squeezed her so tightly she realized he was as overcome with emotion as she was, and her heart went out to him. "What about you?" she asked. "Are you glad? It means another mouth to feed."

He drew back, and she could see his eyes were suspiciously bright. "We can manage." His grin told her more than his words. "I'm going to hire a woman to help you."

"Can we afford that?" She knew their financial situation as well as he did, but she had been determined to save every extra penny toward buying the horses Nathan wanted.

"We aren't going to take any chances this time." His eyes didn't meet hers.

For a dreadful minute she thought he knew about Ennis and why Callie had refused to have a child. Then she realized that he was thinking of Callie's miscarriages. She nodded. "You're right. I shouldn't be lifting heavy loads." Neither mentioned that it might have been herbs and not work that had caused her to lose the previous babies. Renata put her hand over his. "I want this baby, Nathan. I want it so much I feel trembly all over."

"That's the morning sickness," he teased, but he cupped her face in the palm of his hand and his eyes were full of tenderness.

"Do you know someone we can hire? It's a long drive out from town."

"There's a family west of here that could use the money. The oldest daughter might want to come and help you. They're Irish immigrants and some of their ways are different from ours."

"That's fine with me. A woman who knows Callie might see the difference in me, and a foreign woman might not recognize the mistakes I still make in housework."

"That's why I think she would be good for the job. I'll ride over before supper and ask her parents. It's close enough for her to go home at night, if I give her the use of a horse. Her name is Lucy Kilpatrick."

Renata nodded. "I think that's a good idea." She smiled and put her head back on his shoulder. "I thought I might be pregnant, but I've been so busy lately I lost count of the days. I expected to tell you in a different way than this." She pointed at the chickens who were clucking and pecking at the dirt by the steps. "I wanted to tell you in a way you would remember fondly."

"What makes you think I won't have fond memories of this? Here you are in my arms and we're sitting on our own steps. A lot of men have heard this news under less favorable circumstances."

She lifted her head and kissed him. "I love you. I hope our baby looks just like you."

"I don't know. I think a little redhead would be nice." He stroked her hair and she smiled.

"This isn't getting our work done, is it?" she said regretfully.

"I was only going to mend that front shutter. It'll keep until tomorrow." He glanced at the sky to guage the time. "Maybe I ought to ride over to the Kilpatrick's now. If Lucy can't come to help you, I may need to go into town to find someone else."

Renata nodded. "Maybe you should. But Nathan, remember—if not Lucy, then get someone else who doesn't know Callie too well."

"I'll remember."

Lucy Kilpatrick turned out to be a cheerful, large-boned girl in her late teens who was fond of singing as she worked. Renata liked her at once, and she found herself humming Lucy's haunting Irish songs as she went about her day.

The morning sickness returned every day that week, then disappeared as suddenly as it had started. Renata worried that this might not be normal, but Nathan assured her that Callie had experienced these same symptoms in each of her pregnancies. Renata was glad to hear her new body could adjust so easily to its hormonal changes.

The following week Renata decided it was time to see a doctor, and she had Nathan drive her into town to visit Pete Larsen. Renata didn't have much faith in the limited knowledge of nineteenth century doctors, but she knew she shouldn't take a chance on something as important as a baby. Nathan sat with her in Pete's waiting room, looking as ill-at-ease as she felt.

"They aren't going to shoot us," she whispered to him.

Nathan smiled. "It shows?"

She laced her fingers with his in spite of the sour glances of two elderly matrons who were also waiting to see the doctor. "Do you know what I'm hungry for? Watermelon. Watermelon and fish. Do you suppose you could catch us some fish for supper?"

He laughed. "I never heard of anybody wanting that combination. That's enough to make you sick again."

"I think I'm needing more iron or something. I read somewhere that cravings often mean that."

"The watermelon is easy enough. I'll bring one

in from the slope when we get home. Would you like to go fishing with me?"

"I'd like that. I don't know how. Will you teach me?"

"Sure. I'll even bait your hook."

Renata wrinkled her nose. "I hadn't thought about that." She looked up as a woman in a severe, gray dress opened the door that led into the inner office.

"Callie Blue," the woman said as she looked at Renata. "Dr. Larsen will see you now."

Renata gave Nathan's hand a squeeze and stood up. She was nervous. What if Pete said she wasn't pregnant? Nathan would be as disappointed as she would be.

The woman led Renata into an office and motioned for her to sit on the wooden chair beside the porcelain cabinet. "Are you feeling sick today?" she asked with professional detachment.

"No. I'm here because I think I'm pregnant."

The woman frowned and looked at Renata over her glasses. "You believe you're with child?"

Renata nodded. She had forgotten that a lady wouldn't have used such a clinical term. Using euphemisms had never been one of Renata's strong points.

The woman left, and Renata looked around the office. It was clean but many of the objects there looked unfamiliar. There was a metal examining table and one wall was covered with glass-fronted cabinets that contained various bottles and boxes and syringes. She tried to remember if sterilization was common practice in 1887.

Pete came in wearing a white cotton jacket over his street clothes. He put Renata at ease with a smile. The elderly woman who had escorted her in was at his heels. "Hello, Callie. How are you feeling today?"

"Fine, thanks. I think I'm going to have a baby."

"Is that so?" Pete gave her a searching look. "You seem happier about it this time."

"Of course I'm happy." Her words sounded more curt than she had intended, but she was all too aware of the unsmiling woman who remained by the door. She supposed the woman's presence was required during the examination of a woman by a male doctor. Then it occurred to her that there might not be any women doctors at all yet.

Pete took her pulse and held a funnel-shaped apparatus to her chest and back to listen to her heartbeat without removing any of her clothing. Then he examined her eyes, ears and mouth. "Any nausea?"

"There was last week, but not for the past several days. I feel tired all the time, and I fall asleep earlier than usual."

"That's because your body is changing."

"Then I really am pregnant?" she asked with a smile.

"I'd say you probably are." Pete was watching her closely. "So you've told Nathan?"

"Of course. He's as happy as I am."

Pete said nothing. He went to the cabinet and took down a bottle of liquid. He poured some into a smaller bottle and returned the large one to the cabinet. He handed the small bottle to her. "This is a tincture of muriate of iron, muriate of quinine, and glycerine in a water solution. Since you tend to have the green sickness under normal conditions, you will need them especially now. And don't argue. You're to take them so you'll stay healthy."

Renata gingerly took the bottle. Iron sounded harmless enough. Was quinine? She hoped Pete was a good doctor. "What is the green sickness?"

Both Pete and the woman attendant gave her a curious look. Renata hastily said, "I remember now. I guess my mind must have wandered." She decided this must be another name for morning sickness.

"Do you want me to deliver the baby when it's time?" Pete asked.

"Who else would do it?"

"You insisted on a midwife last time."

Renata was silent for a moment. Callie would have insisted on that since she was so afraid of men. "I've changed my mind. I would rather have a doctor."

"Come into my office for a minute." He led the way into a room furnished like a small parlor with a large oak desk.

Renata noticed the woman didn't follow them. When she entered, Pete shut the door and sat down behind the desk.

"I have a few questions I'd like to ask you." He took out a pad of paper and unclipped a Waterman fountain pen from his shirt pocket. "I have you down as having several miscarriages. We want to be careful this time. No heavy lifting or becoming too tired. When you sit down, put your feet up. Drink at least two glasses of milk a day."

"Do you have any reason to believe I can't carry the baby full term?"

Pete surveyed her over the tops of his steepled fingers. "I saw no reason for you not to carry it on the other occasions either."

Renata waited to see if he would follow up that statement with an accusation. She knew he suspected Callie of taking something to terminate the other pregnancies, and Renata felt guilty even though it had happened to Callie and not to her and even though Callie had believed she had good reason for doing what she did.

"I'm curious as to why you now want a child when you were so adamant before about not wanting one."

"You know how women are about changing their minds," she tried to bluff.

"No, this is more than a whim. You were afraid before. Will you tell me why you no longer seem to feel that way?"

"No, I won't." Renata replied firmly.

Pete turned back to his pen and paper. "I know this is embarrassing to you, but when do you believe you conceived? I need to know in order to determine when the baby can be expected."

"I'm pretty sure it happened in May, probably toward the middle of the month. I've missed two periods."

Pete looked up sharply and she knew she had been too forthright. "May. Let's say May 15th. Counting back three months that would be February 15th. Add one week and we get February 22nd. That's when the baby may be expected."

"Next February," Renata said slowly. That would make the year 1888, and she knew Callie never lived past 1887. "Is there the possibility of a mistake? I mean, could it possibly be due in December?"

"Not if the date you told me is correct. From your physical appearance, I would say you couldn't be four months along, and you'd have to be for it to be here before the end of the year. You look upset. Why?"

"No reason." Renata tried to smile. "Are you sure I'm in good health? Don't you need to do a pelvic exam or something?"

Pete carefully put down the fountain pen. "I've seen a lot of expectant women in my time, and I can assure you that nothing about the condition changes a woman like the changes

I'm seeing in you. I believe you should tell me what's going on here."

"I don't know what you mean." Renata clutched at her cloth purse and didn't meet his eyes.

"I've known you all my life, and I would have sworn you would cut out your own tongue before you would say 'pelvic' or refer to your monthly courses. Every time I've seen you before, you have refused to so much as loosen your clothing or to allow the word 'pregnancy' to be said in your presence. Now you're talking as if you use these terms all the time."

Renata opened her mouth but she closed it again before speaking. How could she risk telling Pete about what had happened to her? She found it amazing that he could discern the change in her when her own parents and sister couldn't. "I can't explain it. Not in a million years."

Pete looked at her thoughtfully. "Nathan will be terribly disappointed if something happens to prevent the baby from coming. He's taken it hard before."

"I know."

"Last time, he was more disappointed than you were—at least it seemed that way."

"I understand." Renata gripped her reticule tighter until it wadded in her hands, then got hold of herself and forced her fingers to relax. "Nothing is going to happen to this baby, not if I can help it."

"I'm glad to hear that." Pete's voice was dry as if he weren't entirely convinced. "It's of great importance for you to be careful, especially for the next couple of months. I mean what I say about not lifting heavy loads or getting too tired."

She nodded. "Are you absolutely positive that the baby won't arrive before the end of the year?"

"A baby born six weeks early has little chance of survival. I've heard of it happening, but it's rare. What's wrong with having it in February? By the time you're up and about and the baby is old enough to leave the house, the weather will have turned warm."

She thought of her friends who had had babies and had been on their feet in a matter of hours. In Renata's day, the sight of newborns in grocery stores or malls was common. "How long do you expect me to stay inside?" she asked out of curiosity.

"You may be up for short periods of time after a couple of weeks. In six weeks or so you can resume most of your normal activities, as long as you take it slow and don't tire yourself. As for the baby going anywhere, that depends on the weather."

"Oh."

"Most women are glad to rest from their chores. You look disappointed."

"That's only surprise you see." Her mind was back on the date. If Callie died before 1888, the baby would die, too. Nathan would lose them both. "Is there any way . . . That is, if something should happen to me . . ." She found it difficult to continue. How could she make the doctor understand her concern without telling him she wasn't really Callie?

"Yes?"

"If something should happen to me—an accident, say—would it be possible for you to save my baby?"

"An accident?" He seemed to tense up, and his voice became cooler. "What sort of accident?"

"I've had a . . . a premonition, a feeling that I may die before the end of the year."

Pete relaxed, and his placid expression returned. "That's not uncommon for a woman in your condition to think. There is no basis for these premonitions, however. I don't believe in them myself."

Renata sighed. There would be no reassurance here, and unless Callie died in the hospital, no doctor would be there to even attempt to save the baby. She shivered and closed her eyes. What would happen to her if Callie died?

Pete stood and cast his professional smile her way. "Don't worry, Callie. You appear to be in perfect health. This premonition won't amount to anything. We'll laugh about it when the baby comes."

"It doesn't seem particularly funny now," she retorted.

"I was just trying to humor you—not because unpleasant thoughts could mark the child, you understand, though I know some fine doctors who do believe it would—but I know worry isn't good for a mother-to-be."

Renata stood and went to the door. If Pete never had made a more thorough examination of Callie than he had done today, he would never have had reason to suspect she had been attacked. Even then, he might not have seen any evidence, except for bruises. But even Nathan had not questioned Callie about bruises. Either Ennis had been careful and had left no marks on her, or Nathan and Callie had always made love in the dark and so hurriedly that he had not noticed. Renata's heart went out to Callie for the predicament that had so neatly trapped her.

Nathan was waiting for her when she walked back into the front room. His eyes searched her face and when he saw her smile, he grinned. Pete came forward and shook his hand. "She's perfectly healthy—for a woman about to have a baby."

Nathan's grin broadened. "It's a fact then?"

"He says it will be born around February 22nd," Renata said. She noticed the two elderly women who had disapproved of her holding Nathan's hand had left the waiting room so she put her arm around his waist. "I'm sure he will look exactly like you."

"Maybe it's a she," Nathan countered. "I have a fondness for redheaded women. Maybe we'll have a houseful of girls, all with hair like their mama."

"Maybe so," Pete said, his eyes on Renata. "You two look happy together. Maybe I have a lot to look forward to in my own marriage."

Nathan hugged Renata. "It takes a special woman to put a grin on a man's face and to keep it there. I can honestly say that I've never been happier in my life."

Renata's eyes met Pete's.

"Stay that way," Pete said. "And by the way, Callie—no horseback riding."

"I can guarantee that I won't go anywhere near a saddle," she promised firmly. "And now, Nathan, we have to go to my parents' house and tell them they are about to become grand-parents."

Chapter Sixteen

"I have a surprise for you today," Nathan told Renata as they finished breakfast. "Molly is coming out."

"Oh?" Renata finished stacking the dishes on the counter beside her wash pan. Having Molly come for a visit was always nice, but it was hardly a surprise.

"I was going to wait for her to tell you, but I know you'll want to have time to fry a chicken. She and Ennis are buying the parcel of land between us and the Kilpatricks."

"They are! When did you hear about this?" Alarms were going off in her head. If Molly and Ennis moved so close, he would be able to get to her all too easily.

"Molly told me yesterday when we drove by to tell her about the coming baby. She said she hadn't mentioned to you that they were considering it, because she didn't want to get your hopes up and the deal not go through. Why don't you look pleased?"

Renata realized she was staring at him as if

he were discussing the end of the world rather than the possibility of her sister becoming a neighbor. "Morning sickness," she lied. "Then it's for certain? They bought the land?"

"The deal was closed yesterday. Here. Sit down until you feel better." He led her to the table, and she sank down onto a chair. Nathan stayed behind her and rubbed her shoulders.

Renata knew this was the perfect time to tell him about Ennis. If she waited until her sister and brother-in-law moved to the land it would be too late. "Nathan . . ." she began, but she couldn't finish. What if he believed the coming baby was Ennis's and not his own? Renata felt her stomach knot, and she tried to relax and breathe deeply.

"Yes?"

"I . . . never mind." She felt as if the walls were closing in on her. Ennis would be only a pasture away! Again she tried to tell Nathan, but she couldn't form the words.

"Molly had wanted us to ride to the site where they are going to build the house, but in view of the coming baby, we will take the buggy."

"What?" New alarms were sounding.

"She thought it would be easier if we rode horseback. You've always liked riding before. She and Ennis are putting the house on the knoll of that hill."

Renata gripped the tabletop as panic rushed through her. A horseback ride with Molly to the knoll of a hill? That was how Callie had died! This was the day!

"I can't go. Nathan, I mustn't go there!"

"Why not?" he asked with an uncertain smile. "We've ridden there often." He thought for a minute. "Or was that before you arrived?"

"You have to tell them I can't go there." She tried to keep the panic from her voice.

"Molly will want to know why. She's so excited about being our neighbor." He sighed. "I guess we'll have to accept Ennis being so close. Maybe after we get to know him better, we will like him better."

"No! Nathan, we will never like him!" She stood and put her hands on Nathan's chest and looked up into his eyes. "They mustn't move there."

"It's too late. They own the land and have put their house in town up for sale. They are coming out today to pace off the location of the new house. Why are you so upset?"

Renata knew she couldn't tell him Ennis had been molesting her since she was 16, nor could she tell him this was the day Callie was to die. The rattle of an approaching buggy drew her attention.

"They're here already. Molly told me it would be closer to lunchtime. Now I'll have to put off fixing the calf pen."

Renata felt as if she were about to faint. She wanted to tell Nathan to send them away, but she knew that would be impossible unless she told him the real reasons. He kissed her on the forehead and went to the door to greet them.

"You're early," he called.

Molly waved. "We couldn't wait any longer. I hope you don't mind. I cooked enough chicken for all of us."

Renata looked around her and felt dizzy. She loved Nathan and their life together. Was it about to end? Was this dizzying sensation the premonition of death, or did it mean Dr. McIntyre was finally succeeding in recalling her back to her own time? She didn't want to leave Nathan! She touched the kitchen table, the porcelain countertop where she washed dishes, the wooden pantry with the roll-top doors. She didn't want to leave!

"Let's go," Nathan was saying to her. "Put the dishes in to soak. They're waiting for us."

As if she were moving underwater, Renata obeyed him. She felt as if she were caught up in a drama that she could only witness as it unfolded. Maybe, she told herself, it was enough to change the fact that she wasn't going to ride horseback. Maybe that would be enough to prevent Callie's death. She put the breakfast dishes in the pan of water and dried her hands on her apron before untying it from around her waist.

"Come on, darling," Nathan said. "What's wrong?"

Renata realized she was standing as if she were rooted to the floor. "Nathan, I don't want to do this."

"Neither do I, but how could I tell Molly no?"

She let him take her hand and lead her through the door. As they neared the buggy she heard Nathan tell Molly that he had had to drag her away from washing dishes. Renata was keenly aware of the crooked smile on Ennis's face as he sat there holding the reins and leering at her. On numb feet she reached the buggy and climbed in beside Nathan.

"Are you all right?" Molly asked. "You're as pale as you can be."

Renata made herself nod. She was sitting behind Molly and could see Ennis watching her out of the corner of his eye. She took Nathan's hand and held it between her icy palms. As the buggy lurched forward, she automatically braced herself against the bumps.

"We'll build a smooth road between the houses," Nathan was telling her. "When I finish, it will be as good as the one that goes to town. I expect it will see nearly as much traffic."

Ennis smiled and turned his head to look at Renata. She hoped she wasn't going to be sick.

Molly and Nathan kept chatting until they reached the spot where the house would stand. Nathan got out of the buggy and handed Renata down. She made her legs support her even though they felt like jelly.

"Come see what a view we will have," Molly said eagerly. "Come to the top of the knoll."

"I can see it from here," Renata told her. She didn't want to go anywhere near the knoll where Callie was to die.

"No, you can't." Molly caught Renata's hand and pulled her along behind her. "Look. From here you can almost see your house. It will be visible from our bedroom window. Ennis said so."

Renata looked from where Molly was pointing to her sister. Maybe she could tell Molly. Even as the thought formed, she knew it was impossible. If she couldn't tell Nathan, she certainly couldn't tell Molly—not about Callie's death, not about Ennis.

Renata forced herself to look about. The knoll was a natural meadow with a few rocks scattered here and there. If a person fell from a horse and her head hit one of those rocks, it could kill her, but on foot there was no danger. Renata began to relax. She was on the knoll and nothing was happening. Maybe this wasn't the day after all.

"Nathan, help me pace off the houses" Ennis said. "The carpenters will start work tomorrow."

"It's pretty up here," Renata told Molly, relaxing a little more.

"Isn't it? I fell in love with it as soon as Ennis showed it to me. It's a good thing I did, because he had already bought it." Molly laughed as if she found it amusing, but her laughter sounded false. Renata wondered if

Ennis had overextended them financially in order to do this.

Nathan and Ennis began pacing out the length of the house. Renata made herself look at the men. With Nathan and Molly so close by, Ennis didn't look all that threatening. He was not as tall as Nathan and certainly not as broad-shouldered. In the sunlight his skin was too pale, and when he removed his hat, Renata saw that his hair was plastered to his scalp with pomade. As if he felt her looking at him, he turned his curiously flat eyes in her direction. Renata shivered and looked away.

"I want my porch swing here," Molly was saying. "I can look out over the meadow when I swing, not that I have much free time to do that. Mama never told me how laborious it is to be a wife. It seems I'm working from the time I get up in the morning until bedtime." Her voice trailed off as if she were thinking of something unpleasant. More brightly she added, "I'll be so close, you and I can shell peas together and make a quilt."

Renata nodded. She was losing that sickening feeling of vertigo and was more aware of the beauty of the location. "You've chosen a lovely place to build. Our house is also on a hill, you know, and we always have a breeze. Nathan says it's too cold in the winter, but we don't have much cold weather in Louisiana. Not like up north."

"That's true, but I half-freeze as it is. I've never liked winter."

"I'm going to love this one." Renata knew if she was still here by the time winter set in she would most likely be here to stay.

"Because of the baby, you mean." Molly added, "Mama said for me to tell you not to refer to it so often. I think you shocked her and Papa by talking about it. Mama told me she never told Papa at all when she was expecting us. She just waited for him to notice."

"She didn't!" Renata laughed out loud. "Really?"

"That's what she said. She also told me to tell you not to talk about names for it."

"Why not? Nathan and I have to agree on a name."

"There's plenty of time for that later. It's bad luck for a baby to have a name at birth. Mama says Aunt Mahitaba lost two babies that way."

"Surely no one really believes that. How terrible if Aunt Mahitaba believes it and thinks she caused such a tragedy."

"I'm just repeating what Mama said. It doesn't hurt to be on the safe side."

"Well, I don't agree. If it's a boy I want to name him after Nathan. If it's a girl, Nathan wants to name her Renata."

"I've never heard that name before. I like it. Where did Nathan hear it?"

Renata shrugged and smiled. "Who knows?"

Ennis knelt and viewed the distance between

Nathan and himself. "I think this looks good. I'll go to the buggy and get the twine and the stakes."

"I'll go." Nathan kicked the grass away to mark the spot where he stood.

They had left the buggy at the base of the hill, and Nathan started down the slope.

"I wonder if I'll have children," Molly was saying. "We've been married a while now and there's still no sign."

"A woman can only get pregnant at one time of her cycle," Renata said. "You haven't been married long enough, that's all."

"How do you know that? About when a woman can get . . . what you said. Mama certainly never told you that."

"You're right. I suppose I read it somewhere."

"Who would ever print something like that?"

Nathan reached the buggy. "There's no twine here," he called back to Ennis.

"I guess I forgot to put it in. Do you have any at your house?"

Nathan shook his head in exasperation. "Sure. I'll go back and get it." He swung up onto the buggy.

"That reminds me," Molly said. "I was out of salt and the store wasn't open early enough for me to buy more. Nathan, wait and I'll ride back with you."

"No!" Renata called, but Molly was already running down the hill to catch Nathan before

331

he drove away. "Molly, wait! I want to go with you!" Molly didn't hear her or didn't notice the urgency in Renata's voice.

Renata lifted her skirts to run after them, but Ennis caught her arm. "Let them go," he growled. "You and I have business to tend to."

She whirled to face him and jerked her arm free. "The only business I have with you is to tell you never to speak to me again." She once more started to run after Molly and Nathan. By now Molly was in the buggy and Nathan was driving away.

"Nathan!" she shouted after them. Her voice wasn't audible over the creak of the buggy and harness.

"They can't hear you." Ennis grinned. "Looks like you and me are here all by ourselves."

Renata backed away from him. "Don't you dare touch me or I'll tell Nathan and Molly."

"No, you won't or you already would have. See? I know you better than you know yourself. If you say anything to Molly she won't believe you, and even if she did, there's nothing she can do about it. I won't let any woman rule me. As for Nathan, how are you going to explain why you never told him before? I've had you since you were sixteen. You can't do anything about it now."

"Yes, I can. I was wrong not to tell, and I'm going to correct that error."

"Have you thought what that will mean?" Ennis jeered at her. "None of your family will have anything to do with you after they hear this news. I'll tell them you enticed me and that I wasn't able to resist."

Remembering about Barbara Downs and how the entire town shunned her, Renata wondered if Ennis was right. "Not Nathan. He would never treat me like that."

"Then why haven't you told him before now? I'll bet he would be real interested in knowing who plowed his field before he got there himself." Ennis laughed, and the sound wasn't pleasant. "How long do you think he'll stand by you when everybody else is shunning you? A man has his pride."

"Nathan isn't like that. We'll move if need be. Make a fresh start somewhere else."

Ennis shook his head. "You can't do that. Nathan put all he had into that farm. He won't be able to just pick up and move like he could if he was a storekeeper or something like that. See? I've thought all this out real good. You're mine, and it's going to stay that way." He chuckled again. "I reckon when you refused to marry me you thought that would be the end of it, but I married your sister—and now I have both of you and I always will."

Renata felt sick all over. It was easy to see how this man had been able to frighten Callie into submission. Renata wasn't timid by any means but even she was afraid of him.

Ennis removed his hat and tossed it to the ground. Then he started taking off his coat.

"We've got plenty of time. They won't be back for half an hour, even if Nathan knows right where to look for that twine. It took us fifteen minutes to drive here from your house." He threw his coat on the ground. "It's going to be real nice having you just fifteen minutes away."

Renata knew the buggy was out of sight and that Nathan couldn't know what was happening, but she called out to him with every ounce of her being.

"Go ahead and yell. He won't hear you." Ennis started to unbutton his pants.

"Stop right there!" Renata knew she would have to protect herself. "You're not going to treat me like this any more."

"I wouldn't bet on it." He came toward her.

Callie had been helpless with Ennis, but Renata had an advantage. She had taken a course in self-defense. When she had signed up for it, she had never guessed she would use it under these conditions, but at least she had been trained. She bent slightly at the waist and wished she could be free of the encumbering skirt and petticoats for only a few minutes. Keeping her eye on Ennis, she started to circle to gain the advantage.

"What the hell are you doing?" he asked with a laugh.

"Come on," she said in a measured voice. He had to attack her before her training would work. She hoped she remembered what to do.

Ennis's smile disappeared. He was tired of taunting her, especially now that she was changing her tactics. He started toward her.

Renata forced herself to wait until he grabbed her arm. Putting all her weight into the movement, she used his own momentum to throw him to the ground. Ennis sat up and shook his head as if he were dazed. With a growl he scrambled up from the ground and charged at her.

Again Renata waited until the optimum moment. Putting her hand on his arm, she jerked, and he again went sprawling behind her. This time a string of curses rained from his mouth as he rolled up onto his hands and knees. Renata began to back away. Her feet found the downward slope, and she wondered if she could possibly outrun him. With the encumbering skirts it seemed unlikely. Could she stall off his advances until Nathan returned? That seemed even more unlikely. Renata hadn't learned that much self-defense, only enough to break a hold and run for help.

She backed away, keeping her eyes on Ennis. He was on his feet now and stalking her. She felt her way carefully, but the ground was uneven. A tree touched her shoulder, and she cried out before she realized what it was. She had left the knoll and was backing into the woods. "Ennis, leave me alone," she said in as threatening a manner as she could.

"That ain't likely. Especially not now. No

woman can throw me to the ground and get away with it."

"I don't want to hurt you," she bluffed. "Don't come any nearer."

"I'll tell you what I'm going to do." Ennis's voice had dropped to a hiss. "First I'm going to take you right here, and if you think I hurt you before, you haven't seen anything yet. Then I'm going to kill you."

"You can't get away with that!" She felt for the trees behind her. "Everyone will know you did it. You'll hang."

"No, I won't. You're going to trip over a berry vine and hit your head on one of these sharp rocks. It's going to split your head clean open. I'll see to that. It's going to be an accident as far as anyone knows."

Renata felt bile rise in her throat. Callie hadn't fallen from a horse at all. Ennis had killed her in the same way he was threatening to kill Renata now. Vertigo returned and with it the silent shriek of passing time. Renata didn't dare turn to run. In the trees he would catch her before she could get away. How far did the trees reach? Was she almost in the open again?

Ennis unfastened another button of his trousers. "It won't do you no good to try to get away from me. You can't back all the way to your house." He charged at her and Renata dodged. His fingers touched her skirt, but she yanked it free and ran back toward the knoll. In the open she was safer.

With a bellow Ennis ran after her. She could hear him gaining and she turned and crouched. When he reached her, she again sent him sprawling.

"Callie!" a voice screamed behind her. Renata looked up to see Molly standing on the knoll. They had come back for some reason. She drew in a ragged gasp of relief. The impact from Ennis's body had knocked the breath out of her.

Renata landed on the ground with Ennis straddling her body. His face was flushed with rage, and he grabbed for a rock. Renata screamed and raised her hands to ward off the blow. She heard another scream in her ears and thought it must be Molly.

Then Ennis was yanked off her. When she dared to open her eyes, she saw Nathan knock Ennis to the ground, haul him up and knock him down again. Ennis was babbling that Callie had tempted him and that it wasn't his fault, but Nathan wasn't listening. By the time Nathan had sent Ennis to the ground a third time, Renata was on her feet and grabbing at Nathan's arm.

"No!" she said. "You'll kill him!"

Nathan's eyes were black with rage, and she could feel him trembling beneath her hands. "No!" she said again.

He blinked as if he were only now realizing what she was saying. "Are you hurt? Did he hurt you?"

Elizabeth Crane

She shook her head. "I'm all right. How were you able to hear me? Why did you come back?"

"I heard you call me. I don't know how I heard it." He turned back toward Ennis. "I'm going to kill him for laying his dirty hands on you."

"No, no! Nathan, listen to me. If you kill Ennis, you'll be the one they hang. He's not worth it." She looked at Ennis, who was sitting up and tenderly touching a cut on his lip. He already had a black eye and his cheek was swelling. "He won't ever touch me again."

"He's done this before?" Nathan snapped his head back toward her. "He's the one?"

Renata nodded. "He forced Callie, Nathan. She never wanted him to touch her. He hasn't been able to touch me."

Molly was staring from them to her husband. She had missed the reference to Callie being a different person from Renata. "You hurt my sister?" she demanded. She flew at Ennis and hit him as hard on the shoulder as she could. "You hurt Callie?"

Ennis warded off her blows and got to his feet. He swayed as if he weren't too sure his legs would hold him.

Renata felt Nathan's muscles bunch under her hand as he raised his arm to point his finger at Ennis. "I don't ever want to see you again. If it wouldn't ruin Callie in this town, I'd have you run out of town on a rail—and you know I can do it."

Ennis backed up a step.

"But Callie's right. If I kill you, it's possible that no one would believe me about what happened. I'm not going to take that chance. If you see me coming, you'd better run the other way, though, because I'm going to knock you down every time I see you."

Ennis scowled, but he was too smart to talk back to a man as large and as full of rage as Nathan.

Molly advanced on him. "I knew you had a woman somewhere, but I thought it was Barbara Downs. I never guessed it was my own sister and that you were forcing yourself on her. I'm leaving you, Ennis—and I'm also going to divorce you."

He glared at her. "You don't dare do that. Your family won't let you."

"I'll even help you do it," Renata said as she stepped to Molly's side. "Together we'll stand up to anybody who tries to talk her out of it."

"I'll drive you to the lawyer," Nathan said as he came to stand beside them. "You'd better leave town while you have the chance, Ennis."

"You don't dare tell anybody what Callie let me do," he bluffed.

"No?" Renata said. "I think we'll take the chance. Rape is a crime, and I'll be sure to see that you're punished."

"You might want to remember what happened to Jonas Sykes a few years back," Nathan said. "He won't be forcing himself on any more women. I wasn't a part of it, but I know the men who were."

Ennis paled and backed farther away. In a last attempt at bravado, he pointed his finger at Renata. "You're to blame for all this. I'll see you pay. You'll pay for ruining me like this."

Renata shivered but said, "I doubt it."

Nathan put his arm around her waist and pushed her gently toward the buggy. "Let's go. A walk back to town won't hurt him."

Renata and Molly hurried to the buggy. Renata couldn't bear to meet Molly's eyes. Even though it hadn't been her fault and even though it had happened to Callie and not to her, she was ashamed. Molly was crying by the time they were in the buggy. Renata slowly raised her eyes and found Nathan looking at her. His face was lined as if he were suddenly older than his years.

"I never tempted him," she whispered. "He was lying."

"I know that. Did he hurt you bad?"

For a moment Renata balanced her answer, then she shook her head. Nathan might still go back and kill Ennis if she told him the truth. She could tell by his expression that he knew she wasn't telling him the truth and knew why she was lying. He got into the buggy and slapped the reins on the horse's back. The buggy lurched forward. Renata refused to look back, but she could feel Ennis's hate-filled stare on her back. Molly blindly reached out for Renata's hand and held it tightly.

Chapter Seventeen

"I'm afraid to go home," Molly said. She was so frightened she was trembling, even though the day was warm. "What will happen to me when Ennis walks back to town?"

Renata and Nathan exchanged a glance. They knew she was right. Ennis had been a hurtful man when everything was going his way. Now he was dangerous. Renata reached behind her and covered Molly's cold hand with her own. "We'll take you to Mama and Papa. He won't dare harm you there."

At Renata's direction, Nathan drove first to Molly's house, where Molly hurriedly packed all the clothing she would need, then he put her trunk into the buggy and drove to the Grahams' house. When they arrived, Molly shook her head and stared at the house where she had been raised as if she had never seen it before. "I can't go in. What will Mama say when I tell her I'm divorcing Ennis? What will Papa do?"

"You have nothing to fear from them," Renata reassured her. "They're your parents."

"You know how angry Papa can get," Molly whispered. She wrapped her arms around her middle and said, "Will you go in with me?"

"Of course. You didn't think we were going to drop you off and leave, did you? I'll help you tell them what happened."

After Nathan tied the horse, he lifted down first Renata, then Molly. When Molly was on the ground, she stood there as if she were turned to stone. "Maybe we're wrong to do this."

"Could you live with Ennis after today?" Nathan asked.

Molly shook her head.

"Then you have no choice. Your parents will have to know about this and the sooner you tell them, the better." He opened the iron gate that led to the front walk.

Renata was concerned that Molly seemed so frightened. Did she know something about her parents that Renata didn't? Or was this a backlash of shock at all that had happened? She again experienced the dizzy sensation that had troubled her earlier, but she knew it could well be attributed to her own shock. If anything, she knew she should be amazed at handling her emotions so well.

At the front door Molly knocked lightly, then opened it. "Mama? Papa? Are you home?"

Ida Graham came out of the back parlor and said, "Back so early? I didn't think you'd finish until afternoon, at least." Then she saw their faces. "What's wrong?"

"Mama, I've left Ennis," Molly said in a small voice.

Ida looked as if she would faint. "William? William, come here," she called to her husband. "I couldn't have heard you right, Molly."

William joined his wife in the foyer. "What's wrong? Is someone hurt?"

"I think we should all go in and sit down," Renata suggested. "We have quite a bit to tell you."

The back parlor was papered in a heavy maroon print and the curtains were gold velvet with silk fringes and tassels. Renata had never felt at ease in this room with all its oppressive colors, and under the present circumstances she felt even more uncomfortable. She took a chair and this time she didn't mind not leaning back; she was too upset to relax.

"Now what is all this?" William asked, his eyes darting suspiciously from one daughter to the other, then to Nathan. "Where is Ennis?"

"He's probably halfway to town by now," Nathan said, then moved next to Renata's chair as if to protect her. "He attacked Callie. There was a fight, and we left him there."

"What!" William leaned forward as if he hadn't heard. "He did what?"

"He attacked me, Papa," Renata said. "Molly

and Nathan had gone to fetch some twine to mark off the foundation of the house and he attacked me."

"You mean he shouted at you, that you had an argument?"

Renata shook her head. "I mean he tried to rape me."

Silence ticked by in what seemed to be an endless parade of unspoken words. Finally William said, "You must be mistaken."

Renata frowned. "I hardly think a woman would mistake such a thing. And it's not the first time he's tried." She decided for Molly's sake not to reveal how long it had been going on.

Ida picked up a fan and began waving it with a trembling hand in front of her face. "My smelling salts, William. I'm about to faint." She looked as if she were about to do exactly that.

William took a vial of ammonia salts from the mantel and thrust it at his wife.

Ida unscrewed the top on the vial and waved it beneath her nose. Her eyelids continued to flutter, but she seemed to be feeling better when she said, "What will people say? Who else knows about this?"

"Only us," Molly said. "It just happened."

"There must be an explanation for it." William was pacing now, his hands behind his back. "Ennis must have had a reason."

Renata suddenly felt cold all over. Ennis had

said he would tell everyone she had enticed him and that they would all believe it was her fault. "Papa, he tried to *rape* me."

"Don't use that word in front of your mother," William sputtered. "I dare say you don't even know what it means."

"I most certainly do! That's ridiculous."

Nathan put his hand on her shoulder to show her he was with her. "I saw what was happening, and Callie isn't mistaken. If you had been there, you'd know it, too. I pulled Ennis off her and knocked him down. I don't think you could call it a fight since he never got in a blow, but he will have bruises to explain."

"I wasn't hurt," Renata said since neither of her parents had asked her, "but he was trying to kill me."

"Well? Which was it? Rape or murder?" William demanded.

"It was both!" Renata exclaimed. "Why are you acting like this? Don't you care about me?"

"Certainly we care," William said. "Don't be foolish. But these are serious charges. There you sit without a mark on you, your dress not torn, your hair no more disheveled than it might have become in a wind. I don't know what to think."

"Papa," Molly said in a burst of courage, "I'm leaving Ennis. I can no longer live with him after this. I've told him that I'm going to divorce him."

"Divorce! Out of the question!" William

roared. Molly flinched away from him.

"No one in my family will ever be divorced," Ida exclaimed. "Never!"

"I can't continue living with him!" Molly cried. "It's impossible. I was there. I know what he did. And I have reason to believe Callie when she says this wasn't the first time he has tried to hurt her."

"Remember the burn on his hand?" Renata asked. "He got that burn from hot grease in my kitchen, not from a coal at the blacksmith's shop."

"He was in our house?" Nathan's voice rose in a growl. "He tried to hurt you there?"

"Nothing happened," she said. "I burned him instead. That was the day I nailed the cellar door shut. Remember?"

"I ought to go back and kill him." Nathan clenched his hand into a fist, and Renata held it to restrain him.

"I don't want him killed. Especially not by you. They hang people for such as that." She put his hand to her cheek. "I couldn't bear it if you weren't with me."

Nathan tamped his anger and stroked her hair, his gesture a bit awkward since he was aware her parents and sister were watching them closely. "I'll do as you want."

"I have my clothes in a trunk in the buggy," Molly said. "I want to move back here."

William rose to his feet. "No, I can't come between a man and his wife in a quarrel."

William seemed determined to disbelieve all Renata had said. "Callie, you know how excitable you are. You've been afraid of your shadow for years. I've known Ennis all his life. I can't believe what I'm hearing."

"You don't believe me?" Renata stood and faced Callie's father fearlessly. "You'd trust the word of a scoundrel rather than that of your own daughter? No wonder Callie didn't trust you to protect her."

Nathan moved hastily to Renata's side and said, "You're upset, Callie. Maybe we had better go. Ennis may come here looking for Molly, and it's best if I don't have to see him. I'm not sure I could control myself if I do."

Renata wanted to say a great deal more to William, but she knew she would say too much if she said anything else at all.

"Papa, will you take my trunk out of the buggy?" Molly asked. "Can I stay here?"

"No. You go on home and let me talk to Ennis. You can't do anything so hasty as to move out of your home. Why, this morning you were happy because you were moving so near Callie and you were saying how this would make the two of you neighbors."

"This morning I didn't know what I know now."

Renata turned to Molly. "You can come home with us. We'll put you in the spare bedroom. I'll help you find a lawyer tomorrow. Returning to Ennis would be dangerous, and the worst thing you could do. Believe me, divorce is better."

She could hear William and Ida making angry noises, but Renata ignored them, taking Nathan's hand and marching out of the house. She had a curious ringing in her ears, and she felt as if her nausea was returning. Once she was in the fresh air and out of Ida's oppressively decorated house, she felt better. As Nathan handed her and Molly into the carriage, Renata heard a door slam as if William were putting a footnote to his rejection of their story. She didn't care. She had never particularly liked him anyway.

Molly cried softly all the way to the farm. Renata was afraid that they would meet Ennis at every turn, but the road was empty. The farm had never looked as good to her as it did that day. Her house was gleaming white in the sunshine, the flowers were blooming in the beds along the walk and picket fence, and in the pasture she saw Janie's foal kicking up his heels and running in a circle.

She put her hand on Nathan's leg. Emotions were about to overcome her, and she wished she could let herself cry as Molly was doing. Nathan covered her hand with his own and was supportive in his silence. Renata smiled at the thought that she knew him so well now. At one time she would have felt apart from a man of so few words. Now she felt secure that they could communicate without the need for words.

At the house, Renata and Molly went inside while Nathan took the horse and buggy down to the barn. Molly looked down at her trunk on the floor and began to cry harder.

"Come upstairs," Renata said comfortingly. "Nathan will bring up your things when he gets to the house."

"My head hurts so badly. Do you have any cologne water I could put on my handkerchief?"

"Of course." Renata wished she had an aspirin. Cologne water wasn't strong enough for what they had been through that day. She left Molly in the spare bedroom and went to get her bottle of rose water and a fresh handkerchief. "Here. Now lie down and put it over your eyes."

Molly sat on the chair while removing her laced shoes, then climbed onto the bed. Renata pulled the curtains to darken the room. "How's that? Better?"

Molly nodded as she placed the handkerchief over her forehead. "Is Papa right? Am I making a mistake in leaving Ennis?"

Renata hesitated for a moment, then came to the bed and sat on the edge. "Molly, I'm going to tell you something that will hurt you, but if you are considering going back to him, you must know it. Ennis first raped me when I was sixteen. He's used me as he pleased ever since." Molly gasped, and Renata reached out and took her hand in a comforting gesture. "Nathan doesn't know about this, and I want to keep it that way. You saw him today. He would kill Ennis with his bare hands if he knew the whole truth."

"Why did you never tell anybody?"

"I was afraid. I listened to Mama and Papa just as much as you do." Renata knew this was true. She didn't have to be a psychologist to understand why Callie had been afraid to tell anyone or what the outcome would have been if she had. "If they didn't believe me today with you and Nathan there to verify the truth in my story, they wouldn't have believed me at sixteen."

"You tried to warn me," Molly said slowly. "That's why you refused to talk to me when I told you I was going to marry Ennis."

Renata nodded.

"Why didn't you tell me?"

"Would you have believed me? What excuse could you have given to Mama and Papa for calling off the marriage? I was afraid of becoming an outcast like Barbara Downs."

Molly was silent for a moment. "I guess you're right."

"I was even afraid that if Nathan found out, he would want no more to do with me." A faint smile crossed Renata's lips. "I guess I was afraid of everything."

"I can understand that. Right now I'm scared to death. How will I hold my head up in town?"

"No one need know the real reason you left Ennis, and only you and I know how long Ennis has hurt me." She found herself slipping easily into the euphemistic term. "I never want anyone to know that."

"Then Nathan wasn't your first," Molly exclaimed. "How did you explain that?"

Renata had wondered that herself. "Nathan loves me. He pretended not to notice." Knowing Nathan as she did now, she was sure this was the truth.

"I'm afraid, Callie. I don't know a single person who has ever been divorced."

"I know. But Nathan and I will stand by you. In time maybe you'll meet someone else and this time the love will be real."

"Never. I'll never remarry."

Renata smiled. She knew from having met Emma Blanders that this wasn't true. Molly would be all right. "I'm going downstairs now. Do you need anything else?"

"No, just rest. And Callie, if Ennis comes, don't tell him I'm here."

"No, we won't. Anyway he would be afraid to show his face around here."

She went downstairs to the kitchen where the breakfast dishes were piled and waiting for her. Renata pushed up her sleeves and went to work. By the time Nathan came into the house, she had the kitchen spotless.

"I'm sorry it took me so long, but I put Ennis's horse in the pen with ours and I had to wait to see if they would fight." He looked at Renata across the room. "Now that we're alone, I want the truth. Did he hurt you?"

"No, I'm only shaken up." She patted her middle. "The baby's fine."

"I wasn't worrying about the baby."

"I know. I'm fine, too. Really I am." She laughed. "You should have seen the look on Ennis's face when I threw him onto the ground."

"You threw him down? How could you possibly do that?"

"I took a self-defense course. Thank goodness it all came back to me."

"Women have to defend themselves in the future? Someone actually teaches them how to fight?"

"It's a different world, Nathan. Very different.

Molly slept all afternoon and was awake only long enough that evening to eat a small supper before going back to bed. Renata decided that sleep would be best for her, so she and Nathan let Molly rest.

"There's something I want to tell you," Renata said as they sat in the back parlor, watching the evening grow dark outside the windows. "I was supposed to die today."

"I beg your pardon?"

"I wasn't sure of the exact date of death on Callie's tombstone, but I knew it was to be this year." She held up a hand to stop him from speaking. "No, let me finish. For a long time I didn't know what year this was—by the way, why don't you have a calendar or an almanac or something?"

"I do. It's hanging in the barn."

"Anyway, when I found out the year is 1887, I remembered that as the year of Callie's death, but I didn't know the month and day. I did know, however, from reading some papers left by Molly to one of her children that Callie died from falling from a horse. That's why I was so glad when Pete told me not to ride horseback. I wasn't sure what excuse I could give you, and I didn't want you to worry."

"Not worry! Damn it, Renata, I *should* have worried! I couldn't protect you if I didn't know there was a need to."

"Since I wasn't going to get on a horse, I didn't think I needed protection. This morning when you described where Ennis was planning to build his house, I realized this was the day." She paused. "I know now that Callie didn't die in a fall. Ennis killed her just as he was about to kill me today. He apparently would have lied about Callie falling from her horse. Molly was so afraid of him that she would have gone along with the story even if she suspected something different."

Nathan stared at her. "I don't know what to say. I want to find Ennis and kill him with my bare hands. The man is a bastard." He realized he was talking to a woman and added, "Sorry."

Renata smiled. "You're right. He is."

"When I think how close I came to losing you . . ." Nathan couldn't finish the thought.

"But you didn't. Don't you see? I was able to change things. I kept Callie from dying and that must mean I'm here to stay." The recurrent dizziness came over her again, and she rubbed her temples. "This time you'll have a beautiful, healthy baby. Maybe we'll have a houseful of them. I can stay, Nathan."

Outside in the darkness Ennis was watching them. His face was swollen and sore from Nathan's fists, and he was in a rage such as he had never felt before. Revenge was the only thing on his mind. He had looked everywhere for Molly, but she had evidently gone running to her parents. Because she would have told them what had happened, he was afraid to go there and get her.

He rubbed his hand along the barrel of the rifle. This time he would silence Callie for good. If she ever told what he had been doing to her all these years, there was no predicting what the men of Lorain would do to him. He would be lucky if they only hanged him.

Callie moved forward, and he could see her talking to Nathan in ernest. Was she telling what he had done to her? Since Nathan stayed seated and looked relatively calm, Ennis thought it wasn't likely.

He almost enjoyed watching them, knowing

that Callie would be dead before he left this place. To hold their fate in his hands made him feel powerful and Ennis had always liked power. He lifted the shotgun and sighted along the barrel, then lowered it. Not yet. He wanted to wait until she was a perfect target.

As he watched he thought about the consequences of his actions. He was going to kill Callie. There was no doubt about that. But if he killed her first, Nathan would come rushing out with his own gun, and Ennis himself might get shot. He didn't want that.

Ennis lifted the gun again and this time he trained it on Nathan. Taking a deep breath to steady his aim, he began tightening his finger on the trigger.

Renata was feeling very strange. The ringing in her ears had returned, and the dizziness was such that she wasn't sure she could stand or walk. As if from a great distance, she heard Nathan ask if she was ill. She thought she answered him, but she wasn't too sure. The room was going out of focus and becoming oddly transparent. Where the fireplace had been, she glimpsed a white wall and a television. Nathan wavered in her vision, and on that white wall she saw a sign bearing the words, "Oxygen in Use," such as she had seen in hospitals.

"No," she whispered. "No!"

"Renata? What's wrong?" Nathan started to get out of his chair and come to her. In that instant she heard a loud noise like a gunshot. Nathan was thrown back, and she saw bright red as the sound echoed in her ears. The room and Nathan vanished, and she was screaming when she opened her eyes.

She was in a hospital room. A television was mounted on the wall and the door was set back just as she had glimpsed it. A tube was running from her arm to a plastic bottle hanging on a rack beside her bed. She tried to stop screaming but she couldn't.

Nurses came running. They seemed as startled as she was. "Where am I?" she demanded. "Is this a hospital?"

"Be quiet, Miss O'Neal," the older one said. Turning to the other woman, she said, "Call Dr. McIntyre. Hurry."

"It's three o'clock in the morning," the nurse protested.

"He won't mind."

Renata tried to calm herself, but she was terrified. Three o'clock in the morning? It should still be evening. What had happened to Nathan? How did she get here?

In less than an hour McIntyre was by her side. His face was drawn and he looked worried. "Renata? Do you know me?"

"Of course I know you," she snapped. "How did I get here?"

"Do you remember coming to my office?"

She nodded. She was having to fight hard not to cry.

McIntyre came closer and pulled one of her feet from under the sheet. He ran his thumbnail down her instep, and as Renata's toes curled in response, she pulled away. "How many fingers am I holding up?"

"Three. Get me out of here."

"Take it easy. You've given us quite a scare. You're muscles are apt to be weak."

"Why?" she demanded.

"You've been in a coma for four months."

Renata stared at him. "What?" she repeated softly.

"I hypnotized you and for some reason couldn't bring you back. I've never heard of anything like that happening. How do you feel?"

"Irritated. Send me back."

"That's out of the question."

"Dr. McIntyre, I just saw Nathan being shot. I have to go back and see if he's all right."

McIntyre patted her hand and studied her face. "You imagined all that. You didn't go anywhere."

"You're wrong. I've been with Nathan all this time. I'm . . . I'm carrying his child." Even to Renata the words sounded insane. "Don't look at me like that. It's true."

"You believe yourself to be pregnant?" McIntyre took a clipboard from under his arm and made some notes.

"Not me, not this body—Callie's." She closed her eyes. "Never mind. Just send me back."

"You've had a difficult time these past four months. Several times we thought we were going to lose you. Your fiancé has threatened to sue me for every cent I have. The medical board is investigating me. There's no way I'm going to hypnotize you again."

"I'll sign a paper. You can have witnesses that I'm willing. Hell, I'm demanding it!"

"Demand all you please, I'm not risking it again." He straightened up. "Your reflexes are good. You seem to be coherent and rational, except for believing you're pregnant. I think we're out of the woods."

Renata's eyes filled with tears. She had been through too much that day. "I want to be alone."

"I'll leave now. Should I call Mr. Symons now or wait until the morning?"

"Bob?" She sighed. "Let him sleep." She turned her face away until she heard McIntyre leave.

She slowly flexed the arm that wasn't tied to an IV. Her legs moved sluggishly as if they weren't used to the effort. She held her hand up and moved the fingers, fingers that were longer than she was now accustomed to seeing. She pulled a strand of hair around so she could see it. Instead of pale auburn it was dark and only as long as her neck. She ran her hand down her body under the sheet. She was wearing a hospital gown and was thinner than she remembered being. Not only did she miss Nathan, she missed being Callie.

Hot tears slid down her cheek. Was Nathan seriously hurt? The thought was pointless. Even if he had been wounded and not killed, he would be dead now. All that had happened over 100 years ago. She still ached for his touch and the sound of his voice.

McIntyre was wrong. She knew he was, just as she knew she would never be able to convince him of it. She hadn't imagined all that had happened to her. She smiled wryly and wiped away her tears. She wasn't imaginative enough to create a world filled with objects she had never heard of and with people who were so real. Somehow she had to get back.

Outside the room she could hear the shushing sound of a nurse's shoes as she passed down the waxed corridor. The hospital had a faint humming sound that she supposed was due to the central heat or air, depending on which month it was. She remembered it was cold when she went to McIntyre's office, so she assumed it must be late spring. That was the first season she had seen as Callie. She had never been so stricken with homesickness in her life. No matter how far she went from home, it was always possible to return there—not, however, if the home was 100 years in the past.

She looked at her hand again. She wore no rings and the nails were clipped short, probably to keep her from scratching herself involuntarily. Moving slowly she turned on the light above her bed, then turned it off. At one time she had thought she would be glad to see electricity again.

The seconds ticked by, but now she had no sensation of time rushing past as she had felt before. She assumed that was because she was now in her own time. Oddly enough, she felt as out of place here as she originally had as Callie. It was as if she belonged to both and to neither. The headache grew worse, and she pressed the button to ask the nurse to bring her an aspirin. She decided she might as well take advantage of modern-day pain killers.

The nurse brought her two aspirins and a small paper cup of water. Renata found it difficult to swallow, but she said nothing about that to the nurse. Instead, she asked, "Can you take the needle out of my arm?"

"I have to wait until morning. The doctor didn't leave orders for that."

Renata sighed and lay back. "It doesn't matter." Nothing mattered if she couldn't be with Nathan. She ran her hand over her stomach and remembered their unborn baby. Was Callie alive to have the child and to raise it? No, that had all happened long ago. She doubted anyone had ever been so confused. If Callie wasn't shot as well as Nathan—and it was a simple matter to guess Ennis had pulled the trigger—what would she think about discovering herself to be pregnant? Or maybe Callie had been aware of it all along, since Callie was also Renata.

Renata rubbed her eyes. If only she could sort things out. If only she didn't feel so disoriented. Part of it, she knew, was because of her poor physical state. The rest of her confusion, she supposed, must be normal for someone who had just traveled from one century to the next in the blink of an eye. Right now she could only gather her strength and get out of the hospital. Then she would convince Dr. McIntyre to hypnotize her again so she could go back. Somehow she had to return.

Chapter Eighteen

Renata stood in her own doorway thinking her apartment might just as well belong to a stranger. Her familiar furniture looked different somehow, too stark and modern, and somehow plastic. She went inside and shut her door, then put her purse on the end table nearest her. Everything had been dusted. Bob must have hired someone to come over and clean.

She wandered into the kitchen and touched the microwave. As Callie, she had missed these conveniences, but she would trade them all for ten minutes with Nathan. A glance in the pantry told her that she would have to shop soon. At the moment everything seemed to be too much of an effort.

Going to her bedroom, Renata slipped off her shoes and put them in the closet. She was tired already and she hadn't done anything but ride home from the hospital. Although she knew this was because she was having to reactivate muscles that had started to atrophy, she also missed Callie's body and its ability to work all

day without tiring. Her own body was familiar to her again, though she had bumped her
head on the suspended television in her hospital room—something that Callie could have
easily walked under. In time she would regain
her strength.

She lay on her bed and gazed up at the white
ceiling. Being surrounded by off-white walls
dissatisfied her after living with Callie's cheerful wallpaper and soft colors. She wondered if
her apartment manager would let her paint,
but that, like almost everything else, seemed
to be too much trouble.

When her phone rang, she sighed. It could
only be Bob or her parents. Her parents had
come rushing to her side in the hospital, but
they both worked so had been able to stay only
one night. Renata knew she ought to call them
that night to say she was home from the hospital.

"Hello?" she said as she answered.

It was Bob. "Hi. How are you feeling? I called
the hospital and they said you had already left.
I was going to drive you home."

"There's no reason for you to leave work to
do that. I took a cab."

"You sound blue. Are you taking the antide-
pressants Dr. McIntyre prescribed for you?"

"Yes." She could have told Bob they weren't
going to work. She had seen Nathan shot before
her very eyes only days ago, and she was mourn-
ing his loss. But there was no need to hurt Bob

by being too honest. "Are you coming over later?"

"I hope to get there after dinner. I have a committee meeting immediately after work."

She reminded herself that dinner was at night, not noon. "I'll be here," she said with pretended lightness.

"Renata," he said, "I'm glad you're okay."

"Thanks." She tried to say she was glad to be back, but the words stuck in her throat. If it had been up to her, she wouldn't have come back at all.

"Well, I'd better get off the phone. The boss doesn't like us making personal calls during business hours, you know."

"Okay. I'll talk to you later." She hung up the receiver and lay back on the bed. Her company had hired someone else while she was in the coma but had told her they could use her as a temporary worker for a while. That wasn't like having her old job back, but it would give her time to find a permanent position in another office.

Renata closed her eyes, rolled to her side and curled into a ball.

For days she put off going to the graveyard behind the little chapel. She was afraid of what she might see there, but at last the need to know overcame her trepidation. The walk from her apartment to the chapel was pretty. Azaleas and dogwood were blooming alongside the spring flowers, but she barely saw them. Across the street from the chapel she stopped. The building looked the same as she remembered. The cemetery beyond was dotted with flowers and gray headstones. She let her feet carry her across the street.

Finding the plot with the black wrought-iron fence was no problem. Making herself go close enough to read the markers was the difficult part. What she found was exactly as she feared it would be. Instead of Callie having died young, Nathan had died in July of 1887. Callie had lived for 52 lonely years. She looked around the graveyard and noticed there were several tombstones with the name of "Blue." Callie must have had a son, who in turn had sired children of his own. Nathan's line had not died out entirely. That was comforting, at least, but she couldn't help but wonder whether the little boy had looked like Nathan and whether he had Nathan's gentle nature. She hoped he had been a comfort to Callie in her loneliness.

Renata felt a dampness on her cheeks and realized she was crying. Since her return, she found she cried as easily as had Callie. Impatiently, she pushed the tears away.

She had gone back to work the second day after her release from the hospital, not because she felt like working, but because her medical bills were astronomical. She still tired easily, and depression was a major problem. Every-

body at work, like everyone else she knew,
pretended the coma had never happened.
They were all so forcibly cheerful around her
that Renata wanted to scream. She leaned her
head on the cool bars of the black fence and
wished she could change things—anything. If
she had never seen Nathan she would be happy
here, or if she had been able to stay with him
she would have been happy. Her eyes returned
to the weathered stone that bore his name and
she was reminded that even if she had stayed
in his time, she wouldn't have been with him.

She read the names on the other headstones.
Ida Graham, William Graham, Mahitaba Graham. All people she had known. Renata had
argued with Ida and William only two weeks
before. There were two older graves in the enclo-
sure and three newer ones, whose names meant
nothing to her but whose presence signified the
on-going lives of the Grahams. Renata had done
the impossible and gone back in time, and no
one but Nathan had ever realized it.

"If I did it once, I can do it again," she told
herself fiercely.

She turned on her heels and headed for
home. As soon as she was in the apartment
she dropped onto the couch and tried to relax,
her palms upward and her eyes closed. She had
known for years how to meditate, and up until
now she had found it both easy and refreshing.
Now her mind refused to be still.

She concentrated harder. Nathan's face rose

in her mind, and she held to it. His voice sounded in her memory, and she ached from wanting him. With all her might she tried to hypnotize herself into going back with him.

After an hour she gave up. She wasn't able to do it because she wasn't sure what words Dr. McIntyre had used to send her back. She considered calling him, but he had refused to repeat the hypnotism under any circumstances. Renata watched the sky outside her windows darken as evening progressed. Somehow she had to convince Dr. McIntyre to help her.

A knock on her door made her jump. She had forgotten Bob was coming to pick her up. She glanced at her wristwatch. He was punctual as usual.

She let him in and hurried into her bedroom to comb her hair. They were only going to his house for dinner so there was no need to change her clothes. Jeans were dressy enough for an evening at home. She studied her reflection as she applied lipstick and told herself she had to tell Bob tonight that she wouldn't marry him. Gratitude had prevented her from telling him before now, but she knew it wasn't right to let him believe things could be the same as they once were between them.

Bob drove her to the new house he had purchased while she was in the coma. Renata liked it even less now than she had before. When she first learned he had bought it, the idea depressed her further. If he loved her as he had so often said, how could he buy a house he knew she disliked? Nathan never would have.

She got out of the car and looked at the beds of grass sitting on the dirt of the still new lawn. In the streetlight they looked like nests of black spiders. The red maple tree was guy-wired upright and was standing at attention two-thirds of the way across the lawn. Several small shrubs had been stuck in the ground beneath the plate glass window. "Why did you buy this house?" she asked.

"Because I like it," he said, surprise registering in his voice. "Why else?"

"Didn't it matter to you that I don't?"

"Renata, a house is a house. You wouldn't have liked anything built in this century, and I don't want to live in a museum. New houses require less upkeep. I don't want to spend all my time renailing boards and repairing pipes."

She made no comment.

At the front door, Bob fit his key into the lock. "I'm back," he called out.

"Someone else is here?"

"Mom is eating with us."

"Great." Renata tried, but couldn't put much enthusiasm into the word. This was the night she had planned to tell Bob she couldn't marry him.

Bob's mother came around the corner of the den. "Hello, you two. You certainly took your time in getting here. I was afraid the meat would burn."

Bob spoke before Renata had a chance. "You've already put it on? I would have done that." Bob took the long-handled fork from her. "You sit down and take it easy. I'll do the cooking."

Mrs. Symons went to the couch and used the remote control to turn on the TV. The sit-com that came on was one Renata had never liked. She told herself Mrs. Symons couldn't possibly have known that. Rather than watch it, she followed Bob outside to the grill.

All the backyards on this street butted up to the backyards on the adjacent street, with only an occasional fence separating the yards. All of the lots here were perfectly square and sterile. Renata crossed her arms over her chest and tried not to remember the lush greenness outside Callie's house.

"You ought to go inside and talk to Mom," Bob suggested. "She was saying earlier that you never talk to her. Why, you never even said hello when we came in."

"She didn't speak to me, either," she pointed out. "Cook my steak a bit more. I don't like it rare."

"It's better this way." Bob continued taking the steaks off the grill. "If you order steak well-done in a nice restaurant, the cook knows you have no taste."

"This isn't a restaurant and I don't care what a stranger may think about me. I always order my meat well-done."

Bob kissed her cheek. "Just try it this way." He headed for the house.

Renata bit back her retort and followed him inside.

Mrs. Symons had set up snack trays in front of the television. "I hope you don't mind eating in here, but I just love this show."

Renata forced a smile. She helped Bob serve three plates and carried hers into the den. Bob handed one to his mother and took a seat on the recliner. Renata recalled the table full of food she had prepared for guests in Nathan's house. The thought made Bob's steak and potato dinner seem like a snack. She told herself to be thankful, since she no longer did enough hard work now to burn off the extra calories.

When the sit-com was over, Mrs. Symons said, "How are you feeling, Renata?"

"Fine, thank you. I still tire easily, but that's to be expected. I'm having some trouble readjusting to a work schedule, though. I have a job interview set up for next week."

"With whom?" Bob asked.

"Downs and Downs." She wondered if they were descendants of Barbara Downs's family.

"Good firm." Bob cut another piece of steak and popped it into his mouth with his fork turned over as if he were British.

"I've been by the cemetery," she said.

"What cemetery?" Bob asked.

"Good heavens, what a morbid subject," Mrs. Symons said with a laugh. "Oh, I'm sorry, dear.

Do you have family buried there?"

Renata was silent for a minute. "In a way."

"Not the cemetery you used to go on and on about," Bob said.

"Yes. The headstones are different now."

"That's impossible." Bob jabbed his fork into his baked potato. "You're imagining things."

"No, I'm not. Why won't anyone listen to me? I'm trying to tell you it all really happened. I was back there for four months. Because of it, the events of history were altered."

Bob and his mother exchanged a look. "I don't think this is the time to discuss it," he said.

"No, I suppose it isn't." Renata put a bite of steak into her mouth. It was too rare. Without a word she got to her feet and took the plate into the kitchen and put it in the microwave. As she waited for it to cook, she tried to control her temper. She could hear Bob and his mother talking in low voices, but because of the noise of the television Renata couldn't tell what they were saying. She was positive, however, that she must be the subject of their conversation.

When her steak was done, she took it back into the den and finished eating. Then she helped Bob carry the dirty dishes into the kitchen and put them into his dishwasher. "Your mother doesn't like me," she whispered.

"Yes, she does. She just worries when you say such odd things. Anyone would."

"Has it ever occurred to you that I may be

right? That I really was in 1887?"

"Renata, we both know that's impossible."

She took a deep breath. "I can't marry you," she said bluntly.

"This is no time to talk about that, either."

"It's never the time to talk about anything with you lately. Whether you like it or not, we have to find time to discuss our future."

"Fine. We'll discuss it. But I'm not going to let you throw our marriage away on some whim." He faced her, and she saw that he really did care about her. Pain was in his eyes.

"It's not a whim, Bob. I realize now that I'm not bringing as much into this relationship as you are. You deserve better."

"I don't want 'better.' I want you to be as reasonable and logical as you once were. I want us to settle down, have a child and get on with our lives."

"We have to talk," she repeated, then said, "Later." He was right that this wasn't the time to get into the reasons why she was breaking their engagement.

For the next three hours she made polite conversation with Bob and Mrs. Symons with the television accompanying them in the background. When Bob stood as a signal that he was about to take Renata home, Mrs. Symons said, "Good-night, Renata. Bob, I'll wait until you come back before I leave."

Renata said her good-night and went outside with Bob. If they married, this was probably how they would spend most of their evenings. It might be comfortable for Bob, but she wanted more. When he walked her to her door, she didn't ask if she could see him the next day.

Renata drove through Lorain, looking at the houses she could recognize from 1887. There were more than she had thought. Until now she had avoided finding the one Callie had shared with Nathan, but the time had come.

She drove out of town on a road she hardly recognized from the dirt one she had traversed in a buggy. The town had spread out, and when she saw the house, she wasn't sure she was at the right place. What had been fields and woods was now scattered with houses and an auction barn. She stopped her car on the roadside and looked at it.

The years had been kind. It had been kept up nicely and had a fresh coat of paint. Instead of being white it was now pale yellow and had dark green shutters, but a swing still hung from the porch ceiling. Someone had added a new room to the side and the tin roof was now shingle, but the house was still recognizable.

Not knowing what she would say to the owners, Renata drove up the drive, which seemed much shorter than she remembered, and parked in front of the picket fence. For a minute she sat there, noting the differences and changes and wondering about the intervening years the house had seen.

There were no more chickens pecking at the dirt and the yard was mowed grass now, but the flower beds still held jonquils and she wondered if they were from the bulbs she had planted. Beyond she could see the trees that lined the stream, but the water had lessened to a mere trickle.

Resolutely, Renata got out of the car, walked up the stone walk and knocked on the door. The porch ceiling was now white instead of robin's egg blue, but the railing where she and Nathan had watched the approaching storm was intact. When the door opened, Renata jumped.

"Yes?" the woman asked warily.

"My name is Renata O'Neal." On inspiration she said, "My family used to live in this house."

"Oh? What was their name?"

"Blue. Nathan Blue. It was a long time ago. Over a century."

The woman's face brightened. "You're doing genealogical research, then. I see. My name is Marge Anderson. Come in."

Renata was amazed how easy it had been. She stepped into what had been the formal, front parlor the last time she had seen it. Now it was a living room decorated with "country" collectibles. Wooden ducks and pigs and cows seemed to be everywhere.

"I did some research on the house just after we bought it," Marge was saying. "I recall the name Blue because it was unusual to me." She laughed. "We were new to the area. Now I know it's fairly common in Lorain."

Renata nodded. She hadn't made the connection earlier. If the name "Blue" had been passed down and if Nathan had only a sister, Callie's baby must have been a son and it must have survived. She felt reassured that all had gone well. "I've not lived here long myself. I know it's terribly pushy of me, but could I look around the house?"

"I suppose so. It's not as clean as I usually keep it, but if you don't mind, I don't either."

"It's looks wonderful to me," Renata said with a smile. The house was spotless.

With different furniture the rooms seemed out of proportion to Renata's eyes. The high sideboard was gone from the dining room and the ceilings seemed unusually high. Someone had installed ceiling fans in all the rooms, and Renata was reminded of how hot the summer had been when she had lived here.

The kitchen was the most changed of all. A new stove, refrigerator and dishwasher had been installed. What had been a large room was now cramped but convenient, and the ducks and pigs and cows she had seen in the living room decorated these walls as well. The table that had stood in the center of the room was now a work island. A chrome and glass dinette set stood in the new addition that jutted out where the side porch had been. Renata recalled how she and Nathan had sat on those steps the day she told him she was expecting his baby. The floor slanted slightly as if it was feeling its age.

"There was a well on the porch through that door," Marge was saying. "I think it must have been here when the Blues owned the house, but it had gone dry long since. We have small children so my husband sealed the top for safcty's sake."

"Good idea." Renata touched the walls and remembered how they hadn't always been painted and plastered. The wallpaper with its delicate colors and patterns had been replaced with textured sheetrock.

"The den is back here," Marge said as she led the way back through the central dining room. "We think it must have been a downstairs bedroom since they would have already had a living room up front."

"It was the back parlor," Renata said automatically. "They only used the front one for formal occasions."

"How do you know that? Family records, I suppose. Say, if you have a diary left by Callie Blue I'd love to read it. I'd take good care of it."

"I'm sorry, but she never left one. I know that because it was common practice from what I've heard." Renata reminded herself that she had to be just as careful now as she had been in the past.

Marge laughed and pointed to the corner nearest the window. "The house has a colorful past. They say someone was shot there. The story is that he died and the killer was never caught. I don't know if it's true or not. Most old houses have stories like this, and I suspect most of them are tall tales."

"The killer was never caught?" Renata felt anger rising. Ennis had ruined Callie's life and gone free. The injustice of it rose like bile in her throat.

She went to the spot where she had sat and watched as the room had faded and Nathan had died. It was so changed now as to be almost unrecognizable. She was glad of this. No ghosts of memories rose to haunt her from that terrible night.

"Would you like to see the bedrooms?" Marge asked. "I don't usually take company up there, but you're welcome to look."

"Thank you. I'd love to see them." Renata hoped she was up to seeing the room she had shared with Nathan.

Marge led the way up the stairs. The plain oak railing had been replaced with a more elaborate one, and the steep stairs were angled at a safer incline. Renata had often worried about falling down them.

At the head of the stairs, the alcove had been turned into a sun room with white wicker furniture and a bookshelf. "I like what you've done with the house," Renata said, realizing that she did, except for the overabundance of pigs and ducks. "I can tell you must love it."

"I do. My husband wanted to move out into the country, but once we saw this, he resigned himself to living in town."

Renata smiled. At one time this had been well into the country.

Marge led her first to the room where Molly had gone to take a nap after leaving Ennis. Here the walls were papered, but in a stripe pattern rather than in lilacs, and boy's toys were scattered everywhere. "See? I told you it was a mess."

"Children need a place to play."

"This is the master bedroom. When we put in central air and heat it became much more comfortable. The people who owned it before us had a window unit, but it made so much noise it kept us awake at night."

"On a hill like this there is always a breeze," Renata said. Nathan had told her that.

"True, but it's a hot one in the summer."

There was no reason to linger longer and Renata didn't want to alarm the woman after she had been so kind as to show her the house. "I want to thank you for letting me see the place," she said as they went back to the stairs. "You'll never know how much this has meant to me."

Her eyes fell on the attic door. A memory arose. She hurried to open it and stepped inside.

"That's only the attic." Marge was at the top of the stairs and was frowning slightly.

"I'm coming." Renata reached up and her fingers found the paper stabbed to the joist with the red hat pin she had bought so long ago. Without showing it to Marge, Renata slipped it into her pocket. "Sorry. I guess I was turned around for a minute."

Marge didn't look as if she believed her, and Renata was glad to escape to her car and drive away.

As soon as she was out of sight of the house, Renata pulled over and stopped. With trembling fingers she took the pin and note from her pocket. The paper was brown and crumbly on the edges and the shaft of the pin was rusted, but the lady bug was as bright as ever once Renata rubbed the years of accumulated dust away. The note read, "Renata O'Neal, 1885, I was here."

She put the note and pin on the seat beside her and drove to Dr. McIntyre's office.

An hour later she had almost convinced the doctor that this was proof she had been back in time. "It's my handwriting. Look." She wrote the same words on the note pad on his desk and put the writings side by side.

"I don't deny that, nor do I deny that the paper and pin are old, but you could have found them somewhere and written on it just before you came to my office."

"I would have to be deranged to do that. And

look at the ink. It's faded brown from age. Have you ever seen a ballpoint pen that would look like that ink?"

McIntyre frowned and leaned nearer. "The lines are rather broad for a ballpoint pen."

"I'm telling you, I found it in the attic of the house I lived in with Nathan. If you don't believe me, call Marge Anderson and ask her if I was there."

He sat down at his desk and thumbed through the telephone book. As he dialed the Anderson's number he stared at Renata with a definite frown. "I don't know what to make of this. Hello?" He turned toward the phone. "Is this Marge Anderson? This is Dr. Sam McIntyre. I'm trying to locate a Miss Renata O'Neal and someone told me she might look you up. Was she? An hour ago. All right, Mrs. Anderson. Sorry to have bothered you." He hung up and studied Renata.

"See? Now will you hypnotize me?"

"I'm very tempted to do as you ask, but I would have to have a witness and my secretary is gone for the day."

"I could call Bob. If I hurry, I can catch him before he leaves work."

McIntyre nodded his assent and Renata dialed the number of the accounting firm where Bob worked. Within minutes she had convinced him to come to the doctor's office.

"He's not happy about this," she said, "but I have to satisfy my curiosity. I have to see

Nathan one more time." She was afraid that if she told McIntyre she was going back to save Nathan's life, he would refuse to hypnotize her.

They waited for Bob's arrival and made desultory small talk as if neither was willing to let themselves relax too far. When Bob arrived, he was clearly upset.

"I won't allow you to do this, Renata," he said. "Look what happened last time."

"I eventually came out of it and I'm fine. I promise I won't be gone long. All I want is one hour." She added, "I'm going to do it whether you approve or not, Bob. It's something I have to do."

As McIntyre showed Bob the pin and note, Renata reclined on his couch and tried to make herself as comfortable as possible. Her heart was racing with excitement. She was going to see Nathan. She was going to save his life.

McIntyre sat in the chair beside the couch and started the tape recorder. As he began counting her down, she saw Bob glare at them and bite at his thumb as he always did when he was upset. She closed her eyes and let the doctor guide her back to Nathan. Rather than listen to his suggestion that she find herself by the stream as she had before, Renata fixed her mind on a July evening at sundown.

Chapter Nineteen

As Dr. McIntyre's voice grew faint, Renata became aware of another voice that rose, then fell. As she concentrated, the voice grew stronger. Over her wave of dizziness Renata heard Nathan say, "When I think how close I came to losing you . . ."

As if she were watching a performance, Renata heard her own, Callie's voice, say, "But you didn't. Don't you see? I was able to change things." She concentrated harder and found herself with Nathan in the back parlor of their home.

The clock on the mantel ticked softly, and she could hear night insects chirping outside the window. "I kept Callie from dying and that must mean I'm . . ." Renata stopped, trying to orient herself. Desperately, she fought off the dizziness that still assailed her.

Nathan looked up at her expectantly. "Must mean what?" he prompted.

Renata gave a frightened cry and leaped from her chair. Without explanation she ran for the door that led onto the porch. Ennis would pull the trigger at any moment. She flew out the door and let it bang shut behind her. The night was as dark as pitch, but she knew where Ennis must be. She had gone over this time and time again in her mind before she was able to convince McIntyre to send her back.

She hurtled herself off the porch and toward the deepest shadows where a grapevine hid Ennis. First she saw only the dark outline of a man, then the glint of lamplight on the gun barrel. He was kneeling exactly where she had thought she would find him, and he was pointing his rifle at the window where Nathan was clearly visible in the light.

Renata screamed Ennis's name as she threw herself at him. He cried out in fright and surprise. Renata grabbed his coat as he tried to twist away, and she clawed at his face and hands. He slapped her and her ears rang, but she refused to release him. Over the noise she and Ennis were making, she heard Nathan shout her name.

The gun went off and for a moment she was dazed. Ennis tried to shake free but she held on tighter. Then Nathan was beside her, wrestling Ennis to the ground. Renata stepped out of the way and felt in the darkness for the shotgun. Finally, her fingers scraped the barrel and she picked it up. "I have his gun!" she cried out.

Her eyes were adjusting to the dark at last, and she could see Nathan hit Ennis. When

Ennis threw up his hands in a gesture of surrender, Nathan let his fist drop. He got off Ennis and hauled him to his feet. "What the hell were you doing?" he demanded of the man.

Ennis shook his head sullenly.

"He was going to shoot you. Look. From here he had a perfect view of our chairs."

Nathan glanced in the direction of the window. "How did you know to come out here, Callie?"

Renata gave a shaky laugh. "Call it woman's intuition."

Nathan took the gun from her and shoved Ennis toward the house. "I'll tie him up, and we can lock him in the root cellar where I know he won't be able to get away. I'll ride to town and get the sheriff."

They went inside, and Nathan bound Ennis's hands securely, then half-shoved him down the steps to the cellar where Ennis had once before tried to break into the house. Renata followed, her skirts gathered close to prevent herself from tripping.

"What was that? Did I hear a shot?" Molly's voice sounded almost hysterical.

"Down here," Renata called to her.

She heard Molly hurry to the top of the stairs, then stop when she saw Ennis. "He tried to kill Nathan," Renata said. "We were able to stop him."

"I still think it was a miracle that you knew he was out there and that he had a gun," Nathan said as he tied Ennis to a pole that supported the ceiling of the cellar room. "You couldn't see him from inside the house."

"I'll explain later."

There was a banging on the door, and Molly gave a terrified shriek.

Renata and Nathan hurried back up the steps. "Who's there?" Nathan shouted as he took Ennis's gun from Renata's hands.

"Open up! It's Sheriff Barnes."

Nathan went to the kitchen door and opened it warily. The sheriff stepped inside. "I heard a shot," Barnes said. "What's going on? Anybody hurt?"

"What are you doing out here at this hour?"

"William Graham came to see me. He told me there was some trouble today."

"Papa came to see you?" Molly stepped forward. "He really did?"

"Ennis Hite tried to kill me this afternoon," Renata said in a firm voice. She had to make the sheriff believe her. "Just a few minutes ago he tried to shoot Nathan through the window."

"Is this true?" Barnes demanded of Nathan.

"I have him tied up in my cellar. I was about to ride to town and get you." Nathan motioned for Barnes to follow him into the cellar.

Barnes went down the steps and stared at Ennis. "What have you got to say for yourself, Hite?"

Ennis glared at him and turned his head away.

"Why would he try to kill you, Mrs. Blue?"

"He was trying to rape me and I resisted." Renata wasn't about to mince words with the sheriff. She didn't know how long she would be able to stay, and she had to be sure Ennis would be convicted. "It wasn't the first time, either. I was afraid to tell anyone. I see now that I was wrong." She looked Ennis straight in the eye. "I'm willing to tell the whole story in court."

Ennis obviously believed her. "She tempted me," he shouted in his defense. "Always swishing her skirts around me and giving me those looks. She made me do it!"

Barnes shook his head. "I've known Callie Blue all her life. She never did any such thing. Why she's so shy she hardly speaks to a man at all."

Renata was finally glad of Callie's fear of men. "You have to lock him up. He'll come back and kill us all if you don't."

"You don't have to worry about that." Barnes went to Ennis and released him from the post but kept his hands firmly tied. "He won't be able to hurt anyone again."

"What did Papa tell you?" Molly said.

"He said Ennis tried to harm your sister. We talked for quite a while, and he mentioned some other things about Ennis that made him suspicious. All this fit with other things I know about him, and I thought it would be a good idea if I rode out and asked the Blues some questions while everything was fresh in their minds." He looked at Ennis. "I never thought I'd find him here."

"What Callie said was true," Molly told him. "I've had reason to fear Ennis myself."

"Now, Mrs. Hite, I'm bound to tell you that you can't be made to testify against your own husband."

"Can I if I want to? And he won't be my husband for long. I'm divorcing him." Molly lifted her chin as if to dare the sheriff to dispute her word.

"Divorce." Barnes mulled this over. "Then I reckon your testimony would be as good as that of any other witness. Of course you can't testify in court, but I can repeat your words and be sure justice is done."

Molly nodded and lowered her head.

"You can call me as a witness," Nathan said. "I can tell you enough to be sure the jury knows what really happened." To Renata he said, "I can't guarantee they'll hang him as he deserves, but at least he'll be locked up for a long time."

Renata glared at Ennis. "Good." She went to the stairs and led them up into the kitchen.

"I guess I had better be on my way," Barnes said as he took Ennis firmly by the arm. "Nathan, if you would be so good as to come in tomorrow, I'll get you to sign the papers."

"I'll be there. I'll help you get Ennis on his horse."

Renata's eyes met Ennis's one last time and this time she didn't feel any fear. She had overcome him. Nathan was safe.

Molly put her hand to her forehead as Ennis was taken away. "I'm faint with all this. I can't bear to think of all that's happened today. This morning started so happily."

Renata nodded. A great deal had happened to her since she had started this morning, more than Molly would ever know. "Maybe you should go up and try to rest. When Nathan comes back in, we will be doing the same."

"Yes, I'll do that. Imagine Papa going to the sheriff like that! I never would have believed it."

Renata didn't comment. She still found it hard to believe, too. Had William given more credit to his daughters' words after he had had time to think them over, or was his denial a way of protecting their mother's sensibilities? Renata knew she would never be able to understand how the typical Victorian man's mind worked.

Nathan returned and took her into his arms. "Are you sure you're all right? When I saw you run out like that and heard the shot, I was afraid you were dead." He buried his face in her hair. "I'd rather lose my own life than to lose you."

"Don't say that. I couldn't bear it if you were harmed." She held him tightly. "You have no idea what lengths I would go to in order to protect you."

"We're safe now. Ennis won't be loose for a long time, if ever. The people of this parish take a dim view of a man who would try to hurt a woman." He looked into her eyes and stroked the curve of her cheek. "Let's go to bed, Renata. We've had more than enough excitement for today."

She wanted to beg for more time with him, but she knew it would be no use. She wanted to spend all the time she had left with him in his arms.

As if the thought made her hold on the past more tenuous, she felt the dizzying sensation again. She pressed her hands to her face. It was too soon! She couldn't have been here a full hour!

"Renata? What's wrong?"

"I . . . I feel Dr. McIntyre calling to me. I don't want to go! I don't want to leave you, Nathan!"

He held her tighter. "No! I won't let you leave me. Not now, not ever!"

She saw the room waver and panic struck her. In a matter of moments she would be gone, and this time she would never see Nathan again. Anger sparked to life in her. It was too unfair! She wouldn't lose him again! With all her might she resisted McIntyre's call.

"Look at me, Renata," Nathan commanded. "Look at me."

Her eyes met his and she gazed at him steadfastly even though the room was growing faint.

Elizabeth Crane

"I love you," she said. "I refuse to leave you."

From the corners of her eyes she could see the outlines of McIntyre's office replacing the more familiar shapes in her kitchen, but she kept all her attention on Nathan. Even when she heard McIntyre shout for help and the faint echoes of Bob's voice raised in alarm, she didn't waver from Nathan's gaze.

"We're losing her," McIntyre shouted from far away. "Call an ambulance!"

"Renata!" Bob was saying. "Renata, wake up!"

"No," she whispered, "I'm staying here. I'm staying with Nathan."

"Fight it," Nathan commanded. "Don't leave me, Renata!"

With all her might Renata shut out the other voices, refusing to believe in their existence. Nathan was her reality and she wanted no other.

"Where's that ambulance?" McIntyre bellowed. "She's going! I can't find her pulse!"

Renata smiled and held Nathan tighter. McIntyre's voice was growing faint, and she could scarcely make out what he was saying. "I love you, Nathan. I'm going to stay with you, and we're going to have a beautiful baby son."

"A son?" His face smiled, but his eyes were still worried. "How do you know that?"

"I just know." Now she could hardly hear McIntyre at all, and the kitchen was becoming more real than the doctor's office. The whirl of rushing time was loud in her ears, but she ignored it. "And after our son, we will have more children. I want to have a houseful, and I want them all to look exactly like you."

She felt a tremendous release, and she swayed in Nathan's arms. Something had happened! Slowly she looked around. She was still in their kitchen with Nathan's arms about her. Renata put her hand up and touched her ear. The rushing sound had stopped.

"Renata, are you all right?" Nathan sounded worried and she smiled to reassure him.

"Yes, I'm fine." She stepped back and touched her body, then his chest. "I'm still here."

He nodded, his eyes uncertain.

"I'm not sure how I managed it, but I'm still here." Her eyes were wide in amazement. In spite of her determination, she hadn't really believed she could overcome McIntyre's commands to return to the twentieth century. "It worked!"

"What do you mean?"

"I can't hear the doctor or Bob anymore. I can't see his office. I'm really here." She moved experimentally. She felt more at home and more real than she had ever felt before. She felt as if this was the only place she would ever be again.

Renata rushed back into Nathan's arms. "I'm really here. Don't you see? I never have to leave!"

Nathan held her tightly. "No, you'll never leave me. Fate wouldn't be that cruel. Now that I've found you, I'll never let you go."

She nodded. This time it was really true. With misty eyes she looked around the kitchen. She was willing to trade all the conveniences of the twentieth century for a chance to haul Nathan's water out of a well and to cook on a wood stove and to pound and boil dirt from his clothes beside a stream. She had to laugh.

"What's so funny?" he asked, his voice tender with love.

"It will be years before you'll know what I've given up in order to stay with you."

"You have no regrets?"

"None." Arm in arm they walked through the house and blew out the lamps. Taking the lamp they used to light their way upstairs, she said, "Let me tell you again about electricity."

Epilogue

Renata Blue parked her car on the shady street and looked both ways before hurrying across and into the cemetery that flanked the chapel. She hadn't told anyone where she was going. Her family would think it was odd for her to have come to a cemetery on a day such as this.

She found the graves she sought easily. She came here often. The stones, weathered to the point of being all but unreadable, stood as sentinels watching over the well-tended graves they marked. One read "Callie Renata Blue" and the other "Nathan Blue." For all of Renata's 22 years she had listened to the family legends about this couple. For one thing, they had lived longer than most of their generation and had died within weeks of each other. It was said that when the first of them died, the other one did not want to continue alone and had willed himself or herself to die as well, so they could be together again. Renata could no longer remember which had been the first to go, and the dates on the stones had long ago been obliterated by the ravages of time.

The cemetery was filled with descendants of Callie and Nathan. It seemed as though each generation since had supplied another young Nathan, Callie or Renata. Legend had it that the first Nathan had called his wife by either Callie or Renata, interchangeably, although a local genealogist had been quick to point out to her during an inquiry she had made about the family's background that the name "Renata" had not been found anywhere in written records of the family except on the tombstone.

Renata sat on the bench one of her ancestors had placed near the graves. The stone felt cool through her clothes, and even though she felt as if her heart were bursting with the excitement of the coming days, something about being here always filled her with a sense of quiet peace as though the passage of time meant nothing here.

Speaking in a whisper, she said, "I'm going to be married, Grandma Callie." This was the name her mother had used for Callie; it was how she was generally referred to in the family. "Grandpa Nathan, Mom says he reminds her of you. He's tall and has dark hair like in the old tintype of you Mom has over her fireplace." Renata paused and smiled as she tried to imagine what Grandma Callie and Grandpa Nathan had looked like when they were young, but she could only picture them as a comfortable elderly couple who, like many truly married couples, had grown to resemble each other in their twilight years. In her mind she always saw them smiling and comfortable in their enduring love.

"That's why I wanted to come out here and tell you. Nat says I'm silly to carry on so about my Travis, but little brothers can be insufferable." She pushed her long, pale auburn hair back from her face and her gray eyes became thoughtful. "I won't be Callie Renata Blue anymore after I marry Travis. I wonder if I should keep my maiden name. Some girls do, you know. Or maybe I'll use it as a middle name for my first child." She smiled and hugged herself at the idea of having a child of her own. Her child and Travis's.

"Were you ever thrilled over being in love?" she whispered to the grassy graves. "Did you ever feel what I feel when Travis says he loves me?" Renata grinned. It was impossible to imagine Grandma Callie and Grandpa Nathan young and filled with passion. Renata thought they would probably be shocked at the idea. She had read that people in Victorian times were like that. Of course they had both lived well into the present century, but by then they would have been getting on in years. Renata was of the opinion that no one past the age of 30 was capable of feeling an overwhelming passion. She couldn't imagine her own parents being giddy with love, much less her great-great-grandparents.

"Travis says his family once lived here in Lorain, but I met him at college," Renata continued. "I think there may be some kinship way back there somewhere. I'm kin to practically everyone else in town. You know," she mused, "the first time I met Travis, it was as if I had known him before. I think I may have known him in a past life. I guess you never heard of such a thing, but it's called reincarnation. Mom and Dad say that's silly, but when Dad met him, he kept saying Travis reminded him of someone, too. He said he thought it was someone he had known when he was a boy, but who knows?" Renata shrugged happily. "I guess there's nothing to it, but I like the idea that I might have known and loved him before."

She glanced at her wristwatch and stood up quickly. "I have to run. I told Aunt Emma I would go see her before Travis comes over tonight. If I don't hurry, she'll think I forgot." With a smile broad enough to encompass the green grass and sky above, Renata hurried away.

The jonquils at the bases of the tombstones, descendants of the ones the first Renata had planted in Callie's scraped yard, bobbed their heads as if in silent laughter at some cosmic joke.

BITTERROOT

VICTORIA CHANCELLOR

Bestselling Author Of *Forever & A Day*

In the Wyoming Territory—a land both breathtaking and brutal—bitterroots grow every summer for a brief time. Therapist Rebecca Hartford has never seen such a plant—until she is swept back to the days of Indian medicine men, feuding ranchers, and her pioneer forebears. Nor has she ever known a man as dark, menacing, and devastatingly handsome as Sloan Travers. Sloan hides a tormented past, and Rebecca vows to use her professional skills to help the former Union soldier, even though she longs to succumb to personal desire. But when a mysterious shaman warns Rebecca that her sojourn in the Old West will last only as long as the bitterroot blooms, she can only pray that her love for Sloan is strong enough to span the ages....

_52087-7 $5.50 US/$7.50 CAN

MIRIAM RAFTERY

Taylor James's wrinkled Shar-Pei, Apollo, is always getting into trouble. But the young beauty never expects her mischievous puppy to lead her on the romantic adventure of a lifetime—from a dusty old Victorian attic to the strong arms of Nathaniel Stuart and his turn-of-the-century charm. One minute Taylor and Apollo are in modern-day San Francisco, and the next thing Taylor knows, a shift in the earth's crust, a wrinkle in time, and the lovely historian finds herself facing the terror of California's most infamous earthquake—and a love so monumental it threatens to shake the foundations of her world.

_52084-2 $4.99 US/$6.99 CAN

TIMESWEPT

REFLECTIONS IN TIME

ELIZABETH CRANE

Ms. Crane has spun "a web of love that transcends the boundaries of time." —*Romantic Times*

THE DREAM

Renata glanced up at the groom. As she had known, his eyes were brown, a soft brown that held dreams and warmth.

"Do you, Callie, take this man to be your husband?" the preacher was saying.

She nodded as if she were in a dream, her eyes on Nathan. "I do."

The room was growing fuzzy, and the preacher's voice was receding. Only Nathan's face was clear. She leaned toward him to tell him that she would remember, that she would never forget.

"Renata? Are you awake?"

She opened her eyes and sat up. The chair clicked into a sitting position. Renata rubbed her forehead as she looked around. Where was the preacher? Where were the people and the fussy Victorian room? Most important, where was Nathan?

Other *Love Spell* Books by Elizabeth Crane:
TIME REMEMBERED